Bedtime Erotica

for FREAKS

(like me)

Lexy Harper

Bedtime Erotica *for* FREAKS (like me)

Ebonique Publishing

First published in Great Britain 2008

Copyright © 2006 Lexy Harper
All Rights Reserved.
www.lexyharper.com

Published by Ebonique Publishing, London.
ISBN-13: 978-0-9556986-2-0

CONTENTS

To freaks (like me) wherever you are.

VANESSA

*H*er pussy wet its lips in anticipation as her man, Lester, walked through the front door of her one-bedroom flat followed by two strange men. Lester's 5'10" frame was superb, but it *wasn't* the sight of her current man that had her pussy salivating; it was the thought of having three cocks all to herself.

"Vanessa baby, meet Tim and Derrick," Lester drawled and walked over to kiss her.

"Hi guys." She smiled, very pleased to meet them.

"Hi Vanessa," Tim replied, coming over to give her a long, deep kiss.

She absentmindedly returned his kiss, her eyes eagerly trained on Derrick's crotch as he fumbled with his fly. Seconds later he unceremoniously pulled out his cock.

I hope some of it's hidden.

Just as she began to wonder if Tim had come to make love not fuck, he stepped back from her—kissing her like she was his fucking woman! He too pulled his cock out and she shifted her eyes from the disappointment of Derrick's cock to encounter an even bigger disappointment. She wanted to chase them both out of her damn flat. They could star in their own porno movie: *Small and Smaller.*

Minutes later, she tried to keep Tim's cock from falling out of her mouth as Lester buried his deep in her ass and Derrick pushed his as far as it would go into her pussy, which wasn't far enough. Her first gang-bang was turning out to be very disappointing. She had to squeeze her pussy muscles tightly to feel Derrick's cock, and giving Tim head was like sucking her thumb. She felt like laughing every time he tried to grip her cropped hair and plunge the thumb into her mouth.

How could Tim agree to a gang-bang and pull his cock out in front of other men without feeling self-conscious?

A cock like his should *only* be shown to his doctor or a woman who really loved him. Lester's big cock in her ass was the only reason she didn't call the whole fucking thing off!

***

"Did you enjoy it, baby?" Lester asked as they climbed into bed after taking a shower together as soon as the other guys had left.

"It was alright, but where the hell did you find those two small-cock guys?" Vanessa didn't want to sound ungrateful but it would have been better if he had fucked her himself and let the other two watch.

"Tim's cock was small wasn't it?" Lester laughed and it started her off. Seconds later they were laughing so hard it hurt.

"Okay, let me give you a nice big cock to make it up to you." Lester stuck his tongue in her ear as he reached down and stroked her clit.

"Are you *still* horny?" she asked in surprise, he'd cum twice during the gang-bang.

"You know I always need some pussy right before I sleep."

He pulled her into position, quickly pushed his cock into

her and fucked her doggy-style.

***

Lester had his own flat but spent most evenings at hers—fucking her. He was unemployed but when she'd met him a year ago it was like finally meeting the man she had dreamed of: her fuckmate. His cock was big and he loved sex just as much as she did. After a hard day's work, a round of sex with him was better than a massage.

Recently they had been living out her sexual fantasies: they had started with fucking in a public place; moved on to her fucking another woman while he watched; then to him pretending to rape her and finally, a week ago, she'd told him about her 'gang-bang' fantasy.

They'd gone for a picnic in Hyde Park one Sunday, two months ago, for the 'fucking-in-a-public-place' fantasy. Lester had pulled her onto his lap as soon as they'd finished eating homemade fried chicken, potato salad and coleslaw. He'd spread her gypsy-style skirt over his lap, put his hand under it and stroked her clit until she was dripping. Then he had opened his fly and pulled her onto his hard cock right in the middle of the park. He had slipped his hands under her light summer jacket and pinched her nipples as she'd rotated her hips against his crotch.

They had both cum noisily. Then she had nonchalantly pulled herself off him, and waited for him to button the fly of his jeans before she stood up and straightened her clothes. A nearby couple had eyed them suspiciously but both she and Lester had ignored them, gathered the blanket and the basket, and left. The outraged couple had stared after them, their mouths opened in shock.

Noticing that a few people had looked down at Lester's groin as they'd gone past, she had finally looked down too— there had been a wet patch on the front of his light blue jeans. They had laughed helplessly as they'd made a dash for her car which was parked a good hundred and fifty metres away.

The 'fucking-another-woman' fantasy hadn't turned out as she had hoped. When Lester had brought the woman over she had seemed a little familiar but it wasn't until Vanessa had fucked the woman and she'd left that Lester had solved the mystery for her—Tessa was his ex-girlfriend.

What kind of nasty bitch would agree to do something like that?

How he'd managed to persuade the woman to come to her flat was beyond Vanessa. Tessa was good-looking and had a great body but she kept acting like she was posing for a camera or being filmed—like a C-rated porn star. While eating Vanessa's pussy she had kept looking up to the corner of the room. It had irritated the hell out of Vanessa. If the woman was going to eat her pussy the least she could do was pay attention to what she was fucking doing. Then the woman had wanted to fuck Vanessa with a dildo. Vanessa had informed her that if 'any fucking with a dildo' was going to be done, that she, Vanessa, would be the one strapping on the dildo and not the other way around. Tessa had agreed, and Vanessa had strapped up. Tessa's loud unrealistic moans had put Vanessa right off and when the woman had had a fake orgasm Vanessa pulled the dildo out of her in relief. Lester had wanted her to also fuck Tessa's ass but for Vanessa the fantasy was over, so he'd done it himself, with his own cock.

The 'rape' fantasy had completely blown Vanessa's mind. She had come home tired from work one Saturday evening and as she put her key in her front door, someone had grabbed her from behind and pushed her into the flat. Before she'd had a chance to get a glimpse of her assailant, she was blindfolded and pushed onto the sofa. She hadn't panicked, sure that it was Lester. *Until* the man had spoken with one of the strongest Jamaican accents she'd ever heard—Lester was Dominican!

When she'd worriedly called his name the man asked, "who the fuck is Lester?" and told her to "shut the fuck up!" His body had pressed her into the sofa and he had felt heavier and bulkier than Lester. He had roughly stripped her naked and squeezed her breasts before pulling her legs off the sofa and positioning himself behind her. Her pussy juice had started flowing when he had first grabbed her, but when doubts about his identity had begun to creep into her mind she had found herself tensing up. The man's cock had felt big and hard as he pushed it past her fear-tightened entrance and up inside her with one quick thrust. When he came he left his cock inside her as he played with her pierced nipples, without saying a word.

When his cock hardened again he put it against her asshole but she'd been so tense he couldn't get it inside her. Then Lester had whispered the sweetest words she'd ever heard into her ear, 'Relax, Vannie baby.' She'd collapsed weakly in relief and let him give her one of the most memorable backshots of her life.

Later he had laughed when she told him she had begun to worry that it wasn't him after he had used a different accent and had fucked her so silently—Lester was a man who liked to let you know that he was enjoying your pussy. Just the sweet memory of the fantasy was enough to make her pussy wet wherever she was.

***

The next Friday she left the hair salon, where she worked as a stylist, tired but filled with anticipation—Lester had promised her another gang-bang. She hoped the guys would be more hung than the last two.

It had been an unusually busy day at the salon and she felt a bit sweaty. A quick shower and she'd be ready for all comers.

She heard their voices before she opened the door. Two of the four jumped up and rushed forward to meet her, sandwiching her between their hard bodies as soon as she entered her small living room.

"Boys, I need a shower…" she arched her neck as the guy behind her pressed his mouth against her neck and squeezed her breasts "…then I'll be right with you."

"Guys give her a chance to shower," Lester recommended, trying to bring some order to the proceedings.

The guy in front of her ignored Lester as he pushed his hand under her short skirt and into her thong. He ran his hands over her shaved pussy and wet his fingers in the moisture oozing between her already swollen lips. He pulled his fingers out and licked them clean before pushing them up inside her. "I prefer musky pussy."

Vanessa opened her legs wider and smiled up at him. "Knock yourself out, sugar."

He knelt on the floor, pushed her skirt up and tongued her clit as he continued to finger-fuck her. Meanwhile, the guy behind her opened her top and freed her small breasts, each with a silver nipple ring through its centre that matched the one through her clit. Immediately, the other two guys hurried over to join the fun. One guy slipped the tip of his tongue through a nipple ring and pulled on it before he flicked his tongue expertly around her dark nipple. She rubbed her hand over his cleanly shaven head as she watched him, shuddering deliciously at the thought of his tongue working on her clit with equal expertise. The other guy, who was barely taller than her 5'3", just opened his mouth and took as much breast as he could into it and sucked—nipple ring and all.

The guy behind her decided that he needed some action.

He pushed her skirt up over her ass, spread her cheeks and started to rim her asshole. Vanessa wrapped her arms around the two guys sucking on her breasts, closed her eyes and savoured every sensation. It was heaven being squashed between four hard bodies and having four tongues, thirty-two fingers and eight thumbs on various parts of her anatomy at the same time.

The guy in front straightened and pulled his cock out of his jeans. Vanessa let go of Short Guy, reached down and stroked it. It wasn't very long but it had girth; a pussy-plugging cock. She leaned back a bit and guided it between her pussy lips.

"Go on, sugar, fuck that musky pussy."

The guy pushed into her with one quick thrust and started to ram into her like he was a jack-hammer.

"Slowly, sugar, *slowly*," she warned. "Your friends will have none of this pussy if you make me sore."

The guy was too far gone to slow down, he just kept hammering away.

"Delroy, slow down man!" Lester, the pussy-warden, tried to get the man to ease his pace but it was as if Delroy had gone deaf the moment he pushed his cock inside her. Thankfully, he came seconds later.

"Now guys, can I have my shower or is there anyone else for musky pussy?" Vanessa asked as Delroy straightened.

"I'll have some musky ass." The guy who had been rimming her ass stood up and bent her slightly forward. She reached behind and ran her hand along his cock as he positioned it against her ass. She glanced behind to ensure that her brain had received the right message from her hand. It had—his cock was a nice reasonable size.

"Spit on that cock first, sweets, or you won't get it into my asshole," she advised as she held onto the two guys still playing with her nipples and braced herself.

The guy separated her pussy lips and pushed his cock slowly inside her. After a few strokes he pulled it out and pressed it against her asshole.

"How many inches do you have there, sweets?" Vanessa asked as he tried to work the head inside her.

"Seven," he panted as he pulled back slightly and pushed forward again.

Trust a man to add an extra half inch!

Vanessa *knew* cocks and his was no more than 6½". She'd had bigger cocks up her ass before but he wasn't making much headway.

"Stay still and let me work myself back onto you." She quickly realized the trick to a successful gang-bang would be to control the guys. Left to it, Mr Musky Ass would rip her asshole before he got his cock inside her. Vanessa swiftly rotated her hips, got the head inside her and continued to impale herself onto him.

"There!" Vanessa said as she felt his balls slap against her pussy lips. "Now *do* your thing, sweetness."

The guy held her hips and started thrusting backwards and forwards. He also came too quickly. She hoped it wasn't going to be a night of short-fucks.

Lester had been sitting in a chair pumping his cock, watching the action. He jumped up and said, "Let's move this to the bedroom."

"Yes, I think it's time for my shower." Vanessa didn't mind serving her own man slightly musky pussy or ass but it seemed common courtesy to wash them before offering them to strangers.

"I'll join you." Short Guy started taking his clothes off.

The other guys crowded round the glass-fronted shower cubicle and watched as he pressed her up against the tiles and fucked her from behind. His cock, like him, was short and taking her from the back while standing didn't make the most of it. But he had staying power. That was always the way—men with the little dicks took too long to cum; the ones with the big dicks came too quickly. She put her arm behind Short Guy and pushed her finger in his butt to speed up his progress. He came within seconds.

The last guy, Mr Cleanly Shaven Head, was waiting, naked, with an open bath towel in his hands as she stepped out of the shower. Earlier she had noticed how tall and well-built he was and as he wrapped the towel around her she caught sight of his erection. It was long and thick with an exceptionally bulbous head—her favourite kind of cock.

Talk about saving the best for last!

She looked up at him and he gave her a wicked wink before quickly drying her off and swinging her up in his muscular arms.

"Okay guys, my turn." He walked over to the bed and placed her on it.

The other guys moved around the bed. Mr Short Guy quickly moved in to suck on her nipple again.

"By the way, Vanessa, I'm Michael." Mr Cleanly Shaven Head smiled as he fingered her clit. "I thought I should at least introduce myself to you before I introduced my cock to your pussy."

"Hi, Michael!" she gasped as he dipped his head and tongued her clit. He gently worried the ring in her clit, making her remember why she got it pierced in the first place. Then, he straightened and slowly pushed that wicked cock of his into her pussy, staring into her eyes as he did so. When he pulled his cock back to plunge inside her again, they both groaned.

"Hold onto your hat, sweetheart, it's going to be a bumpy ride." He winked at her again as he started gyrating his hips, belying his words, giving her the full length of his cock in a smooth, rhythmic motion. She clasped her legs around his hips and enjoyed the ride.

Then Short Guy wanted another round of pussy.

Didn't you see the size of the cock Michael just pulled out of my pussy?

He stuck his short cock into her pussy and started a furious ramming. Her pussy had been humming after Michael's cock, Short Guy quickly brought it down from its high. Luckily, Michael seemed to sense that she was getting a little bored and said, "Ease up, Kent. Let me get to her sweet ass."

Kent rolled over onto his back. She straddled him, slipped his dick inside her and leaned over to give Michael full access to her ass. He immediately spread her cheeks and started to rim her. Her pussy clenched tighter and tighter around Kent's cock with each stroke of Michael's lethal tongue, and Short Guy soon came with a loud groan. Lester, who had been directing the fucking up until then, decided to get some action for himself. He took up Kent's vacant position as Michael continued to rim her, preparing her asshole with a couple of fingers then sticking his big cock inside it.

The *ultimate* DP!

But right afterwards Tyrone, Mr Musky Ass, had himself another piece of ass and instantly spoilt the memory of Michael's sweet anal fuck.

Delroy, Mr Musky Pussy, seemed to really prefer musky pussy—he sat on the bench for the rest of the game. Lester and Michael finished the night on a high-note by giving her another DP—Michael in her pussy; Lester bringing up the rear. She would have preferred it the other way around but they still made her cum twice before Lester and finally Michael came. Lester then signalled the end of play and led the guys to the living room for chilled cans of beer.

Vanessa had a long shower and came back into the

bedroom to find that Lester had stripped the bed and put on fresh sheets. She crawled under the duvet naked and instantly fell asleep.

She was awakened by something heavy pressing against her stomach. She turned onto her side to try and dislodge it. It tightened and pulled her back against a warm body.

"Are you awake?" Lester whispered in her ear.

"No!" she denied sleepily.

"Come on, Vanessa," he pleaded as he fondled her breast.

"I'm tired," she protested and tried to roll away from him but he held her tightly.

"My cock is hard, I have to fuck." He pulled her leg over his, reached down and fingered her clit.

She didn't understand how he could be horny again. He and his friends had fucked her only hours ago. She liked fucking but there was fuck time and there was sleep time. This was fucking sleep time. One drawback of having a trifling niggah for a man was that he fucked her nicely until the wee hours of the morning and later, when she struggled out of bed to shower and dress for work, he turned over and went right back to sleep.

"Lester, I am too tired," she protested again as he fingered the ring through her clit. She could have been talking to herself; he pushed his cock into her from behind.

"I need some pussy bad." He pulled her hips closer to him but she was too tired to move. After a few thrust he rolled her onto her stomach and got his cock deeper inside her. She dozed lightly as he fucked her. He came, rolled off her and pulled her back against him.

***

When she got home the following Saturday she found Lester, Tyrone, Kent, and Delroy drinking beer in her living room as she walked in.

No Michael.

"Lester, why are your friends in my flat?" she asked angrily.

"They're here to fuck you," Lester replied.

"You had better be joking!"

"I am your man—you'll do whatever I say!" Lester grabbed her arm and twisted it behind her back before she could blink. "Delroy, come get some musky pussy before she takes a shower."

"No!" She tried to pull out of Lester's tight grip but he held her firmly.

Mr Musky Pussy, jumped out of his chair, took her from Lester and pressed her against the wall. He kissed her and then sucked on her neck.

"I think I'll try a piece of musky ass this time," he whispered in her ear, then turned her around and pushed her over the back of her leather sofa. She started to struggle and soon they were both out of breath.

"Come and hold her for me," he panted to the other guys.

Tyrone held her down as Delroy rimmed her ass, then pushed his fat cock into her asshole. Kent slid onto the sofa and kissed her while he fondled her breasts. Delroy seemed to fuck only one way—hard and fast, he lasted about the same time as he had done the previous week. Tyrone didn't give her asshole time to close before he pushed his longer dick inside and gave her an almost equally quick, hard fuck. When he was finished Kent pushed her to her knees and made her suck his short cock, then forced her to swallow his cum.

"I want fresh pussy." Lester grabbed her arm and pulled her along to the bathroom.

He soaped and rinsed her body quickly before turning the water off and ordering her out of the shower. She grabbed a towel but he picked her up and tossed her on to the bed while she was still damp. He held her hands down, nudged her legs apart with his knee and plunged his cock into her. The other guys stood around the bed, stroking their cocks as they watched him fuck her. As soon as he vacated her pussy Kent took his place. Delroy, Mr Musky Pussy, seemed to think the pussy was musky enough after two fuckings so he had some next. Tyrone had another helping of ass as Lester made her sit on his cock.

***

"So how was the double fantasy?" Lester asked as he rubbed her dry with the slightly damp towel he'd just used himself.

"Baby, it was wild!"

When he had mentioned combining the 'rape' and the 'gang-bang' fantasies she had almost cum at the thought. It had been almost as good as she'd anticipated, the only letdown was Michael not turning up. She hadn't asked for him specifically because she knew it would make Lester jealous. But when she had asked him to bring the guys back she'd assumed Michael would definitely want to come back for some pussy and ass, he seemed to enjoy them enough the last time.

***

Three weeks later, Lester sat on the bed and watched Vanessa as she undressed. "Do you fancy another gang-bang?"

"No."

"What's the matter with you? You are getting a little boring." He sulked like a little boy.

Though she'd enjoyed the last gang-bang, she knew it would have been even better if Michael had been there. She had tried to casually slip his name into one of their conversations but Lester had just said something about

Michael not being cool and changed the topic.

"It's weird but now that I've lived out all my fantasies, I'm fine."

"Well start thinking of a few new ones because I am getting bored of the same straight sex every day," Lester complained, sounding totally pissed off.

"I thought you were doing them for *me*."

"*I* enjoy them too."

"Don't *you* have any fantasies?"

"The only fantasy I have is to see you and a group of girls fuck each other."

"That *isn't* going to happen again. That bitch Tessa spoilt *that* fantasy for me."

"If I get different girls, would you do it?"

"I don't know, Lester. I prefer men."

"Come on, Vanessa, I need something different."

She had noticed a change in Lester—he had gone from a man who used pussy as a sleeping pill to one who now turned over many nights and slept without fucking her.

"Okay, I'll do the girl-bang but *I* will be the one who fucks them," she conceded.

Lester had lost some of his appeal since she'd met Michael but she still enjoyed the fucking he gave her when he could be bothered. She didn't know if she would ever meet Michael again or even if he wanted to be her new fuckmate. Had he been as impressed with her pussy and ass as she had been with his nimble fingers, bulbous cock and clever tongue? She didn't want to lose both corn and husk, i.e. drop Lester without knowing whether or not she had a chance with Michael.

***

As soon as the women turned up on her doorsteps she regretted her decision to do the girl-bang. Two of the women Sheila and Hyacinth were both in their late-thirties and looked it. The third was *Tessa*! When she pulled Lester aside and asked him why the bitch was here, he told her he wanted a four girl-bang but couldn't find another woman, other than Tessa.

Vanessa decided that she didn't like any of them well enough to put her mouth on their pussies *or* let them put theirs on hers. So, she strapped on a dildo and stood at the side of the bed, hands on her hips like a big, bad butch, and let them get on with their shit.

Tessa, the porn star, came to the edge of the bed and started to suck on the dildo as if it were a real cock, occasionally looking up at Vanessa to see if she was enjoying it—she felt like spitting in the bitch's eye. Then Tessa turned around and backed on to the dildo and started her loud moaning and groaning, looking up in the corner again. Vanessa decided she was going to fuck her in the ass this time, so she pulled the dildo out and quickly shoved it into her asshole. The dildo went in so quickly Vanessa nearly overbalanced. She grabbed Tessa's hips and gave her some deep, hard thrusts. The bitch had the nerve to behave as if she was in pain.

Sheila pulled Tessa's mouth down to her pussy while Hyacinth sat on Sheila's face. Lester came over to the bed and gave Hyacinth his cock to occupy her mouth. The room was soon filled with grunts, groans and moans. Everyone was enjoying themselves except Vanessa; she was so bored she almost fell asleep at one point. Finally Lester came, pulling his cock out of Hyacinth's mouth to let his spunk spurt all over her breasts and stomach. The others all followed him with faked orgasms but Tessa still took the crown for her explosive orgasm. Vanessa didn't bother to fake shit—she just pulled the dildo out of Tessa's ass and moved away before the woman accidentally hit her with one of her flaying limbs.

After the women had dressed and left, Lester turned to Vanessa and said furiously, "The least you could have done was look like you were enjoying yourself!"

Then he stormed out of the house, slamming the door behind him.

She didn't see him for four days and the night he came back he didn't fuck her. Or the next. Or the next week. Or the next month. She knew he was definitely getting pussy elsewhere because he was a horny bastard. But frankly she didn't give a shit—all she wanted was Michael. Sadly, she had absolutely no way of making contact with him, or his bulbous cock.

***

One Friday, she was in the middle of attaching a weave to a client's hair at Dream Weavers, the salon where she worked when the door chimed and someone walked in. She automatically glanced up to see who it was.

Thank you, Jesus!

Michael was wearing a charcoal suit that accentuated his broad shoulders and made him look taller than 6'1". All the women in the salon suddenly sat up straighter, pulled their stomach in and pushed their chests out. All five of the other stylists paused to check him out.

He's mine, bitches. DOWN!

He caught sight of Vanessa, smiled and sauntered over to her. She heard the ill-concealed groans of disappointment.

"What time do you get off?" he whispered in her ear.

"About half six," she replied and bit his earlobe playfully.

"Okay, I'll be back for you." He kissed her neck, nipping her skin lightly before turning to leave.

Her poor pussy had been acting like it had lost its best friend these past four months, nothing Vanessa did consoled it—now it was doing a Hip! Hip! Hooray! in her drawers.

"Girlfriend, you do get some good-looking men," April,

one of the younger stylists shouted across the floor to her. "I have to borrow that pussy of yours."

April was a light-skinned sister with looks that were usually seen in fashion magazines and full breasts most women would kill for. Her current man was loaded but sixteen years older than her, short and balding. She had been jealous as hell when she had first seen Lester; Michael was even better looking and in his designer suit, he looked the business. April was greedy—she wanted it all—a young, good-looking man with dough. Unlike Vanessa, who didn't mind working for her own money, once her man fucked her right.

"Girl, I could rent you my pussy for a small fee but you would have to also borrow my hips and my lips." Vanessa smiled smugly across at the other stylist.

"Why would I have to borrow your hips?" April demanded, ready to start cussing. She was a bit sensitive about her narrow hips and flat behind.

"Because it is the combination of my sweet pussy, the way I move my hips and use my lips that keeps them coming back." Vanessa brought her hand up and held it in front of her mouth to demonstrate her last point.

"Ugh!" April turned up her nose like she was smelling something bad.

Probably her stink mouth! Girlfriend was beautiful but her breath could peel the bark off trees and she loved to come right up in people's faces to hold a conversation.

"Yes, ladies, *I* give head!" Vanessa announced loudly to all present.

The salon was in uproar for the next few minutes. Vanessa looked at the women shuddering and squirming in their seats like giving head was a bad thing.

Pretentious bitches!

She could tell most of them gave fucking head. Some of

them gave head so regularly they had cock-shaped mouths. One client, in particular, a primary school teacher who has been sleeping with her best friend's husband for years, was shaking her head and looking as though she wanted to throw up at the thought of sucking a man's dick.

Hypocritical bitch!

Vanessa was sure if the man died tomorrow and there was no way of identifying him, forensic scientists could take a mould of the teacher's mouth and it would be a perfect fit for his cock, if he'd died with a hard-on. His wife also came to get her hair done at the salon and Vanessa suspected that the tight-assed bitch wasn't sucking her husband's dick, so her best friend was doing it for her.

"*Ladies!*" Vanessa waited for silence. "Put your hand up if you *don't* suck your man's dick."

Only two women didn't put their hands up. Vanessa was shocked to note that one of them was a middle-aged woman who came to have her grey hair blow-dried and styled once a month. That's why the woman's husband was always smiling when he came to drop her off or pick her up—old girl took care of business! Or maybe the woman was a bit deaf and hadn't heard the question.

The other woman wisely hadn't bothered to waste energy putting her hand up because no one would have believed her. Not only was her mouth cock-shaped, the muscles around her mouth were highly developed. The question to her would have been not *if* she gave head but how many times a day. She was young and didn't smoke but she already had crease-lines around her mouth.

"I know some of you bitches are lying to me but let me give the rest of you some advice—suck your man's dick before someone else does it for you!" Vanessa warned. The teacher rolled her eyes and it got on Vanessa's last nerve. "It might even be your best friend!"

The teacher's mouth opened in shock but she quickly shut it and sat up straighter in the chair. The bitch thought she was slick, the first time she had come to the salon her borrowed man had boldly collected her afterwards. Then her best friend had seen her fantastic weave and wanted hers done at the same salon. A week later the same man had dropped them both off. He had kissed his wife goodbye as the teacher sat in the backseat looking on, kissless. The woman's husband still occasionally collected the teacher but usually at the corner away from the salon. The teacher was always talking to him on her mobile phone and Vanessa had to constantly ask her to hold her fucking head properly. Sometimes if the bitch really annoyed her, Vanessa deliberately tugged her hair to get her attention.

After a few minutes the women settled down again—the stylists going back to their styling and the clients to whatever they were reading or saying before the topic of cock-sucking had come up. Vanessa shook her head.

When will Black women learn? Own up to your shit, sisters! Personally, she thought the reason why Black men, including her two drop-dead gorgeous brothers, were dating outside the race was because they mistakenly thought Black women didn't give head. Very few men knew that Black women were among the best head-givers in the world! There's nothing a man likes to see more than his hard cock between a pair of soft, juicy lips. Which women have the juiciest lips in the world? Damn right! Whenever Vanessa met a man she let him know straight away that head was on the menu and that she expected him to munch on her pussy. She could never understand that one-sided shit—men who wanted you to suck their dick but won't eat your pussy. Or women whose men would eat them like their favourite meal but they wouldn't so much as kiss their dicks in return.

Years ago her friend, Tamara, had confessed that

although her husband ate her pussy, she couldn't bring herself to suck his dick. Vanessa immediately advised her to get down on her knees and address the issue head on. She even bought Tamara an instructional DVD but her friend ignored her warning. After four and a half years of marriage and two children, Tamara's husband left her and started screwing another woman whose mouth was definitely cock-shaped. Tamara took it hard, finally she had dusted off the DVD Vanessa had given her and had spent several days watching it over and over again. Her husband used to visit the children regularly and one Sunday about a month after he had left her, Vanessa baby-sat the kids while Tamara put on her sexiest frock and served him his favourite food. After the main course she crawled under the table and had his cock for dessert while he ate a slice of raspberry cheesecake. The next day when Vanessa dropped the kids off Tamara told her that her husband had confessed that the blowjob was the best he'd ever had. He moved back home the next day and three years later they are still together. Tamara now wears her lovely, cock-shaped mouth with pride.

***

The rest of the afternoon dragged on, Vanessa's pussy was jumping but the hands on the clock weren't. Finally, the last customer left the shop. She quickly turned the lights off and locked up. She had worked at the salon since she'd left school at the age of sixteen, seven years ago. The owner had recently bought another salon and had given Vanessa the responsibility of closing up this shop at the end of each day, without increasing her pay by a single penny. Several salon owners had head-hunted Vanessa over the years but she was saving to open her own salon in two years' time. She wanted to be her own fucking boss by the time she was twenty-five.

Michael rode up on a powerful-looking motorbike a few minutes later, looking sexy in black leather. She walked over and pressed herself against him. He gave her a deep kiss before he pushed a red helmet on her head and said, "Hop on."

She hiked her skirt up and swung her legs over the seat. Wrapping her arms around him, she flattened her breasts against his hard body and held him tighter than she needed to as the bike sped away. She had no idea where they were heading and didn't particularly care—all she knew was that wherever the journey ended some good fucking began.

"Keep your helmet on until we get to my flat," Michael instructed as he parked his bike in the underground car park of the tower block. She turned and looked at him, ready to say, "fuck you" when he explained, "Lester lives on the seventh floor."

"Okay," she agreed hastily. The last thing she needed was Lester acting the jealous boyfriend, thwarting the fantastic fucking she was anticipating.

"This flat belongs to my brother, Levi. He's on a two-year teaching contract in Mozambique so I am renting my house in Islington and living here while he's away," Michael explained as they rode the graffiti-covered, urine-scented lift. "I recently got into the property business and needed every spare penny I could get my hand on to buy my first two properties."

The tenth floor, two-bedroom flat was extremely tidy, furnished in a minimalist, very masculine style in black and ivory.

"You're a *very* hard woman to find," Michael complained, closing the door and kissing her hungrily.

"How did you find me?" she asked when he finally pulled his tongue out of her throat.

"Last night I remembered Lester had mentioned that you worked in a hair salon. I spent the whole morning calling the ones listed in the Yellow Pages. When the receptionist at your salon confirmed that I'd found the right one, I took the rest of the day off and rushed right over!"

"I am so glad you found me." She pressed herself against him to show her gratitude.

"I'll make you even gladder in a few minutes," he said as he winked at her. "You want something to drink?"

"Just a mouthful of your cum." She ran her tongue over her lips in anticipation.

"I meant *before* that."

"All I need is a shower."

"Girl, I want this pussy so bad I'm about to do a Delroy!"

"I'll be two seconds!" she promised, stepping out of her skirt.

"I can't wait that long! I'll do a Kent." Naked, his cock already as stiff as a poker, he pushed her in the direction of the bathroom. She reached back and stroked his cock, familiarizing herself with the bulbous head.

"You'd have to cut your dick in two to do a Kent," she moaned as he worked it inside her less than five minutes later as they stood under the shower.

"Fuck, Vanessa!" Michael groaned as he finally buried his cock to the hilt. "Hasn't Lester been fucking this pussy lately?"

"He hasn't fucked me in months. I need some good cock."

"You've come to the right place, baby. Your pussy will be sore when I'm done tonight, trust me." Michael pushed himself against the wall of the shower cubicle and she used the extra space to tilt her ass and push her pussy right back at him. Slowly, he withdrew his cock and then quickly plunged it back into her. "Damn girl!"

***

"Let me get the chains," he whispered as he pushed her

onto the bed and walked over to his wardrobe.

"Chains? Very kinky!"

"I bought these specially for you." He pulled out a pair of thin silver chains with alligator clips attached to the ends, which he clipped onto the rings in her clit and nipples. Smiling wickedly down at her, he began to gently pull on the chains, expertly adjusting the tension until she was writhing on the bed. Suddenly, he held the chains taut for a few seconds and she came instantly. He undid the clips and stood stroking himself as she watched. When she sat up, he stepped closer and she wrapped her lips around his milk chocolate stick. She had to open wide to give him head but she loved the sensation of his smooth, silky cock-head gliding along her tongue. Usually she gave men blowjobs, controlling the depth she took their cocks into her mouth but she let Michael fuck her mouth. He held her head and thrust into her mouth with short, rhythmic strokes while she caressed his ass and balls. When he finally pulled himself away, his cock looked angry—big and hard, the bulbous head almost purple. Michael stared at it for a second or two as though it belonged to someone else. "You give good head, baby."

He climbed on top of her and she held his gaze as he thrust into her slowly. "Lester must be on crack to neglect this pussy."

"A regular drug-user!" she agreed as he withdrew it almost completely.

"Don't worry, baby. I don't do drugs." Michael covered her lips with his as he started to pummel her pussy with firm, deep strokes, occasionally breaking the kiss to suck on her neck or nipples.

Damn, the fucking man could fuck!

"Mi-chael, I'm cumming!" she screamed only minutes later.

He started to plunge his cock into her faster and harder. She wrapped her legs around his hips and rubbed her clit against his curly pubic hairs every time he thrust forward. She bit his shoulder as she came. He joined her seconds later, collapsing on top of her.

She stroked his shaved head as his cock pulsed to readiness inside her. He eased his weight up, pulled her off the bed and bent her over in front of him. She held onto her ankles as he pushed his cock into her again. The flow of blood to her head intensified the pleasure of his thrusts. Minutes later, when he pushed his finger in her asshole she almost lost consciousness as she came. He pulled her up against him, bending his knees as he continued to thrust into her clenching pussy. She wrapped her arms around his neck, laid her head back onto his shoulder and tilted her ass upwards so that he could plunge into her as deeply as possible.

"Baby, oh baby…," Michael whispered against her neck as he gave her the full length of Mr Mushroom Head. Her pussy fitted over his cock like it was made specially for him and though he tried desperately to last a bit longer, he came within a dozen thrusts. His cock was hardening again even as he eased it out of her. "I can't seem to get enough of you."

"My ass is feeling a little neglected," she complained.

"I was just about to get to it." He positioned her on the bed, opened her cheeks and rimmed her. Pushing two fingers into her pussy, he lubricated them and squeezed them into her ass. "Shit, baby, Lester has really *not* been looking after you!"

"Tell me about it!"

"Have no fear, Uncle Michael's here," he promised as he started to vigorously finger-fuck her ass. She reached between her legs to stroke the bulbous head of his cock, her pussy clenching at the thought of that big head inside her.

"I think I'm ready for Mr Mushroom Head."

He dipped the head of his cock into her pussy for some juice, opened her cheeks and put it against her asshole. He moved his hand from her hip to stroke her clit as he lodged the big head inside. He pressed forward slowly, using short, penetrative thrusts as he rotated his hips and got his cock right up inside her. He stayed still for a moment, then withdrew almost completely and quickly buried it deep again.

"My ass is going to be so sore I'll need a fucking doughnut ring," Vanessa moaned as he withdrew to thrust forward again.

"You want me to stop?" Michael teased, treating her to another wicked thrust.

"Baby, this ass has been dying for your cock, just *bend* it up."

Michael fondled her clit more firmly as he increased his tempo.

"Nice, Michael, so fucking *nice!*" she groaned, pushing her ass back at him.

***

"Is that your own salon?" Michael asked as they lay sipping Hennessy.

"I wish it was!" She tweaked his nipple. "I am still saving to open my own salon."

"*Come on*, you and Lester must have a fortune stashed away by now."

"Oh yes, me and Lester are *loaded!*" She laughed.

"What do you do with all that money?"

All which money?

"We spend it of course!" She laughed again. Then she remembered the bone she had to pick with him. "Why didn't you come to the other gang-bang?"

"If I wanted to be a porn star I would do it for money

not pay money to do it."

"What do you mean by that?" She was really beginning to think he wasn't right in the head, that maybe the fucking *had* damaged his brain. She knew her pussy and ass were deadly but were they lethal enough to make him lose his marbles?

"Lester didn't tell me copies of the DVD were going on sale. He had given me the impression that no one else would see it but us."

"Michael rewind—DVD on sale?" Vanessa stared at him, thinking that his brain had definitely affected and wondering if she should call 999 before he started to suffer even more side effects from over-fucking her dangerous pussy and ass.

"Don't try and play me, Vanessa! Lester said you were the one who wanted £50 from each of us."

"You *paid* Lester to fuck me?" she asked incredulously.

"We all did."

"What DVD?"

"Lester taped the whole thing and he sells the DVDs online."

"Michael *tell* me you are fucking joking!"

"Vanessa, I am serious." He got off the bed and walked over to his desk. He switched his computer on and sat down. "I'll show you."

It took a few minutes for the computer to boot-up and for Michael to logon to the Internet. He clicked on a website from the link in his Favourites, then double-clicked to view the catalogue of amateur porn for sale. There were ten DVDs—she was the star of four of them.

"I have one of them…if you want to have a look."

"Sure, why not?"

Things couldn't get any fucking worse.

But they did. As soon as she saw Tessa walk into the

bedroom in the opening shot of the DVD she thought, *that fucking BITCH!* Tessa had known she was being taped—and exactly where the camera was hidden—she had been looking directly at it the whole fucking time! Vanessa watched in seething silence. When Lester came into view she noticed that while Tessa had been posing for the camera, Lester had been trying to avoid it. He had fucked Tessa's ass with his head carefully turned away from the camera.

"I thought you knew." Michael could tell that she was pissed off!

"Which flat is Lester's?" she asked with deadly calm. She had never been to his council flat; he had never invited her and she'd had no interest in a small probably dingy flat in a high-rise building.

"What are you planning to do?" Michael eyed her suspiciously.

"Beat his ass up and get my fucking property."

"*You* beat Lester up?" Michael smiled.

"Watch me!" She was so pissed off at that moment she could terminate The Terminator if he fucked with her.

"I'll hold him and let you kick his ass." Michael grabbed his keys and they headed through the door. They used the stairs instead of the pissy lift. Michael rapped loudly on Lester's door. No answer. He rapped again and stood back for a minute before slipping a plastic fob attached to his key ring through the doorjamb. The door swung open as he explained, "I did this when I forgot my keys—the cheap locks on these doors are crap."

Everything in the flat was brand spanking new! In the smaller of the two bedrooms they found Lester's porn-making factory and a pile of DVDs.

Michael started looking for copies of the DVD featuring their gang-bang.

"We don't have time to check each one so we are taking

all this shit! I'll check the other bedroom," Vanessa declared.

Michael stopped looking at the labels and started to pack all the DVDs into a black refuse bag. Vanessa went into the adjoining bedroom. She knew that Lester would never put his money in a bank—it had to be in the house somewhere. She came across a briefcase hidden in his laundry basket. It had a combination lock but she guessed the combination correctly the first time. Lester's memory was like a sieve, he would use something he wasn't likely to forget—like his date of birth. She gazed at the neat bundles of £50 notes in shock for a few minutes before she started stuffing them into the waistband of her skirt. She left the four loose notes that had been on top the bundles, closed the briefcase and hid it where she had found it.

She smashed the mini-porn factory with a hammer from Lester's toolbox. She thought of wrecking the entire place but then she remembered the good times they'd had when she'd first met him, and changed her mind. She and Michael took every last DVD and left Lester a note signed by The Blafia, a notorious group of organized Black criminals from Brixton, warning him if he continued to sell DVDs his cockless body would be found floating down the Thames. Lester would be scared shitless—if they'd said his headless body it would have been less scary for him—Lester would much rather lose his head than his cock!

They rushed back to Michael's flat with two black bags bulging with DVDs. They stashed them under the bed in Michael's spare room and Vanessa quickly caught a cab home. Thankfully, Lester wasn't at her flat. She hid the money in the bottom of her cooker with the baking trays her mother had given her when she had first moved into the flat, but which hadn't since seen the light of day.

She wanted Lester out of her flat immediately, but she had to find him to kick his ass out. He was likely to be in a pub somewhere; he loved to drink. The first time she had seen him he had been in the local pub with Tessa. As soon as Tessa had left he'd come over to Vanessa's table. She'd told him to "piss off" but he had sat down and explained that Tessa was an ex-girlfriend who was now married, that they were just friends.

On a hunch Vanessa walked down to the same pub. Bingo! She found Lester sticking his tongue in Tessa's ear. They both looked like new money, dressed in expensive designer gear. Tessa was sporting shiny gold earrings, Lester a new gold watch and both wearing heavy gold chains. Perfect!

"Lester what are you doing here with Tessa?" Vanessa asked, trying to sound like she gave a damn.

"Fuck off, bitch!" Tessa snarled, loud enough for the whole pub to hear. "I let Lester fuck you for a while but now he's back with me!"

"Lester?" It was only the thought of all the lovely, hidden money that stopped Vanessa from reaching across the table and slapping the shit out of Tessa for giving her lip.

"Don't fret, babes, we had a good thing for a while but now it's over," Lester drawled.

"Can you come and get your things from my flat tonight?" Vanessa pinched her arm hard and squeezed a small tear out of her left eye as she said the words. "And I'll like my key back."

"Here's your key, babes." Lester pulled it from his top pocket. Previously it had been on his key ring—he'd obviously planned on handing it back to her very soon. "Pack my clothes and we'll be around to collect them when the pub closes."

Vanessa walked out of the pub slowly, like a woman who had just lost her last friend but as soon as she was out of view, she punched the air with her right hand. She rushed home and hastily threw his things into his rucksack.

He came around at eleven fifty, casually took the rucksack from her, put his arm around Tessa and said, "Later, babes."

Tessa turned at the gate, looked at Vanessa standing forlornly in the doorway and laughed like a hyena.

Good luck with your trifling niggah, bitch!

She hoped they wouldn't fight too much over the two hundred pounds she had left in the briefcase. At least it was an easy sum to divide; they would have needed a calculator if she had left an odd number of bills. Tessa would probably kick him to the kerb when she realized that their venture into the porn industry had attracted the attention of The Blafia— no one, not even the police, fucked with them.

She laughed as she locked her door and went to retrieve her money.

Nine *lovely* bundles. Twenty-two thousand, five hundred fucking pounds!

She'd stood on her feet working in the hair salon, six days a week to pay the bills while the trifling niggah had been living large! Well, he'd had his fun, now she would have hers. Michael planned to destroy the DVDs which featured their little gang-bang. No problem. She would sell the rest wholesale and split the proceeds with him. She intended to have Michael's big, bulbous cock as often as possible but she wasn't going to tell him shit about the money she'd found in Lester's bedroom. She didn't intend to share it with him or anyone else. Lester had taught her it was every man and woman for themselves. The money was just enough for her to open her own little place on a nice busy high street in a couple of months' time. She already had the perfect name for it—Fake It!

She was the best stylist at Dream Weavers, but the owner didn't appreciate her skill. Hell, she was the best in the UK by miles—she kept her own hair short because no one else could hook hers up half as good. She wasn't going to quit her job just yet, she would get her shit together and when she was ready to rock-and-roll she would take all her regulars with her because she was the reason they came to the salon in the first place. Her weaves were so good many men still had no idea the long hair they loved on their women came out of a plastic bag. Vanessa's first motto was: you bought it—it's yours, so wear it with fucking pride! Her second was: don't be cheap and try to wash your fucking weave at home yourself—bring it and let me hook it up for you real!

She wasn't pissed off that Lester had charged the guys—her pussy was worth the money. She wasn't pissed off that he had taped the action—she'd always wanted to be a movie star and damn she looked good on film. She wasn't pissed off that he was selling the DVDs—she admired his entrepreneurial skills. But she was fucking furious he hadn't given her one penny—that was just not fucking right!

***

Many couples tape themselves having sex—I never understand that shit! Personally, I don't trust anyone that much. If you want to see what you look like having sex buy some mirrors. A pissed off ex-boyfriend or ex-girlfriend could transmit your sex tapes around the world via the Internet in seconds!

*****

AMANDA

"I don't fucking believe it!" Her eyes nearly popped out of her head as she stared at the 6'4" guy in the Bhatman costume striding confidently in her direction. There was only one guy in the world with shoulders that broad, a waist that trim and legs that muscled! A masked woman in a Bunny costume touched his arm and he turned to speak to her briefly before continuing onwards. Yes, there was definitely only one guy in the whole fucking world with an ass like that! Mr Jeremy Alexander. Alexander, the Great! He sat in front of her every day at work and didn't know she was alive.

"Hi Pussycat, is there a hole in that costume where I can stick my dick?"

Even if she hadn't recognised his sexy body there was no mistaking that deep, velvet voice. She almost turned around to see who he was addressing before she caught herself.

"Where's Throbin?" she drawled, imitating her mother's Guyanese accent instead of using her usual Black British dulcet tones. "It usually takes two guys to satisfy me."

"Trust me, Katwoman, my cock is big enough for me and two other guys."

"Okay, Bhatman, let's go *but* I warn you if you have less than 8" you'll have none of this cat tonight or any other night."

"I have a 9" cock," he boasted and grabbed it through his costume.

It *did* look big and it wasn't even hard yet. She reached for his hand and led him to one of the first floor bedrooms.

"Now drop, unzip or whatever you have to do," she commanded with a crack of her whip.

He unzipped a small, cleverly concealed zip and freed his cock.

Nice! Very nice!

"Okay so it's big," she conceded. "Does it work?"

"Put your mouth on it and find out, Pussycat."

She pressed her stopwatch as she dropped to her knees and took him into her mouth. His thick cock hardened in seconds and she opened her throat and let it slip right inside. She mouth-fucked his cock before she reached into the costume and freed his balls. She gave them some head before she went back to his cock. All the while he was moaning and groaning, clutching at the air with his hands. He came in two minutes twelve seconds. Not bad but she had to work on her technique, she was getting a bit rusty.

"Damn!" He sounded disappointed with himself.

"Don't worry. I'll have this big boy up again in less than twenty seconds," she promised. It took her twenty-four to get it rock-hard. Shit! She was really losing her touch!

"Now where is that hole we were talking about earlier?" he asked as he stroked his stiff cock.

"It's right under my tail." She perched on the end of a writing table and opened her legs wide as she unzipped the circular breasts flaps. "Open me up, Bhatman."

He opened the zip and pushed the flap aside.

"Your pussy is very wet," he remarked as he fingered her.

"Giving head always makes me wet, big boy."

He pressed her back against the desk as he pushed his cock through the opening of her costume.

"You've got a very tight pussy, Katwoman," he panted as he tried to work his cock-head inside her.

"No, you've got a big cock, Bhatman." She pinched her nipples as he finally worked his cock into her.

He stopped, brushed one of her hands aside and covered her nipple with his mouth. She cupped the back of his head and stroked his nape.

Was this really happening? Did she actually have Jeremy's cock deep inside her pussy?

"Damn, your pussy is extra tight. I am going to fucking cum any minute!" He straightened and pushed his cock the rest of the way inside her. Before he could do ten thrusts he came again with a loud, *"Shit!"*

"Don't worry about it, Bhatman." She started to get up. "My pussy has that kind of power over men."

"No! No! We are not done yet." He pushed her back against the top of the desk. "Give me a chance to show you what I can do. I swear this has never happened to me before!"

"Okay, Bhatman. Usually, it's two strikes and you are out, but I'll give you three." She lay back down and opened her legs wider.

He leaned down and started to tongue her clit as he pushed a finger inside her pussy. She held on to the desk and raised her hips to meet his lips as he started to maul her clit. Just as she was about to cum he straightened and plunged his cock into her with one quick thrust. She groaned and came instantly.

"Now lie back and let me take you for a ride in the Bhatmobile." Holding her ass, he didn't give her a chance to get her wits about her before starting to thrust his cock inside her. When he felt himself about to cum, he quickly withdrew. To cover the fact that he had almost cum again, he pulled her up and turned her around. "Turn over for me, let me get this pussy from the back like a tomcat."

He pushed his rigid cock back inside her and whispered in her ear as he started thrusting again, "I could fuck this tight pussy all night."

Yes! Fuck me, Jeremy, fuck me!

She was going to be sore for the next month but she didn't give a shit! The Great was fucking her and the fucking was great! Just the thought of the chiselled face she'd been gazing at longingly for the last three years made her cum on his next forward stroke. He grabbed her ass and ground his cock into her as he came too. He lay against her for a minute before he eased his weight off of her.

"Bhatman, I am so glad I gave you another chance at the crease, you hit a home run, shugs."

"Katwoman, I think this pussy was made just for this cock."

"Superguy told me that last week and today I saw him fucking Blonder Woman."

"You are the only woman I want to fuck in here."

"That's sweet, Bhatman, but I must go and suck on a few more cocks before the night is through. Variety is the spice of my life."

She walked out of the room and left him still stuffing his cock back into his costume.

When he came out of the room she was on her knees in front of Bare Devil.

***

On Monday morning, she walked into the office and found four of her male colleagues huddled around Jeremy's desk.

"Good morning, guys," she said brightly, instinctively guessing what, or more precisely whom, they were gossiping about.

"Good morning, Mandy," they mumbled in unison, and promptly ignored her as they went back to their conversation.

"I am telling you guys, this woman's pussy is the tightest I have ever come across and I have had a few virgins in my time, but that isn't all—when she put her mouth on my cock I came in less than ten minutes."

Actually, Jeremy, you came twice in ten minutes, but let's not nit-pick.

Amanda settled herself behind her desk and turned her computer on. She should be flattered that he thought her pussy was tight. But her tight pussy hadn't been enough for her last boyfriend to take her on an actual date or for him not to marry someone else. Jackson had ranted and raved about her tight pussy but two years ago he had left her to marry one of his ex-girlfriends. He had still wanted to fuck Amanda and she had told him that he could, "if she started taking crack cocaine and needed money for a hit or she plain lost her fucking mind!" Then the bastard had had the nerve to tell her that he had done her a huge favour by fucking an ugly woman like her.

Amanda was no oil-painting and she knew it, but uglier women had men of their own, why couldn't she? Okay her nose was crooked and if a strong wind blew she could take flight like Dumbo, the elephant. She could never find a pair of spectacles that suited the thick lens she needed. And it certainly wasn't her fault that her eyes were the wrong shape for contact lens—talk about optical fucking discrimination!

No one ever seemed to notice she had beautiful teeth and incredible skin—never had a blemish in her life! And if she found a man she could stop comfort-eating and fuck off the excess weight.

She'd had three boyfriends in her life: the first one Lamar liked to use her as a punching bag until she had busted his kneecap with a rolling pin, the fucker was still walking around with a limp; she'd shared her second boyfriend, Freddy, with a White woman until the woman got pregnant and Freddy got married; the last one, Jackson, had never taken her out in public. She had met him at a party, he'd been a little drunk and had slipped her a finger, when he'd felt her tight pussy hug it, he had immediately wanted to come back to her flat and slip her his cock. He didn't stay for breakfast the following morning but the next Friday night he had come over just after ten in the evening. He had fucked her and left just after midnight—starting the trend that continued until he married someone else.

None of them had ever said they loved or even liked her but the one thing they did say was that her pussy was unbelievably tight. Okay, Lamar was her first man so she'd assumed as she was only sleeping with him she should be a close fit for him. Freddy's cock was smaller than Lamar's and he kept complaining that her 'turtle flesh' made him cum too quickly. She'd just assumed because he was born prematurely he did everything prematurely. Then she'd asked her mother what 'turtle flesh' meant. Her mother had laughed and explained that in Guyana the term was used to describe women whose pussies were always very tight. She'd said it was the best kind of pussy to have and Amanda was very lucky. Then her mother had leaned over and whispered quietly in her ear, "You got it from me, honey." But even then she hadn't understood the significance of the 'turtle-flesh' pussy. Her mother, like Amanda, was no pretty gal but her good-looking father seemed to love her mother enough for five men. Growing up, many nights Amanda used to hear her bank manager father talking gibberish when her parents locked their bedroom door and went to bed. It was only when she got older that she realized he did it only when they were having sex.

Jackson was the person who really made her sit up and pay attention. He said he had slept with hundreds of women but none of them had a pussy as tight as hers. She had thought he too was chatting idly until he came back to beg her to let him keep fucking her after he got married. She had looked at him, begging her for pussy like a druggie begging for a hit and realized he was actually going to miss her pussy. She'd taken great pleasure in telling him, "Hell, fucking NO!"

When Jackson left she didn't miss him but she missed the fucking. She wondered how many women there were in London with pussies going to waste *just* *b*ecause men didn't find them attractive enough. Then one Friday night she was thinking if she'd let him, Jackson would have been at her house getting his freak on. *Like that!* the idea for Freaknight came to her. The concept was simple—ugly women who needed fucking could hook up with guys who wanted to fuck. The beauty of it was that the guys didn't know the women were ugly because everyone was in costume. Amanda advertised for women and she didn't beat around the bush. The advert read, 'Women—too ugly to get a man to fuck you? Call me!'

She interviewed all the women personally and any woman she thought good looking enough to find her own cock, she turned down. The women she accepted had to sign a contract never to disclose details of Freaknight to anyone else. Once the women came and saw the number of men on standby to fuck them, they kept their mouths shut—except to give head—and their legs wide open.

Ryan, an old classmate, had designed her website. He was as gay as the day and she had known that fact the moment she'd met him on the first day of secondary school. They had been oddball friends ever since. When she'd explained her plans and asked him to design her website, he told her that he was also going to teach her to give the best head ever, told her that women didn't know shit about giving head. He'd invited her over to the flat he shared with his boyfriend and started his free tuition on his boyfriend's huge cock with no shame in his game whatsoever. He had even wanted her to demonstrate that she understood; she'd convinced him that she did, without sucking his boyfriend's dick. The man had no shame!

Amanda's speciality on Freaknight was giving head. Most of the women came to get cock but Amanda decided she'd rather 'punk' men out as quickly as she could. She had perfected Ryan's technique down to a fine art and whenever they met for dinner or drinks they exchanged tips.

The first Freaknight had had an attendance of fifteen women and seven men but the second meeting held a month later was attended by nineteen women and thirty-five men. The numbers had grown exponentially until Amanda was forced to restrict entry. She now rented a vacant fifty-bedroom stately home in Buckinghamshire on the last Friday of every month to host the event. Admission for men was strictly by invitation, for which they paid a hefty fee—it ensured that only quality cocks came through the door. The women had exclusive membership cards. Amanda didn't pay them—the fucking they got was payment enough!

Her bank balance had been steadily growing. She had already paid off a substantial part of her flexible mortgage and was now even contemplating some plastic surgery. Nothing drastic—just pinning her ears back and realigning her nose.

***

Amanda looked at the clock on her living room wall, it was 7.45 pm. The personal trainer should arrive in fifteen minutes. She had searched the Yellow Pages for a local fitness trainer the morning after she'd had the Great fucking. She was about twenty-five pounds heavier than her optimum weight but when she squeezed herself in her Katwoman costume it accentuated the positive aspects of her body, and hid the parts she didn't want revealed. Mr Fabulous Alexander obviously spent time working on his body; she wanted to be in the best shape possible too.

Phillip, the personal trainer, turned out to be forty-five years old—he had sounded much younger on the phone. But her disappointment was short-lived when he started putting her through her paces. He was extremely good, if she worked with him she would get her body in shape in no time.

Always with an eye for a bargain, by the second week she was throwing in some head and getting the sessions at half price. She decided not to throw in some pussy, at his age even if he gave her the training for free he would still owe her big money. And she didn't want to lose him as soon as she had discovered him, the man was almost twice her age, she had seen the way younger men reacted to the tightness of her pussy—it might give him a heart attack!

***

The next Freaknight Katwoman was keeping an eye on the door, waiting impatiently for Bhatman to turn up. He walked in with two guys from the office, Daniel and Mike. She wouldn't have recognised them if she hadn't personally processed their credit card payments the previous week.

"I see you've brought some friends," she purred, having rushed over to meet them before some hungry hussy grabbed them.

"We heard so much about you, we had to come and see you for ourselves," said Mike, Mr Charm himself!

"Okay, whip them out and let me see."

The two guys quickly presented their cocks for her inspection.

"I am afraid you don't pass the test." She touched Mike's medium cock with the end of her whip dismissively. She didn't like the arrogant fucker and would have found some excuse not to let him fuck her. She had once heard him tell another colleague at work that when God was handing out ugliness she was so greedy she went for a double portion!

She stroked Daniel's slightly fatter cock with her whip. "Nice. You can have some pussy."

Jeremy was standing there looking at her expectantly. "Well, I've had you already so I don't think I'll be giving you any pussy tonight." She suppressed a laugh as his face fell. "But maybe I'll let you keep my ass warm while he's fucking my pussy."

He smiled as she took him and Daniel by the hand. She started walking towards an empty bedroom before she turned and looked back at Mike. "His cock is big, I might need something to bite down on while he's fucking my ass, so you may as well bring your small cock."

Mike followed reluctantly.

She pushed Daniel onto the bed and took his cock into her mouth, he was rock-hard in seconds. "Keep that hard for me, I'll be back."

Obediently he grabbed his cock and started to stroke it.

"While you are here you may as well make yourself useful and eat some pussy." She opened her cat flap and pulled Mike's head into her crotch, then she beckoned Jeremy closer. "Come over, big boy. Let me speak to your microphone."

She looked down at Mike as he ate her pussy expertly. "You are lousy at eating pussy, see if you can do a better job rimming my asshole."

She took Jeremy deep in her mouth as Mike started tonguing her asshole. She had to bite her moans in, Mike was very good but she would never let him know, he was too fucking conceited already.

"Now, cocks at the ready, let's have some fun." She pulled Jeremy's stiff cock out her mouth and climbed onto Daniel.

"Arrgh!" The way Daniel groaned anyone would think she tried to put her cock into him and not vice versa. She decided she didn't want to fuck him after all. She pulled herself off the head of his cock and took it into her mouth.

He came in one minute, forty-seven seconds. Not bad but she could do better.

"You, big boy, get to that ass." She pointed to Jeremy before she turned and looked at Mike. "*You*, bring that cock for me to bite on."

Mike came over and stood in front of her as Jeremy put his cock against her asshole. She took Mike's cock in her mouth and started her stop watch. She was hoping for a new record as she put her hand on his balls and sucked on his cock. Ninety-three seconds—a new record and she decided not to swallow. She pulled her mouth away and held his cock like it was something rotten as he spurted the rest of his spunk onto the polished floor. "Your cum's rancid, you better let a doctor check you out."

Jeremy, in the meantime, was making no headway with her asshole because she kept it tightly clenched. She'd never had anal sex—she was saving her ass for her old age, in case her pussy lost some of its power. Though, her mother swore the 'turtle-flesh' pussy remained tight until death, so she might be able to hold on to her ass-cherry indefinitely.

"You two guys excuse me," she said to Daniel and Mike. "I want to be alone with big boy here."

As soon as they had slunk out of the room, she pulled her ass away from Jeremy. "Next time don't bring your lame friends. One screamed like a bitch before I got my pussy on the head of his cock properly and the other one now holds the record for rapid fire."

"Okay." He looked at her uncertainly, wondering if that was his lot for the night.

"Now eat my pussy right and *maybe* I let you fuck it afterwards. I want to cum at least twice before you stick your big dick in me."

She lay back on the bed and let him suck on her clit. He was even more eager than last Friday and within seven minutes he made her cum twice.

"Okay, big boy, you got the pussy nice and wet, so fuck it." She loved having him obey her every command.

He put his cock against her and pushed the head inside her.

"Damn, Katwoman, where did you get this pussy from?" he groaned as her pussy grabbed his cock in its jaws and held on.

"I bought it in a pet shop," she told him as she found his nipples through his costume and tweaked them. "You want to buy one?"

"I want to buy this one," he groaned again as he thrust his cock inside her, pulled it back and paused.

"The shop had lots of other pussies; some of them were much cuter, some of them were even fluffier. Why buy this one when you can go and choose any one you like?"

"Another one wouldn't bite like this one." He bared his teeth as he tried to stop himself from cumming.

"I guess you are right, I trained this pussy to be a wild cat!" She swiftly rotated her hips and he came seconds later.

"God! Your pussy is turning me into a teenaged boy!" Jeremy couldn't understand it—he was Mr Control and this woman was making him cum at will.

"Shugs, you know you're always better the second time around," she soothed as she sat up and wrapped her lips around his cock.

***

"That woman's a bitch! I can't believe you made me pay all that money just to be insulted."

Amanda smiled as she listened to Mike's words.

"I don't know why you keep going on about Katwoman—you got your money's worth of *other* pussy." Jeremy put his hand behind his head and stretched lazily.

"Yes, but the bitch spoiled the night for me."

"Well, I had a great time myself—the other women were *very* eager to please," Daniel piped in. "You were right about her pussy and that mouth of hers though. If I go back I'll stay far away from her."

"Well, I am not going back!"

No one wants you back anyway, Mike.

"I can't get enough of that pussy of hers. I'll keep going back until she gives me her number," Jeremy said, with a little smile.

"When the bitch dumps you don't ask me to help you drown your sorrows." Mike walked away in disgust.

Have you made that appointment with your doctor yet, Mikey?

Amanda smiled. She'd always tried to be pleasant hoping that people would say, 'she is not pretty but at least she's nice'. Her Katsuit allowed her to be a superbitch, and it felt so fucking good!

"Mandy, can you get me a coffee?" She looked up. Jeremy was holding up his cup, looking expectantly across at her. She looked blankly back at him and he continued, "You make it just the way I like."

The *only* time he ever spoke to her was when he wanted a cup of coffee.

"Get it your damn self!" she hissed at him, leaning over the workstation. He almost fell off his chair. "And my fucking name is Amanda!"

"Sorry!" He smiled at her in apology. "Can I get you one?"

"Yes, please." She smiled in return and handed him her cup. "Cream, no sugar."

She couldn't believe he'd asked her if she wanted a cuppa after she hissed at him like a snake! This bitching thing was working better than she'd imagined.

By the end of the day she saw the rest of their colleagues looking over at her and Jeremy strangely. They were so used to him completely ignoring her, everyone was curious when he suddenly started talking to her.

***

By the next Freaknight she and Jeremy were actually sharing jokes across their workstations. That evening when he entered looking magnificent in his costume, she decided she was going to give him a nice bit of pussy for turning out to be quite a decent guy after all.

"Hi Bhatman!" She crept up behind him and cupped his crotch.

"Hey, baby!" He turned around and smiled down at her. "Miss me?"

"Sorry, no. Been too busy giving head to give you a thought."

"You know how to made a guy feel bad, don't you?"

"The cattiness comes with the suit, shugs." She sensed she had hurt his feelings just a bit so she decided to stroke his ego. "But I did remember your big cock and the sweet fucking you gave me the last time you were here."

"So are you going to let me fuck you again tonight?" he

asked eagerly.

"I'm free at the moment. Spiderguy just pulled his long leg out my pussy."

She held his hand, led the way up to a vacant bedroom on the second floor and pushed him onto the bed for a 69. She pulled his cock from his costume and gave him the best head she had given anyone since she started Freaknight. She polished his knob for just over ten and a half minutes without letting him cum once although she herself came twice.

When she turned over and opened her legs for him, his cock was rock hard. He entered her and came in six strokes.

"Don't worry, shugs," she commiserated at his crestfallen face. "I'm yours for the rest of the night, so take your time."

He collapsed on the bed beside her.

"Are you going to give me your number tonight?" he asked her as he rolled her right nipple firmly between his fingers.

"I live with a man, shugs, I can't give you the digits."

"What about your mobile number?

"Suppose you call me and he is right there? I can't take that chance."

"I need to see you before next month. Your pussy's got me so sprung I haven't fucked my girlfriend in weeks. When I was fucking her all I keep thinking is that her pussy's nothing like yours. "

"You better fuck her before another man does!" Amanda warned him.

"I don't even care. Right now all I am living for are Freaknights."

"While we're lying, time's a flying. Let's get back to fucking." Talking to him was too dangerous, her accent might slip or she might call him by his real name.

He sat up and sucked on her nipples. She reached down and stroked his cock.

"I would love to see your body out of this Katsuit."

No you wouldn't, Jeremy.

When she went home after each Freaknight she had to exhale fully to peel the suit off her body. It had been a little easier to pull on earlier because she was finally beginning to see some results from her exercise regime but she was nowhere near ready to show her body to Jeremy or anyone else.

"I have never come across a pussy like this before." Bhatman's face looked like he was in pain as he slipped his cock inside her again.

"They are very rare—only one woman in every million has one," she informed him as she started to gyrate.

"Don't move your waist!" He held her hips in an iron grip and started to rotate his waist as he pushed his cock slowly in and out of her.

"Okay, you do what you want with this pussy, shugs."

***

"What are you going to do with two months' leave?" Jeremy demanded as she tidied her desk, six weeks later.

"Have a ball—sleep late, watch DVDs, overeat—the usual things."

"For two months?"

"Are you going to miss me?" she teased.

"Actually I will," he admitted.

"I'll miss you too, babes."

"You better give me your mobile number so I can call you and give you a dirty joke every now and again."

"Okay." She wrote it down on a piece of paper and passed it over the workstation.

"Don't you want mine?" he asked her in surprise as she continued to tidy her desk.

"Only if you want to give it to me. I don't want to cause any trouble between you and your girlfriend."

"You don't have to worry about that, my girlfriend and I have split up. I moved back to my own place last week." He handed her his number on a square of paper.

"Well, it's 5.30—time to go." She grabbed her handbag.

"Do you want to go for a quick drink?"

"Okay."

Was he feeling alright?

Jeremy took a swig of his beer as soon as the bartender placed it in front of him and said, "I want to apologize again for ignoring you all these years."

"It's alright, everyone else did."

"I know but I was sitting the closest to you, I should have made more of an effort."

"It was partly my fault too. I let myself be ignored."

"I can't believe how funny you turned out to be." Jeremy smiled across at her.

She couldn't believe how funny she turned out to be!

"At least you never made comments about me being beaten with an ugly stick or being greedy and going back for a double portion of ugliness," she remarked with a smile.

"You heard Mike's comments?" Jeremy asked, looking apologetic.

"I think he meant for me to hear him."

"I am sorry. But you know Mike."

"He probably has a small cock so he tries to play the big man."

Jeremy laughed. "I can't believe I just heard you say the word 'cock'!"

"Would you prefer dick or prick?"

Jeremy laughed again. "You know the guys think you're still a virgin?"

"Me?" She put her hand on her chest and laughed in

disbelief.

"Yes, once they were even going to try and see who could sleep with you but I told them to back off."

"When was this?"

"About two years ago. We were having a drink at the pub and your name came up."

"What would have been the prize for the guy who slept with me?"

"Maybe I shouldn't have told you." Jeremy's face sobered. "I'm sorry."

"It's okay," she told him. "I just thought no one knew I was alive. I can't believe they'd have a discussion about me when they were sitting around having a good time."

"Actually, I think Mike brought your name up and the other guys joined in."

"Let me guess—Mike said something like: if he accidentally slept with me when he was drunk and woke up in the morning with his cock still inside me, he'd break it off and leave it there rather than wake me."

Jeremy laughed out loud. "Amanda, you are insane. I can't believe you sat at your desk for three years and kept your mouth shut! All the guys in the office are scared of you now. Mike even says you remind him of a woman we met a while back."

Shit!

"What woman?" she asked nonchalantly.

"We went to a sort of meeting and the woman really insulted him." Amanda liked the way he neatly avoided telling her about Freaknight. "Actually it was good to see someone give him a bit of his own medicine."

She looked at her watch, drained her glass and reluctantly got to her feet. "Jeremy, I have to go. I have someone coming over later."

"I'll call you." He got up and kissed her cheek before

she left.

***

"Come on Amanda! One, two, three—" Phillip broke off as her mobile phone rang. "Switch that damn thing off!"

It was ten thirty in the morning and she was already covered in a thin film of perspiration. She checked the number—it was the office and the only person there who had her mobile number was Jeremy.

"Just give me a minute, Phillip." She headed for the bedroom as she pressed the button to take the call. "Hello?"

"Hi! You sound out of breath." Jeremy's sexy voice sounded like brown velvet.

"I was in the middle of a workout."

Phillip put his head around her bedroom door and scowled at her. She ignored him, so he shouted, "Amanda, I'm waiting."

"Don't let me keep you from your workout." Jeremy's voice was suddenly as cold as deep winter.

He sounded jealous!

"Yes, let me go before he gets annoyed. Thanks for calling." She closed the phone and walked back to the living room where Phillip was waiting impatiently.

"Sorry, sweets, I'll make it up to you later." She promised him with a wink—she was going to 'punk' his old ass out for interrupting her important phone call. She was hoping for a new record too!

***

"You didn't tell me you had a man," Jeremy commented as he ran his finger down the chilled glass of beer in front of him.

"You never asked me."

He had called her every day since the day Phillip had rudely interrupted their phone call. This morning he had asked her if she wanted to meet for a drink after he'd finished work, as they had done the previous Friday evening.

"So, is it serious?"

She shrugged and took a sip of her Bacardi and coke. "We are not married. Why do you want to know anyway?"

"I was just curious." He shrugged.

"Curiosity killed the cat, big boy," she drawled, Katwomanesque.

His head snapped up but she looked innocently back at him and he relaxed again.

"How is work?" she asked, changing the topic.

"Boring as hell without you, I can't imagine why you need a two-month vacation."

"I hadn't taken any leave since I started working with the company. My annual leave was just piling up."

"But you could have taken it a week at a time."

"You are just annoyed because you have to work harder in my absence."

"No," he denied, holding her gaze. "I miss you. The days just seem to drag on without you there to give me one of your wisecracks. Mike's been saying that I look like a lost dog without my bitch."

She smiled and suggested, "We could meet again for a drink next Friday."

"Actually I have to be somewhere next Friday."

Me too, big boy.

"Okay then, maybe the Friday after that."

"I guess you'd be too busy with your man to meet me on Saturday instead."

"*Much* too busy." She couldn't believe she just said that! It was as close to a date as she was going to get with the Great and she'd turned it down!

He nodded, raised his glass and took a good swig.

"I'm on a losing streak at the moment. I am interested in two women and they both already have men."

"Why did you break up with your girlfriend?"

"We've always had an open relationship yet when I told her about a woman I'd slept with recently who has the tightest pussy known to man, she asked me to pack my things."

"That'll do it every time."

"Is your man jealous?" he asked, gesturing a repeat round to the bartender.

"As soon as I find one, I will let you know."

"Amanda, do you have a man or not?"

"I am not seeing anyone at the moment."

"So who was the guy on Monday?"

"Just a man I used to pay to give me a regular workout."

"You used to pay a man for *sex*?"

"Why? Would you have fucked me for *free*?"

"Why can't you ever give a straight answer?" Jeremy asked in exasperation and took another gulp of his beer.

"Okay. The guy was my personal trainer but I used to give him head."

She almost ended up with a faceful of beer as Jeremy choked. "You're joking right?"

"No, I am *very* serious. I used to workout with him six days a week and only had to pay him half price. I saved over a hundred pounds by giving him head once a week."

Jeremy sat looking at her as if she'd grown another head.

"If you ever need head, let me know, I'll give you some," she continued casually.

"Amanda, please be serious!"

"I am serious."

"Are you saying you'd suck my cock for me, *just like that*?"

"Yes, but I wouldn't give you any pussy."

"My place or yours?" Jeremy obviously thought she was joking.

"Let's go to your place." She got up, pulled on her jacket and stood looking down at him expectantly. "That way if you miss my mouth *you'll* have to clean the mess up afterwards, not me."

Jeremy stared up at her. "Amanda, don't jerk my strings. I haven't had sex in almost three weeks, I am like a firecracker."

"So let's get out of here before you explode."

Forty minutes later, as soon as they walked into his flat, she pushed him into a chair and knelt in front of it. She quickly opened his trousers and pulled his erect cock out of his boxers.

"Stay well back, let me handle this firecracker—I have been specially trained to defuse explosive devices." She ran her tongue around the head and gathered a drop of his pre-cum. "Tasty."

When she slid his cock into her throat he moaned and put both his hands on her head. She prolonged the 'heading'. She didn't want him to associate it with her fast and nasty performances at Freaknight but she wanted it to be equally good.

He took the hairpins out of her hair one at a time and ran his fingers through her almost waist-length hair as he moaned her name repeatedly. Every time he seemed set to cum she stopped, until finally he couldn't take it anymore, he gripped her head, pushed his cock deep into her throat and exploded.

"Fuck!" he said loudly as he shot the last spurt of his cum down her throat.

She gave his cock a last lick and smiled up at him. "I assume that means you liked it?"

"Fuck!" he said again and leaned back against the chair. "Where did you learn to give head like that?"

"I took a short, intensive course." She looked at her

watch. "I don't want to miss Law and Order, would you like a second spit and polish or—"

"Fuck, yes!" he agreed eagerly.

***

"So Bhatman, you missed me?"

He spun around and looked down at Katwoman, his lips parted in a sexy smile.

"A bit, but I got some head last Friday that was as good as yours."

"I give the best head in London," she bragged. "The only person who could give you better head is another man and I didn't think you swung both ways."

"It was another woman and she was *very* good."

"The bitch must be ugly," she taunted.

"She is not ugly."

"Did you see her in the light?" She couldn't resist the opportunity to find out exactly what he thought of her.

"She is my work colleague."

"Still sounds ugly to me."

"She has perfect skin, a great smile and a sexy body."

She was a little disappointed that he didn't say that she was pretty, yet glad in a way that he had been honest. At least he had noticed her best features and thought her body was sexy. She smiled. "Let's find a bedroom so you can compare our techniques."

She led him to a nearby bedroom but backed out when she realized that it was already occupied. Some women didn't bother to lock the door or use the '**Don't disturb—I'm fucking**' signs Amanda had specially commissioned. The exhibitionist bitch on the bed had probably wanted witnesses to her three-in-one feat; a cock in every opening except for ears and nose.

The next bedroom was free. Amanda pushed Bhatman down onto the bed and freed his cock. She deliberately used a similar technique to the one she'd used the previous Friday and sensed his total confusion. Before he came, she sat up and commanded him to eat her pussy. When he straightened up to stick his cock in her she said, "Enjoy this pussy because I won't be here the next time."

"Why not?"

"I fancy a night-in with my man."

He pulled his cock back and tried to stuff it into his costume.

"What's the matter now?" she demanded.

"I am tired of playing games with you." He turned and walked out of the room.

Shit! She blew it! She had hoped to get a last round of cock before she checked into the Harley Street clinic in the morning. She wasn't going to see him for another six weeks! Scrambling off the bed she ran after him and barely caught him as he was about to go through the door.

"I'm sorry, big boy."

He stood stubbornly at the entrance until she cupped his crotch and whispered, "You are the only one in here I ever let fuck this pussy."

He suddenly grabbed her arm and frog-marched her to the bedroom. He didn't say a word as he pulled his semi-hard cock out and quickly stroked it to readiness. When she opened her zipper he pushed two fingers in her pussy and finger-fucked her as he took one of her nipples between his teeth.

"Oh yes, big boy, yes!"

She decided she was going to let him do his thing tonight. When he pushed his cock into her, she relaxed and let her pussy close gently over it. She wrapped her arms around him and let him drive his cock into her pussy again and again.

***

Two days later as she lay with her face covered in bandages she thought of the sweet piece of shafting he had given her and smiled. *Or* tried to smile. It fucking hurt to move her facial muscles.

She wasn't expecting to be a raving beauty when the bandages came off but she hoped that with her nose back where it used to be before Lamar had pushed it to one side and her ears against her head like regular people, she would look half-decent.

Her plastic surgeon was urging her to have laser eye surgery but she wasn't sure if he had her welfare at heart or was just trying to drum up business for his colleague. He had said she needed some liposuction but she had refused—she had sweated to lose twenty pounds so far, she was willing to sweat some more to lose the rest.

***

Her head still felt strange without the weight of her hair as she walked into the office six weeks later. When the image consultant had suggested cutting her hair short she had immediately said, "no" but the woman had reminded her that she no longer needed it to cover her ears, and Amanda had let herself be talked around to the idea.

Only three of the sixteen workstations were occupied. None of her colleagues looked up as she settled herself in her chair and switched on her computer.

Five minutes later Jeremy walked in. "Amanda!"

He sounded so pleased to see her. She looked up at him with a smile. His eyes widened as he stared at her—his mouth opened but no sound came out.

"Hi, Jeremy."

She could understand his shock—the surgeon had done a fantastic job. He had wanted to give her a slimmer nose but she opted for her old nose less the crookedness. Her ears were against her head where they belonged and she'd had the laser eye surgery. Her short hair framed a face which had suddenly developed interesting angles with her thirty-five pound weight loss. No supermodel but the very best Amanda she could possibly be.

"Fuck me!" Jeremy forgot that he was in an office.

"Your place or mine?" She winked at him.

"Oh—my—god!" Bernice, one of her female colleagues looked like she was about to pass out as she caught sight of Amanda.

Within a minute everyone in the office, except Mike, was crowded around her desk.

"I wouldn't have recognised you on the street." Daniel touched her hair. "You look so good."

"What's going on here?" Pierce, the manager came down from his ivory tower to see what the commotion was. He looked at Amanda blankly before he asked, "Are you new here?"

"It's Amanda!" Bernice informed him.

"Which Amanda?" He still looked as blank as a plank.

"Amanda Knox. She's *only* been working here for the last *three* years," Bernice elaborated.

"Oh! *Amanda!*" His face still had the wooden look and Amanda realized that the man didn't know she existed.

"Yes, Pierce, the *same* Amanda who punched you in the gut when you put your hand up her skirt," she clarified. The man had almost fingered her and forgot. Bastard!

Everyone quickly found their workstations and suddenly got extremely busy. Pierce slunk back to his room and for about half an hour there was complete silence in the office.

***

"I can't believe Pierce tried to feel you up and you let everyone know!" Jeremy was still amused as they left the office that evening.

"I should have reported the old fucker or sued the

company!"

"How long ago was this?"

"It happened a week after I'd joined the company. He asked me to stay and do some extra work and the next thing I know we are the only two people in the office and his hand is under my skirt. I punched him so hard I thought I'd killed him—he went down like lead!" Pierce had caught her at a bad time, she had been in a hitting mood—she had busted Lamar's kneecap only the week before so she had still been in full swing.

Jeremy's face sobered suddenly. "I've been calling you every day for the last six weeks, why didn't you answer your mobile?"

"I wasn't ready for my close-up, darling!"

"I thought something had happened to you."

"Did you miss me or the head?"

"I missed you."

"*Shame* because I was going to suggest going back to yours for a bit of heading."

Jeremy stopped and spun her to face him. "Let's go for a drink. I want to talk to you seriously."

***

"You want to be my man?" Amanda asked shocked, minutes later. "What about the woman you are sexually attracted to?"

"She has a man already."

"Didn't you know that before you told your girlfriend about her?"

"Yes."

"*So* you want her but you would settle for me. No thanks."

"I want you too."

"I see. You want us both?"

"It's complicated."

"Good night, Jeremy. Talk to me when you have simplified your life."

"Don't go!" He caught her hand and pulled her back down beside him. "Okay, I am going to see her next Friday and tell her it's over."

"Don't let me make you do anything you don't want to do. I will gladly give you the occasional blowjob but until you stop fucking that other bitch I am not giving you any pussy."

"If I promise not to fuck her, will you give me some pussy tonight?"

"No, you have to tell her it's over first. Her tight pussy might be sweeter than mine. If I give you some pussy now and it is not as good as hers, you will still fuck her next Friday. You have to take a chance on giving up her pussy for some unknown pussy." He looked so disappointed she decided to give him a little consolation prize. "It's a tough choice, but let me give you some head tonight, it might help you make up your mind."

***

She was feeling fine—the night was young and she could breathe comfortably in her Katwoman costume. She had continued the exercises although Phillip had failed to show after she had 'punked' him in fifty-eight seconds.

There's my man!

Bhatman was just coming through the door, his massive shoulders looking amazing in the suit. She sneaked up to him from the back, as usual, pressing herself against his firm ass.

"Hey Bhatman! Did this big boy miss me?" she asked as she stroked his cock.

"Hi Katwoman." He grabbed her wandering hand. "I need to talk to you."

She turned and walked towards the only unoccupied

bedroom. "What's to talk about, shugs? I haven't seen you in two months my pussy has been crying for this big boy."

"I am seeing someone else and you have a man."

"I was just joking about having a man, shugs. I give the other guys in here head but this pussy hasn't been fucked by anyone but you in the past two years." She took his hand, pushed it into her costume and rubbed it over her pussy. "Feel all that lovely pussy juice, flowing just for your big cock. Are you going to disappoint poor pussy?"

"You told me you had a man, now I have committed myself to someone else."

"Committed—sounds like you are doing time or a crime." She stuck his finger inside her pussy, not that he was resisting. "Come on, shugs, stick your finger in there, feel that wild cat hold on to it."

He pushed a second finger into her and started finger-fucking her as he sucked on her nipple. She stroked his erect cock through his costume before she unzipped the flap and pulled it out.

"Stick that big boy in my pussy right now!"

He pulled himself away, took a step backwards and stood watching her.

"I need to know the truth—do you have a man?"

"Shugs, I swear I'm telling the truth. I'll even give you my telephone number. Don't play with kitty, she is hungry! Feed her your big cock."

He stepped closer, pushed his cock into her and started working it in and out of her. Amanda wanted to squeeze his cock and make him cum in seconds *but* Katwoman wanted a nice long fuck.

Am I actually jealous of myself?
Either way, I'm getting fucked.
Yes, but he chose Katwoman.

***

"Amanda?" She instantly recognized his voice even though he had awoken her from a nice deep, after-fuck sleep. How could he be up already? He was fucking her less than four hours ago!

"Yes."

"Can we meet for a drink?"

"You *fucked* her, didn't you?"

"Give me a chance to explain," he pleaded.

"Let me guess, she *raped* you!"

"I thought she was seeing someone else but she isn't."

"Well I am happy for you. Lucky I didn't give you my pussy then."

"Amanda, I really like you."

"Jeremy, don't worry about it, I'll see you Monday." She disconnected the call.

Well, he got a few brownie points for being honest but none for being pussy-whipped.

***

"Is Daniel a nice guy?" Amanda asked Jeremy casually as the waitress placed their drinks on the bar the next Monday evening.

"Why do you ask?"

"Well he asked me on a date but he is Mike's friend, and Mike's a bastard."

"Daniel is a decent guy," Jeremy admitted, reluctantly.

"Do you know if he has a girlfriend? I was thinking about giving him some pussy after the date but I wanted to check first."

"On the first date?" Jeremy stared at her in horror as though she was planning to murder Daniel not fuck him.

"Well I had been saving it for you but since you are getting it elsewhere I may as well give it to Daniel."

"Amanda, I'm sorry how things turned out. I—"

"Jeremy, don't beat yourself up, honey. I am a big girl, I

will survive."

***

Sunday lunchtime her phone rang. She checked the caller ID. Bhatman!

"Hello?"

"Hi Pussycat, it's Jeremy."

"Who?"

"Bhatman."

"Hi, Shugs. Are you missing the Kat?"

"Yes. So are you going to let me come over?"

"Patience, Bhatman, let's not rush into anything."

"I thought you were ready for a relationship when you gave me your number."

"Shugs, don't get tense. Make yourself comfortable and let the Kat put you in the right mood."

"Katwoman, I didn't call you for *telephone* sex! I thought I'd come over to your place or you'd come to mine for a drink and a chat."

"Shugs, I am a very busy Pussycat but I'll try and squeeze you into my tight schedule soon," she purred. "Oh dear, all this talk about tight and squeezing has put me right in the mood. I'll have to take my drawers off and finger my wet pussy. Talk to me dirty, Bhatman."

"Katwoman, do you realize I don't even know your real name?"

"Shugs, that's part of my mystique. Come on, Bhatman, talk to this pussy. Talk to her nicely and let her know how much you miss her so that next Freaknight she will stroke you instead of scratch you."

***

Jeremy watched Daniel and Amanda leave the office together for the third time in two weeks. He had spoken to Katwoman on the phone twice and both times they'd had telephone sex but with each passing day he realized he'd made the wrong choice. Every time he thought of Daniel fucking Amanda he wanted to strangle him.

The next afternoon he leaned over her workstation. "Are you free for a quick drink?"

Amanda looked up and smiled. "Sure."

"So have you and Daniel slept together?" he asked bluntly as soon as they sat at the bar.

"Only *every* night for the last ten days. He says that my pussy is very nice."

"Oh!"

She tried not to laugh at the look on his face. "Why?"

"I wanted to ask for another chance but I guess it's too late now."

"What happened to the other bitch?"

"I made a mistake and I am going to tell her when I see her. The last time I really intended to tell her it was over but when she told me she didn't have a man, it threw me."

"I was only joking about fucking Daniel. He and I are just friends." She smiled as he reached over and squeezed her hand. "But I am still not giving you my pussy until you straighten your shit out."

"Amanda, I promise!"

"I hope I am not going to get a call from you early next Saturday morning telling me that she fucked you *again*."

"You won't!"

"Shall we seal the deal with a bit of head?" she suggested. *Any excuse to suck your cock, big boy.*

***

"Hey, shugs, I thought you weren't coming tonight."

"Hey Katwoman," Bhatman replied, sounding unenthusiastic.

"Is that any way to greet your woman?"

"We have to talk?" he said seriously.

"Again? The aim of this shindig is to fuck not talk."

"I didn't come to fuck tonight. I want to talk to you."

"Let's find a room, shugs, and let this Kat work the tension out of those broad shoulders."

"All we are going to do in the room is talk, is that understood?" he warned.

"Whatever you say, shugs." She loved it when he was acting Great.

As soon as she closed the door, she dropped to her knees in front of him and reached for the hidden zip in his costume. He evaded her hand and moved away. "Katwoman, I'm serious."

She crawled over to him and grabbed his crotch. He caught both of her hands in his and pulled her to her feet.

"Don't be a spoilsport!" She tried to free her hands but he held them tighter.

"I am not coming back after tonight," he informed her.

"Why? If it's the fee, I'll waive it in your case."

"It's not the fee."

"Shugs, I'll let you come to my house and fuck this wild cat as often as you like."

"Katwoman, if you had made me that offer three months ago I would have jumped on it but now I want to be with someone else."

"Is her pussy as sweet as mine?"

"I don't know."

"You haven't fucked her yet? You risk losing *this* pussy for some pussy you haven't tried? Don't think I'll give you a chance to fuck this pussy again."

"I'll miss your tight pussy but—"

"What about head? Can she make you cum like I do?"

"Yes, she can." He smiled a secret, knowing smile. "Bye, Katwoman."

She waited until he got to the door before she ordered, "Come back here to me, Mr Jeremy Flynn Alexander!"

He spun around and stared at her in confusion.

She walked over to him and cupped his crotch. "Tonight you've done well, shugs, and for that you'll get some *extra* special pussy."

"Amanda!"

"Yes, big boy. If you think Katwoman's pussy was sweet wait until you see what Amanda's been saving for you. This wild cat feels like purr-rring *all night*! ME-OO-OW!"

She reached behind him and locked the door.

"Amanda?"

"Yes, shugs." She held onto his cock through his costume and moved backwards towards the bed. "Let me get out of this catsuit so you can lick me all over."

She took off her costume bit by bit, first the arms, the legs, the breast flaps and then she undid the zip at the back and removed the bodysuit. Finally she pulled the hood off her head. Jeremy smiled when he confirmed that it *was* really her.

"Take off your costume, Jeremy honey. I want to lick you too."

Bhatman unzipped his costume, stepped out of it and stood in front of her. Fuck! His big cock stuck out of his toned, dark chocolate body like an extra limb.

He came closer to her and bent to take a hard nipple into his mouth and tease it with his tongue and teeth before he straightened and whispered in her ear, "I'll be the 6, you be the 9."

He climbed onto the bed and pulled her on top of him. His cock tasted so sweet she almost took a bite out of it. Fucking him as Katwoman had been fantastic but knowing he knew who she was blew her mind. Apparently it had the same effect on him, his cock was so hard one false move and she could chip a tooth on it.

Jeremy grabbed her ass in his big hands and pulled her

pussy closer to his face. She moaned around his cock as he sucked her clit right into his mouth. He meant business tonight! Minutes later, as her pussy was convulsing around his tongue she pulled his cock from her mouth and ran her tongue round the head. She quickly plunged it back into her throat and he groaned against her clit as his cock spurted his cum down her gullet. She gave his cock a last pump with her hand and caught the last drops of his cum before she crawled up his body and kissed him.

"Your skin feels like silk," he remarked as he ran his hands down her back and cupped her ass. He held her gaze and said arrogantly, "This pussy is mine now—no one else touches it and you don't give anyone else head, either."

"Shugs, no one ever ate my pussy the way you do and your cock makes it purr. I love sucking on your big cock and swallowing your tasty cum. Treat me right and I am yours 110%."

"I want to hear you purr, again." He held her hips and placed her onto his rigid cock. He hissed as she slowly sank on to it. "Fuck, Amanda, where the hell did you get this tight pussy from?"

"I inherited it from my mother." She smiled as she lifted herself fractionally and slid back onto him. "Don't worry, shugs—be nice to me and I'll ride you nice and slow."

She rode him slowly for a minute or two, her tight pussy holding him like a cashmere glove. "But piss me off and I'll ride you cowgirl-style." She locked her pussy onto his cock and quickened the tempo of her hips. His cock hardened even more but just before he came she relaxed her pussy, slowed down and kissed him. "So, be very nice to me."

"I will," he promised as he sucked one of her erect nipples into his mouth.

"That's all I ask, shugs."

Amanda smiled. Finally the 'turtle-flesh' pussy had done

its work and it was a job extremely well done. Jeremy was truly and utterly pussy-whipped!

***

The 'turtle flesh' phenomenon does exist and is quite rare. A woman who has this kind of pussy is a 'jewel' among women and can use the power of her pussy to keep a man in her bed once she gets him there. I am not telling you if I have this kind of pussy or not, but let's just say that a few men have cried when I have denied them my pussy.

*****

GERALDINE

*S*he knotted the white sheet around Wesley's hips and gave him the bottle of milk. "Mama's going to do some chores. Finish your milk and have a nap."

He nodded obediently as she pulled the duvet up to his neck.

Wesley was one of her regulars, he came to see her at least once a week and paid her very good money. Best of all she didn't have to fuck him. Sometimes he would cum even before she started to baby-talk him. She'd first met him when she used to stand on street corners in short skirts and high heels, freezing her butt off looking for business. Back then she used to sit in his lap on the backseat of his large BMW and let him suck on her breasts.

She had given up street corners four years ago when she'd had to start jostling for space with a bunch of young Eastern European women. It had gotten to the point where some nights she was lucky if she pulled a trick, but a few of her regulars like Wesley had always come back. Then late one night she'd been idly flicking through channels on her television and had caught the end of a documentary on prostitution. One of the women—a fat, rather ugly, middle-aged ex-cleaner had claimed she made £1000 a week just babying men in her home. Geraldine had thought, if she can do it, so can I!

***

Ten years ago, Geraldine had been a high-flying executive before she had stolen a tiny bit of money from her employers. Okay, two million—tiny compared to the billions the company was worth. The director had paid himself the exact amount as his annual bonus and hadn't worked half as hard as Geraldine, so she had rewarded herself. The company hadn't even missed it until a nosy auditor had discovered it. The bastards had made her serve two years for it. Luckily, she had used most of the money to buy a five-bedroom house in Kensington using a fake name. They had seized her Ferrari and the contents of her rented luxury flat but she had managed to hold onto the house. After prison no one wanted to hire her, not even the clients whom she had done excellent work for in the past, the ungrateful bastards. The money in her safety deposit box soon disappeared after she came out of prison and couldn't find gainful employment.

At 32 and quite beautiful, she'd made good money when she'd started tricking. Two years of prison hadn't harmed her looks much; three years of street walking had nearly fucked them up.

It had taken her some time to build an elite clientele working from home but now she easily made upwards of £2,500 each week, some weeks she made twice that amount. She only slept with a small handful of her clients because most of them had very specific fetishes or fantasies. There were certain risks involved, she had been slapped unconscious by one of the first tricks she had turned from the comfort of her home. The man had caught her unexpectedly, his first slap had left her almost semi-conscious and he had continued to slap her repeatedly until she had blacked out. She'd lost an entire week's work while she waited for the swelling of her face to go down.

Then the bastard had had the *nerve* to darken her doorstep two weeks later. He'd waited just outside her door until she had stepped out to go shopping and had dragged her back inside. She'd smashed her knee so hard into his groin she doubted his balls had ever fully recovered their original shape. While he was bent over, cupping his injured jewels, she had grabbed the riding crop she had used only the day before to punish a school teacher, and whacked him around the head a few times. Then she had pushed him out of her front door, her foot planted in the middle of his ass and called the police to cart him away. He had tried to tell the policemen that she was a prostitute but the size of her house, the exclusive neighbourhood, her posh voice and mannerisms made them think the man wasn't right in the head. They'd promised to take him straight to a mental hospital for assessment. He was probably still rotting there.

***

She switched off the TV and went to see if Wesley needed another bottle or some babying. Once he'd started coming to her house he'd finally told her what he'd really wanted. Now he was quite happy with a bottle instead of sucking on her breasts.

As soon as she hit the door the smell hit her! What the fuck?

Is that shit I'm smelling?

"Wesley?" she called out questioningly as she walked over to the bed. The smell got stronger.

"Mama, baby had accident." Wesley said around the thumb in his mouth.

"YOU SHIT IN MY SHEET?"

"Baby sorry." Wesley started to look worried as she stood at the side of the bed and glared down at him.

"Mama is going to make baby very sorry!" She picked up her riding crop from the side of her bed and beat the little shitter through his sheet-cum-napkin until he started whimpering. "Now get up, go into the bathroom and clean yourself off! And when you are finished, clean up the fucking bathroom as well!"

Wesley jumped up and hurried into the bathroom in his shitty napkin.

What the hell could he have been thinking?

So she let him pee or cum in the napkin but why would the little fucker think she was going to wipe shit from his ass? If he made her late for her next client, the magistrate, she would give him another good spanking. Usually he was a very well-behaved baby, not as demanding as some of the others. He liked to be bottle not breast-fed, which was fine with her because it left her free to do her housework. She stripped the bed and changed the sheet although the shit hadn't managed to leak through the napkin he'd been wearing.

Twenty-five minutes later he came out of the bathroom naked, looking like a big apologetic baby.

"Come to mama!" He was sweet really, and she didn't want him too traumatized, the money he paid her each week came in quite handy.

He came over and sat next to her, bending to rest his head on her chest. She looked at the time; he only had another ten minutes left but maybe she could make an exception today.

"Let me put you back to bed and you can stay for an extra half an hour."

She put a fresh napkin on him, gave him another bottle and baby-talked him until it was time for him to go. When he'd put on his suit and again looked the part of the successful young executive he was, he gave her an extra £100 for being such a naughty baby.

She hurried to the bathroom after he'd gone and was surprised to find it almost spotlessly clean. His shit must have had a pebbly consistency so he hadn't made a mess. She thought of telling him to drink more water and eat more fruit but then thought of him having another accident. Maybe not! She much preferred him to be constipated than for him to mess her sheets up.

She quickly set the scene for the magistrate's seduction and was ready when he knocked on her door.

He put on the underwear she had laid out and then the new size 24 dress, which she had bought from Evans with the money he had left specifically for that purpose on his last visit. He liked to wear a new dress every month—the girlier, the better. He pulled his wig from his briefcase and put it on—the fantasy probably began the first day he pulled it on in his chambers.

Geraldine came in dressed as a priest, a bottle of red wine and two glasses in her hands. She bent to kiss his cheek and asked in a deepened voice, "Do you like the flowers, my dear?"

"Yes, Father, they are lovely." He fluttered his eyelashes at her as he took a long-stemmed yellow rose from the vase and sniffed it.

"Would you like a glass of wine, my dear?" she asked.

"Just a drop, my parents don't allow me to touch alcohol."

"Go on, my dear, they won't know," she encouraged as she poured him a full glass and then one for herself.

She sat next to him on the bed and as they sipped the wine she sneakily undid the dress, reached into his bra and felt his nipples. They hardened as she tweaked them firmly.

"Oh Father, what are you doing? You are making me all a-tingle!" He blushed prettily.

"Relax, my dear. These little nipples of yours are ready for a man's touch."

"But I am only eighteen, Father."

"You are a woman, my child, and ready for womanhood," Geraldine told him as she slipped the high-waist panties down his hairy legs. "Now bend right over, my dear."

She threw the hem of the dress up over his broad back as he knelt on a low-bench and leaned over the bed.

"You have such a lovely womanly ass, my dear," she complimented as she pulled a latex glove on her right hand and poured some lubricant on it.

"What are you doing, Father?" he groaned as she pushed two gloved, lubricated fingers into his asshole. "I am a virgin."

"Not for much longer, my dear," she replied as she pushed a third finger inside him.

"Father, please stop! My parents won't approve," he implored as he spread his saggy butt cheeks so that she could thrust her fingers deeper.

"If we don't tell them, they will never know." She gathered the robe awkwardly with her left hand and revealed the dildo she had strapped on earlier. She finger-fucked his ass briskly for a few seconds and then put the head of the dildo against it. "Now, my dear, I want you to be very brave while I rid you of your virginity."

"Oh, Father, what will happen on my wedding night if you take my virginity now?"

"Your husband will be relieved he doesn't have to do the tiresome task himself."

"Okay then, Father, do with me what you must."

She pushed the dildo forcefully against his asshole and the head slipped inside. They had progressed over the years from her fingers to bigger and bigger dildos because he liked to feel the *pain* of losing his virginity.

"Oh Father, your big penis is tearing my little vagina in two," he moaned.

"Be patient, my dear, the pain will soon go and all you will feel is pleasure as I push my cock in and out of your lovely, virginal pussy."

"I see what you mean, Father." He started to moan. "The pleasure is beginning to overtake me now. Don't stop, Father."

Geraldine fucked him hard, remembering the other bastard of a magistrate who had sent her down for the two-year stretch in the rat-infested hotel at Her Majesty's pleasure.

After he left, she added the £750 he had given her to the pile of notes in the box hidden in her underwear drawer. He paid her £500 for the ass-fucking and the remainder to buy a new dress, roses and vintage wine for the next seduction. He lost his virginity to her on the first of every month regardless of the day it fell on. He had even come around to *lose* it on New Year's Day; she had obliged but charged him double for her trouble.

He was happily married to the same woman for over twenty years and had three teenaged children. Geraldine had once slipped into the back of his courtroom and seen him in action. He had looked a normal well-adjusted man as he sat there presiding over a murder case.

She'd made £1,850 in the last two days. Not bad, and she still had the retired cop coming in two hours. He liked her to dress as a prostitute and then he'd come along and bust her. Very original! Although the first time he had turned up in his uniform she had almost peed herself thinking, *shit, I'm busted!* He hadn't told her on the telephone what he wanted her to do or mentioned the fact that he would be wearing a police uniform.

He liked to clap handcuffs on her and interrogate her for a while before she offered him some pussy in return for her release. Then he would fuck her from behind while she was still wearing the handcuffs, either by bending her right over or pushing her up against a wall. He obviously missed his old job!

Thankfully his cock was small. There was nothing Geraldine hated more than being fucked.

***

Gerald walked into the bar and looked around. His eyes glinted as he spotted a slim woman at the bar on her own and headed straight for her. She looked about twenty-three, just the way he liked them—tender. This could be his lucky night for some young pussy.

"Hi, sweets, what's a nice girl like you doing in a place like this?"

"Maybe waiting for a guy like you."

"What are you drinking?"

"Hennessy."

"Bartender, a double Hennessey for the lady and I'll have a Bud, please."

"I love a generous man." She smiled at him as she emptied the remains of her glass into the one the bartender placed in front of her.

"You won't find a man more generous than me, especially in the bedroom. I am so generous women call me Sugar Daddy because I give them so much sweetness." He took a pull of his Bud. "I give women extra good loving."

"I deserve some good loving. My boyfriend comes home tired from work every night—too tired to give me any kind of loving. Sometimes I think he's seeing another woman but his paycheque's fat at the end of the week."

"All work and no play makes Sugar Daddy fuck your woman. Want to come out to my car for some sugar?"

"My boyfriend's very jealous. He would kick my ass if he found out."

"How would he find out? Are you going to tell him? Because I am certainly not going to."

"I don't know."

Sensing that she was tempted, he continued, "We don't have to have sex. If you let me tongue your pussy, I would be a very happy man."

"*All* you want to do is lick my pussy?"

"That's *all* I want to do. I like to see women smiling, and as soon as I walked in here tonight I noticed that you weren't—that made me very sad."

"How far away is your car?"

"It's parked right outside. We could move to a quieter spot in the car park and you could keep a look-out while I worked on your clit."

"Okay." She downed the brandy and got off the barstool.

He watched her small behind as he followed her out.

Damn! He'd been hoping for a plumper ass as the size of her tits had already disappointed him.

"Let me park over there behind that Red Peugeot," he said as he started the car. "Just take off your jeans and knickers and leave the rest to me."

She slipped her tight-fitting jeans and her tiny thong off before lying back and opening her legs wide. "Gimme some sugar, daddy."

He reclined both seats, squeezed himself into the space and put his lips on her clit. All the talk of eating her pussy hadn't aroused her much, she was hardly wet. He tongued her clit for a while but when he tried to push two fingers in her pussy he couldn't get them in. He wet his fingers in his mouth, gathering as much of his saliva as he could on them before pushing them inside her.

"Give me more fingers, daddy, I want to feel like you are fucking me with your cock."

Gerald wet another finger and squeezed it into her pussy.

Her pussy was surprisingly dry for a woman of her age. Maybe this was why her boyfriend didn't fuck her often.

"Come on, daddy, give me all of them."

"Your pussy is tight, honey, I don't think I can get another finger into it."

"My boyfriend hasn't fucked me in almost two and a half months. Shit, I'm like a virgin again!"

"Open your top and let Sugar Daddy suck on your nipples while he finger-fucks you."

She pulled her short top up to her neck. She wasn't wearing a bra, her breasts were small but droopy. He clamped his lips on the nearest one and almost immediately he felt the moisture start to flow in her pussy.

Why hadn't the stupid woman told him that he needed to suck on her nipples not her clit!

He increased the speed of his wrist.

"Yes, daddy, give me sugar. Fuck my pussy. Fuck it. Fuck it." She lifted her hips off the seat and started a serious 'whiining' against his fingers.

Lucky no one can see into the fucking car, Gerald thought, grateful the car had tinted windows. *The bitch has completely forgotten she's supposed to be on the look-out.*

"Oh, daddy, I'm gonna cum." She raised herself further out of the seat and shuddered. "I'm cum-ming."

When she lowered her ass back down on the seat, Gerald straightened and pulled his fingers out. "Is that enough sugar for you?"

"Daddy, that was extra sweet!"

"I told you I'm a very generous man."

"By the way, my name is Hazel."

"Hazel, that's a perfect name for a woman with your

beautiful eyes. Mine's Gerald."

"Gerald, I will be back at the bar next week waiting for some more of your sugar." She straightened her clothes and opened the car door. "I have to get in before the boyfriend comes home."

Gerald watched her walk to her car before pulling off. She hadn't turned out as he'd hoped. He wanted to suck on a pair of luscious breasts, tongue a nice juicy young pussy and probably fuck it afterwards. He headed for another bar and looked around it before buying a drink. Except for two drunken older women sitting together, all the women had partners. A nice, barely-legal young woman caught his eye but her boyfriend's arm was wrapped around her slim shoulders. No chance!

He was going to have to pay for his young pussy tonight.

He cruised along a familiar street, looking at the bored faces of the hookers waiting for their next trick. He ignored them, he didn't want over-fucked pussy.

Then he spotted a young mixed-race woman and cruised alongside her.

"What's your name, sweetheart?"

"Tiffany."

"How old are you?"

"Twenty." She looked a bit older maybe twenty-two, but she was fresh on the street. He could almost smell the newness of her pussy.

"How long have you been doing this kind of work?"

"Tonight's my first night and you are my first trick."

He wouldn't normally believe anything a hooker told him but he cruised the area often enough to know she had to be very new.

"Okay, jump in and let me take you for a little spin." She looked a little uncertain. "Come on, baby, you can trust me."

"I don't do anal," she blurted out nervously.

"Then you are in the wrong job, baby."

She stepped back hurriedly from his car.

He quickly reassured her, "No, no, I want to suck on your tits, eat your young pussy and maybe push my cock inside it. I'm not interested in your ass."

"Okay." She walked around the car and quickly slipped inside it. "You have a place?"

"I have somewhere quiet for us to park." Gerald started the car and moved smoothly off. "*Never* go to a trick's home with him. I think you need someone to show you the ropes."

"Are you some kind of pimp or something?" Tiffany's eyes opened in alarm as she turned to look at him.

"I'm not a pimp, baby. Relax."

They drove in silence until Gerald turned into a deserted industrial area.

"It looks a bit too quiet here." Tiffany peered into the darkness around them nervously.

"That's why we are here. No one will disturb us."

He switched the engine off and turned to her. "Let me see your tits."

She pulled her V-neck top downwards and revealed a pair of full, firm breasts. Gerald's mouth watered.

"Very nice." He reached over and squeezed her right nipple. It stood out stiffly. He leaned closer and rolled his tongue around it. She moaned and he pulled it into his mouth and sucked on it. Wrapping his hand around her breast, he moulded it as he tugged on her nipple. The nipple elongated and hardened. When it achieved maximum distension he pulled his lips off and complimented, "You have beautiful tits, baby. Turn and let me suck on the other one."

She offered her left breast, nipple already semi-erect. He wrapped his lips around it and bit firmly. She gasped and tried to pull away but he held her tightly, raising his head briefly to say, "Punters are going to do all sorts of things to you, so you better get used to the idea."

She closed her eyes and he took her nipple between his teeth again. He teased it gently until it was pebble-hard again and she was moaning.

God, she really has nice fucking tits!

"Now let me see your cunt." Her head jerked at the word 'cunt', so he re-phrased, "Go on show me your pussy."

She wasn't going to last ten seconds on the streets if she didn't learn fast. She pulled the dress up and pulled her thong aside.

"Take it off."

"I'm *not* getting naked!"

"I meant your *thong*."

She took it off and held it in her hand.

Gerald reached over and pressed a button and the seat slowly reclined. When it stopped at its optimum position he spread her legs and put his hand on her pussy. She flinched but didn't say anything as he parted her pussy lips and pushed his finger inside her. Her pussy was moist and the young folds hugged his finger. He pulled his finger out and smelled it. Her pussy was fresh—she definitely hadn't been fucked yet tonight. He licked his finger as she watched him warily. He wet another finger in his mouth, spread her pussy lips with his free hand and pushed both wet fingers inside her. He tried to kiss her but she turned her head. He sucked on her neck before going back to her breast. He pulled hard on her erect nipple as he pushed a third finger into her pussy, liking the way it resisted.

Nothing like young, tender pussy.

He heard the sound of her nails digging into the fabric of the headrest but she didn't make a sound as he worked his fingers deeper. He wished he had taken her back to his place when they had first moved off, it would have been better to have some comfort while he fucked her.

"Turn around for me, baby. I want to fuck your tight pussy from behind."

She turned and held on to the top of the seat. He pushed her dress up and his breath caught in his throat as he revealed her firm, plump ass. He fondled the fleshy contours briefly, tempted to push a finger into her tightly puckered asshole but resisting the urge. She would be very lucky if her next trick didn't stick his cock between those cheeks.

He rammed his *cock* into her with one quick stroke, admiring her for not screaming as her whole body jerked at the suddenness of his entry. He held her hips and thrust into her with fast, deep strokes enjoying the friction of her slick pussy walls against his thick, hard *cock*. It forced her open with every stroke as he fucked her in total silence for a minute or two, just slamming in and out of her again and again.

"Please stop," she pleaded, her voice sounding tearful. He halted his thrusting and pulled his *cock* out of her. He packed it away and pulled his zipper up. When she turned around there were no tears on her face but she looked very upset. "Can you take me back, please?"

"I haven't finished fucking you yet."

"Your penis is too big. You don't have to pay me, *just* please take me back."

"It's a cock sweetheart, and we are not leaving here before I get some more pussy," he threatened.

"I'm too sore!" She looked at him defiantly. The fire in her eyes made his pulse race.

"If I am your first trick of the night and you are sore, how are you going to survive a whole night of turning tricks?"

"I am not turning any more tricks tonight, I am going

home."

"Why are you on the streets anyway?"

"I got into a bit of trouble back home in Leicester."

"Unless you murdered someone you'd be better off in jail. Walking the streets of London at night is very dangerous."

"I am *not* going back to Leicester!"

"The streets are too rough for a girl like you. You wouldn't last a week."

"Can you just take me back?"

"Here, take this." He offered her two £50 notes.

"Thanks," she said gratefully, quickly slipping the money into her small purse. If she was very careful the money could last her for the next month. Maybe by then she could get a job and not have to turn any more tricks.

"My sister works from home and she is looking for another girl to share her house," Gerald said, breaking into her thoughts. "I think you would be perfect."

It would be safer but she had completely gone off the idea of tricking. "I don't—"

"At the moment she has too many clients and needs some one to help her do housework," Gerald elaborated. "You wouldn't have to fuck any of her Johns but I would come once or twice a week for a taste of your sweet pussy."

"I don't think so!"

"I'll pay for the pleasure and trust me, you'll get used to my big cock once I keep fucking you regularly."

"I'll never get used to—"

"Trust me, you will." He smiled at her encouragingly. "Think about it...you wouldn't have to get into strange men's cars and put your life at risk every night...you would have your own room."

"Thanks but I can't, my friend and I are turning tricks together."

"So where is she *now?*"

"She went off with a guy."

"Exactly, there is little loyalty between whores, and the sooner you learn that, the better. Let me give you a ride home. You can think about it overnight and let my sister know in the morning. Here's her mobile number, call or text her if you decide you want to stay with her and she'll come to collect you." Gerald handed her an embossed card and then started the engine. "Now tell me where you live."

***

"Let me show you to the bedroom." Geraldine took the heavy bag from Tiffany as she tried to manoeuvre herself through the front door. The hallway was painted a dusky salmon and a large mirror gave the illusion of spaciousness. Geraldine headed up the stairs and pushed the second door on the left open. Tiffany followed wearily, her eyes lighting up when she saw the neatly-made double bed in the elegantly furnished room. It was like a palace compared to the hovel she'd been living in for the last five days.

"Thanks for letting me stay with you, Geraldine."

"Don't mention it, sweetheart. It was the least I could do when Gerald told me about your situation." The older woman smiled at her. "Rest for a while, you look tired."

As soon as Geraldine left the room, Tiffany lay back on the bed and closed her eyes. She was totally exhausted; she hadn't slept properly in almost a week.

Last week she was just another nineteen-year-old, living with her parents, anxiously awaiting the results of her A-Level exams and sneaking her boyfriend in for sex almost every night. Then, last Saturday morning she had gone to one of the designer stores in the Town Centre with Mary, a friend from college. They had seen a to-die-for top for £375 and had taken turns trying it on. It had fitted too snugly around Tiffany's bust but looked much better on Mary.

Since neither of them could afford it, the fit was irrelevant. Finding nothing under £100 in the shop, Tiffany had suggested that they check out the nearby branch of Next instead. When they reached the entrance of the store the alarm had sounded and a young security guard had quickly grabbed Mary. Tiffany had been about to help her friend when Mary pulled a knife from her pocket and stabbed the man, just like that!

They had run to Mary's house as it was nearer than Tiffany's. And as soon as they had gotten indoors, Mary had pulled the top from her bag and showed it to Tiffany, laughing like it was the biggest joke in the world. Tiffany hadn't even seen her steal it.

The next day the stabbing was reported in the local newspaper, the guard had survived but the store was offering a large reward for their arrests. The still photograph from the surveillance camera which accompanied the story was very grainy and indistinct but Tiffany knew there was a slim chance someone might recognize them. In the evening news when a senior police officer from the local squad started talking about attempted murder charges Tiffany knew she was in deep shit.

Mary had suggested running away together to London to stay with her older sister, Rachel.

Tiffany hadn't thought to ask Mary what her sister did for a living or if she had space to accommodate them, she had just packed her clothes, emptied her money box and they had caught the late train to London. They arrived just before midnight and caught a night bus to Rachel's place. It turned out to be a cramped bed-sit which she used to turn tricks. She was pissed off when Mary told her she'd brought Tiffany to stay. Tiffany had offered the money she had brought with her trying to appease Rachel. Mary's older sister had quickly grabbed it and stuffed it down her bra without a word of thanks. Tiffany and Mary had shared a sleeping bag on the floor but every time Rachel returned with a trick, they had to stand in the freezing hallway until she was done fucking.

After four days of sleeping like cats, Mary had suggested that they turned tricks together on the street. Reluctantly, Tiffany had agreed. Rachel hadn't used the money Tiffany had given her to stock the cupboards; they went hungry most days. And the jobs in London that Mary had assured her were plentiful were very hard to find. She had managed to get an application form from a high street store but she would probably die from hunger before the interview stage in three weeks and be buried before the actual start date two weeks later.

She and Mary had gotten dressed for their first night on the streets, both wearing skimpy dresses and lots of make-up. Within ten minutes of them standing at the side of the street a young guy had pulled up in a Vitara and motioned the taller, slimmer Mary over. She had talked to him for a while before turning to tell Tiffany that he only wanted one girl, jumping in the vehicle and leaving Tiffany by herself. Tiffany knew Rachel's address but wasn't sure how to get back to the bed-sit. Plus, she had no money to do so. She was still praying that Mary would come back to get her half an hour later when Gerald had cruised by. He had looked harmless so she'd said to herself, *why not?*

When Gerald had first suggested she move in with his sister she had hesitated. She didn't mind doing all of Geraldine's housework but just thinking of Gerald's big cock made her shudder. When he'd dropped her off at Rachel's place her pussy had been so sore she doubted she would agree to let him fuck her again; the man was hung like a horse! She loved sex but his cock was much bigger than her boyfriend's. But four hours later, standing in the cold hallway waiting for Rachel and her punter to finish fucking, she changed her mind. Business had been brisk for the first four weekdays but on Saturday night Rachel's punters had come in an endless stream. Tiffany had finally had an hour's rest just after five in the morning.

After the sleep-depravation of the last four nights, the thought of having a bedroom to herself again was heavenly. Tiffany had sent Geraldine a text and received an immediate response telling her to be ready in an hour. She had sneaked out of the bed-sit with her belongings packed in a black bag since she couldn't find the rucksack she had brought from Leicester, and waited in the nearby bus stop. The guilt she felt on sneaking out gradually turned to anger. She didn't owe Mary anything; it was *her* fault that Tiffany's whole life had been turned upside down. Plus, Tiffany was still hurt that Mary had left her alone on the street although they had agreed beforehand that it was safer for them to stick together.

Geraldine had arrived at eight, driving a black Porsche Targa. The older Black woman looked so respectable Tiffany couldn't believe she turned tricks for a living. Geraldine's smooth handling of the car and its warm, cosy interior soon lulled Tiffany into a deep sleep. She had opened her eyes as Geraldine switched the engine off. To Tiffany's horror Gerald's Range Rover was parked in the driveway of the large house.

"Does Gerald live here too?" she'd asked Geraldine in alarm.

Gerald hadn't said anything about living with his sister. Him fucking her once or twice a week would be hard enough. *Every* night would be a nightmare!

"No, he only parks here because he doesn't have off-road parking where he lives. He doesn't need his vehicle for work during the week but sometimes he collects it on the weekend."

***

Heaven help her if she put her hands on the man who invented Viagra!   Geraldine moaned and groaned encouragingly as the frail old age pensioner pushed his small, almost-stiff cock into her. He came to her every Monday after collecting his pension from the post office. He was well over seventy and his poor wife had suggested that he visit a prostitute when she couldn't cope with his weekly demands for sex.

Geraldine didn't mind him really. He was a rather nice old man. They usually had a cup of tea and a few biscuits while they waited for the tablet to take effect. He had fought in World War Two and often regaled her with his war stories.

After the OAP left, Geraldine went to the kitchen to put the dirty cups and saucers into the dishwasher. Tiffany walked into the room a minute later. Geraldine turned to smile at her and thought, *oh fuck!*

"Tiffany, how *old* are you?" she asked the young woman in alarm.

Tiffany didn't reply and Geraldine repeated the question.

"Nineteen."

"Gerald told me you were twenty but you look about fifteen or sixteen to me."

"I'm nineteen," she insisted.

"Do you have anything that proves your age?"

"I have my driving licence."

Geraldine let out the breath she'd been holding. "Go and bring it so that I can confirm your age."

All Tiffany had done since she arrived was sleep. Geraldine heard her come down and go into the kitchen late last night while she had been with one of her customers but she hadn't seen the young woman since showing her up to her room. Tiffany had looked older when Geraldine had collected her but now the long rest had literally taken years off her face. The last thing she needed was a minor under her roof.

Tiffany returned with her driver's licence and Geraldine confirmed that she had turned nineteen eight months ago.

Phew!

***

Hazel made an effort to impress Gerald the next Friday evening. She looked even better than she had done the previous week but not as good as Tiffany.

"Hi, daddy, I've been waiting for you."

"A double Hennessey for the lady and I'll have a Coke."

"You're not drinking tonight, daddy?"

"No, but you go right ahead."

He wanted to be fully sober, in case he wanted to fuck Tiffany later.

She threw back the Hennessey in no time.

"Daddy, can we go out to your car now? My pussy's been jumping all week thinking about the sweetness you'd be giving me tonight." She hopped off the stool impatiently.

He downed his Coke and followed her out of the bar.

When they got into his car he turned and said, "Keep a proper look-out this time, the last time you got a bit carried away."

"Sugar, your fingers in my pussy almost made me forget my name, how could I remember to keep a look-out."

"Try and do a better job this week."

He opened her top, pulled her bra upwards and sucked on her nipple.

"Do you want me to stroke your cock for you, sugar?"

"My cock is just fine, baby. I am just here to give you pleasure."

"Sugar, I think I'm going to need some cock tonight.

The fingering was nice but there is nothing like a bit of cock."

"My cock is big, I don't think you can handle it."

"Sugar, I've had two children, my pussy can stretch to fit your cock."

That explained the breasts. Damn! He'd thought that he was getting tender pussy!

"Okay, let's go to the back seat."

Hazel slipped between the seats and was up on all-fours in no time. He followed, fumbling with his zip.

"I'm waiting for that big cock, daddy."

"I'm putting a condom on."

He tried to work his *cock* inside her but her pussy juice didn't provide enough lubrication.

"Shit, Sugar Daddy, your cock is big."

"I told you so." He almost wanted to pack his *cock* away and leave her high and dry. "Let me get some K-Y Jelly."

He reached over into his glove compartment for a tube of lubricant and smeared some over her pussy lips. "This should help ease my cock into your pussy nicely."

She tried to reach back and stroke him but he caught her hand and faced her forward again. "If you want this *cock* you have to try and keep a look-out. The last thing I want is to get busted by the police."

"Okay, daddy, give me the cock, I'll try and be a good girl."

He opened her pussy lips and pushed his *cock* against her, this time the head slipped inside her. Her pussy wasn't tight—it had just needed the lubricant, his *cock* slid easily in and out of her as he crouched over her and humped her like a dog in the limited headroom of the car.

"Yes, sugar, fuck this pussy." She started to gyrate her hips backwards onto his *cock* as he cupped her swinging breasts and rolled her nipples between his fingers. "Oh, daddy, I'm cum-ming!"

***

Gerald had hoped that fucking Hazel would have satisfied his hunger for the night. He'd wanted to leave Tiffany for Saturday night but as soon as Hazel had mentioned having children it had put him right off. Screwing her had been a chore. Yet, he had agreed to meet her again next Friday.

He would rather be shot!

He thought of Tiffany's young pussy and his mouth watered. He looked at his watch. It was after eleven, a little late to go visiting, but he desperately needed young pussy tonight.

***

Twenty minutes later he pulled a bunch of keys out of his pocket and opened Geraldine's front door. Silently, he climbed the staircase and pushed open Tiffany's bedroom door. Tiffany sat up in bed and blinked at him as he pressed the dimmer switch next to the door and the soft light illuminated the room.

"Tiffany, I need some pussy, baby."

He walked over to the bed and with one fluid movement, pulled her oversized T-shirt off over her head. Pushing her back against the bed, he lay beside her and covered one of her juicy breasts with his lips as he slipped her panties off. She didn't utter a single word as he sucked on her nipple for a while, nipping and pulling on the tender flesh as he finger-fucked her. He couldn't believe that he'd fucked her only the week before, her sweet pussy was so tight!

Lying back on the bed he said, "Sit on my face, baby, let me tongue your clit."

Tiffany turned and looked at him warily. Even in the dim light he saw the blush that travelled from her neck to the roots of her hair. "Don't be shy, sweetie. Your pussy is too tight, I need you nice and wet so I can get my big cock inside you."

The mention of the size of his cock seemed to help her make up her mind. She crawled nearer to his head and swung her leg over his face. He held her ass, positioned her to his satisfaction with her pussy right on top of his nose and mouth, and breathed her in.

She smelled so fucking good!

Her legs began to tremble as soon as he started sucking on her clit. He carried on relentlessly and she was near the brink in no time. He reached up and tweaked her nipples. She came, moaning softly as he lapped up her tasty cum juice.

"Good girl," he whispered as he pulled her off the bed and bent her over at the waist, tilting her ass upwards. He unzipped his trousers, freed his huge *cock* and lightly spanked her ass with the stiff length. "Your pussy's dripping—I'll get my cock inside you in no time."

He couldn't remember ever being so eager to get inside a pussy! He pressed the head against her and heard her hiss as it slipped inside her. She laid her head on the bed and moaned softly as he slowly buried inch after thick inch inside her, gently forcing it inwards with the aid of her slippery juice.

"Whiine for me, baby," he instructed as she finally enveloped the last of his thickness.

Tiffany clutched the sheet and obediently rotated her hips as he fucked her with long, deep strokes, increasing the tempo with every thrust.

He pressed himself deeper as he came, reaching under her to tweak her nipples firmly, making her cum too. Reluctantly pulling his *cock* out of her, he stuffed it back into his trousers and zipped up.

"Here's your weekly allowance." He smiled at her as he

handed her a small roll of £20 notes.

"Thank you, Gerald." She took the money, stunned. She hadn't expected so much!

"Your pussy is worth every penny, baby." He planted his knee on the bed, tilted her chin up and kissed her, pushing his tongue deep into her mouth. She hesitated slightly before sucking on it.

Smart girl! He would have fucked her sore pussy again for her insolence! He reached down and tweaked her nipples as he continued to kiss her. Her nipples hardened to stiff peaks and he pulled his lips away from hers to nibble on them.

"I'll come back on Tuesday or Wednesday for some more pussy," he promised as he got off the bed and walked to the door.

She was pulling on her T-shirt as he switched the light off.

***

"Was Gerald here last night?" Geraldine asked when Tiffany joined her the next morning for breakfast.

Tiffany nodded, chewing on a forkful of bacon and eggs.

"He is such a bastard! He pays the mortgage so he feels he has the right to come and go as he likes—it really annoys me. As soon as I get out of debt, I will take my key from him." Geraldine reached across the table for Tiffany's hand. "He likes you, so play along for now until we can do better."

"Okay." Tiffany had enjoyed the tonguing and fingering but not his big cock.

"Today, I want you to 'baby' one of my clients for me. He is a tax inspector in his forties and one of my nicest babies. He likes to be breast-fed but he will take a bottle of milk when he is ready to sleep."

***

Tiffany turned out to be excellent at babying the men

and Geraldine was ecstatic—she didn't mind the less demanding babies but the men who reverted to being helpless babies irritated the hell out of her. In particular, the other magistrate and a government minister who were both regular clients—the more powerful the man, the bigger the baby they became—both of them had to be breast-fed and then cuddled for the full hour and Geraldine found it very tiresome. She had thought they'd object to Tiffany, thinking that she was too young for the fantasy to work but they had both surprised her by having no problem with it, at all. She supposed to a baby any woman old enough to have children of her own was an adult. Plus Tiffany's young, firm breasts were about ten times bigger than Geraldine's budding breasts.

Today she had left Tiffany to 'baby' Wesley. It was his first visit after the shitting episode and she'd already decided if he and Tiffany got on well she would let her 'mother' him in future. Nothing like smelling a man's shit to put you right off him!

She opened the door silently and peeped in to see how they were getting along. It was nice and quiet. Maybe he was napping.

Bastard baby!

He was breast-feeding! In all the years he had been coming to her house she had bottle-fed him because he had specifically asked for the bottle. Now one look at Tiffany's big breasts and he had gone back to the breast. She laughed as she closed the door. She would add an extra £50 to his fee for being such a choosy baby.

Her next client was a school teacher, Dexter, who liked her to dress up as a school girl. At first she had worried about him being a paedophile and had checked the school where he taught. She'd been relieved to find it was an exclusive A-Level college for boys, *all* over the age of sixteen.

He gave her complex mathematical equations to compute which she never did. He would then lightly smack her bottom through white cotton panties before he sat her on his knee and *felt* her up. Then, sucking her nipples through her white cotton bra, he fingered her pussy before finally raising her skirt and pushing his cock through the leg of her panty. After almost two years he had only gone as far as pushing the head of his cock inside her—in his fantasy she was a young girl who couldn't take *all* of his manhood. He was in his late thirties and unmarried, Geraldine figured if he wasn't coming to her once a week to live out his sick fantasy he would be on the street harming young girls, so she indulged him at £100 a time.

***

"Daddy, I have a surprise for you." Hazel held up a key with a hotel's tag on it. "I've booked a room because I want to suck on your big cock tonight."

Oh shit!

"Hazel, I don't like blowjobs."

"Daddy, every man loves head. You probably haven't had the right woman suck your cock. When I put my lips on the head of your big cock you will be begging me not to stop."

He knew he shouldn't have bothered to show up tonight, but he had been restless. He hadn't fucked Tiffany during the week as he had threatened. He planned to fuck her later tonight, but just thinking about it had made him so horny he had found himself at the bar without realizing it.

"Come on, daddy, the room's waiting."

This bitch keeps calling me daddy, maybe her father used to bong her, he thought irritably as he started the engine.

He knew the direction to the cheap hotel by heart; he had taken many whores there before and fucked them in the darkened rooms.

As soon as they got inside the room, Hazel sat on the edge of the bed. "Bring that big cock over here and let me give you the best blowjob you ever had."

"Look, let's turn off the lights, fuck quickly and get out of here." Gerald didn't want to waste too much time with her. *Not* when he had Tiffany waiting with her juicy, young cunt.

"Leave the lights on, daddy. I want to see your big cock." Hazel stripped off her clothes in less than a minute and climbed further onto the bed.

"Okay, let me just use the bathroom and I'll be right back."

Gerald walked in to the bathroom pissed off that he'd let his horniness rule his head; Geraldine walked back into the bedroom with a dildo strapped to her hips.

"What kind of twilight zone *fuckery* is this?" Hazel scrambled off the bed, grabbed her clothes to her chest and stood staring at the huge dildo.

"I fucked you with it the last time and you said no one ever fucked you better."

"Bitch, *if* I wanted to be fucked by a dildo I'd buy one in the fucking shop!" Hazel pulled on her clothes with the speed of lightning and slammed the door behind her.

Geraldine smiled as she went back into the bathroom to don her disguise.

I don't need you, girlfriend! I have young, tender pussy waiting for me at home.

***

Tiffany was sitting up in bed watching a movie on the large, flat-screen TV in her room when Gerald pushed her door open. He dimmed the lights and walked over to the bed.

"Tiffany, I need pussy, baby."

She picked up the remote to switch the TV off but he

stopped her. "Don't you want to see how it ends, baby?"

"Yes…if you don't mind."

"Leave it on, sweetheart. "I'll prepare your pussy while you watch the end of the movie." Gerald climbed onto the bed behind her.

She was wearing a short, sexy black silk nightshirt—she must have been expecting him. He opened the top three buttons, bared her breasts and cupped their weight in his soft hands. He tweaked her nipples and they responded instantly.

Sensitive young nipples, not like those over-sucked teats.

He rolled them firmly between his fingers for a while, kissing her neck as he rolled, sometimes moving to the side to take one into his mouth. When he put his hand between her legs—the crotch of her thong was soaked. "Take it off and spread your legs wide for me, baby."

Tiffany slid the damp thong off, pulled her knees up and let them fall apart. Gerald sat back against the headboard and pulled her against him, using one hand to spread her pussy lips as he slowly slid two fingers of the other inside her.

"Tilt your hips up for me," he urged.

She complied and moaned softly as he penetrated her deeply.

By the time the movie was over he was working his fingers smoothly in and out of her.

"Turn it off now and let me fuck you, baby."

Tiffany pressed the remote and the screen went blank.

Once again he pulled her to the edge of the bed, but this time he positioned her doggy-style on the end of it. The moisture in her pussy glistened enticingly in the dim light and he bent and lapped up some of her honey, tonguing her clit for a few moments before he straightened and pushed his *cock* inside her. He couldn't get used to the way her young pussy walls clung to his *cock* and pushed it back against his clit. He rested for a moment without pulling his *cock* out of her, trying to hold back his orgasm. He needed to fuck her young pussy for a little while longer—it was so damn 'moreish'. He started thrusting his *cock* in and out of her again, enjoying her soft moans as he fucked on for long moments. He felt a little dizzy when he finally came.

"Here's your allowance," he said as he straightened and pulled the money out of his pocket. "I have to be up early in the morning, but next time I'll stay a bit longer and see if I can open up your tight pussy a bit—it's still giving my cock too much of a hard time."

He leaned down and kissed her, then walked out of the bedroom.

Five minutes later the door opened and Tiffany tensed.

"Tiffany?" Geraldine turned on the light and walked into the room dressed in a sexy robe. "Are you okay, darling?"

Tiffany nodded.

"That bastard Gerald's been here again, hasn't he?"

"Yes," Tiffany confirmed.

Geraldine came around the bed and put her arms around her. "His ex-girlfriend told me that the brute has a big cock."

"He does!"

"Are you sore?"

"A bit," Tiffany admitted.

Geraldine pushed her gently back against the bed. "Let me soothe it for you, honey."

Tiffany stiffened and watched her warily.

"Don't be afraid." Geraldine calmed her as she pushed her nightshirt up to her waist. Tiffany hadn't put her thong back on and Geraldine's mouth watered as she spread Tiffany's legs and opened the swollen folds with her fingers. "Just relax, sweetheart."

She covered Tiffany's clit with her mouth and sucked on

it gently. Within minutes Tiffany was rotating her hips against Geraldine's mouth and moaning softly. Geraldine pushed two fingers in her dripping pussy and finger-fucked her until she came.

"Is that better?" Geraldine moved up the bed and kissed her softly.

"Yes."

"Men are so rough. I hate them, don't you?"

Tiffany agreed and laid her head against Geraldine's chest. She caressed Tiffany's back, gradually increasing the stroke of her hand until she was stroking Tiffany's breasts and then her erect nipples.

"You have lovely breasts, honey," she whispered before she covered one of the peaks with her mouth. She reached down and massaged Tiffany's clit. She couldn't resist the urge to bury her fingers in Tiffany's tightness again. "I can see why my poor brother likes to fuck you so much—your tight pussy is so sweet."

"I don't really mind him fucking me," Tiffany moaned as Geraldine pressed her thumb skilfully against her clit and squeezed a third finger inside her. "I just wish his penis wasn't so big."

"If he allowed you to stretch first he wouldn't hurt you so much. Look how easily you are taking three of my fingers."

Tiffany raised her head, tilted her pussy upwards and watched Geraldine's fingers slide in and out of her pussy. "They feel *so* good inside me."

"I am here to make you feel good, honey." Geraldine kissed her and then bent to gently tease one of her swollen nipples. Instantly Tiffany stiffened and started to ram her pussy against Geraldine's fingers.

"Yes, honey, yes." Geraldine increased the pace, pushing her fingers deeper and deeper with each thrust. Tiffany came with a loud groan, her pussy tightly gripping Geraldine's fingers as she kept them buried to the hilt. When Tiffany's pussy finally stopped clenching, Geraldine pulled her fingers free, wrapped her arms around Tiffany and held her. "Sleep now, honey."

***

Tuesday evening the government minister breast-fed on Tiffany's young nipples for almost a full half an hour. Afterwards, she brought her dripping pussy to Geraldine, who gave her a deeply-penetrative three-finger-fuck, resisting the urge to whip out a dildo and give her a thorough 'seeing-to'.

Gerald came again on Friday and gave Tiffany another good hard fucking.

Ten minutes after he left, Geraldine heard a tap on her door.

"Come in."

Tiffany entered the room, "Gerald's been here again."

"Come here, honey." Geraldine held her arms open and Tiffany fell into them.

"I think you get sore because you are not accustomed to having a penis inside you." Geraldine opened her top drawer and pulled out a dildo that was slimmer than Gerald's cock but still big enough to stretch Tiffany nicely. "I think if I _gently_ thrust this inside you every night while I tongue your clit, the next time Gerald comes it won't be so bad."

Tiffany looked a bit uncertain.

"Trust me, honey." Geraldine placed the dildo on the bed as she started tonguing and tweaking Tiffany's nipples. Then she moved down Tiffany's body and ate her pussy while finger-fucking her. Tiffany was barely aware of Geraldine pulling her fingers out and slowly pushing the dildo inside her.

Geraldine deliberately left it buried inside Tiffany as she

went through the throes of her orgasm. Afterwards she pulled it out slowly as Tiffany looked down at her.

"Wasn't that good?"

"It was amazing," Tiffany agreed.

"I told you so. If we try it every night this week, by the time Gerald comes back on Friday you should be able to take his larger penis a bit more easily and in a short while it won't cause you any discomfort at all."

"Thanks Geraldine."

"You don't have to thank me, honey. Now let me suck on your lovely nipples to erase all thoughts of horrible Gerald from your mind. And maybe we will practise with the dildo a little more."

Geraldine sucked hungrily on Tiffany's nipples before she moved down to her clit. When she asked Tiffany if she wanted the dildo again Tiffany gasped, "Yes please!"

Half an hour later, Geraldine smiled as she held a sleepy, satisfied Tiffany against her.

By next week I'll be strapping it on and thrusting it up her lovely, young cunt.

***

Prison had been tough after living the high-life but there was one thing that had made Geraldine wake with a smile every day—the young inmate with whom she'd shared the cell. Daniela was a kleptomaniac; she had even stolen things from Geraldine. But she'd a sweet, juicy, young pussy and a pair of small, firm breasts that Geraldine had spent many hours tonguing and fingering. Tiffany had reminded Geraldine of Daniela when she had cruised up to her. She had planned to tongue Tiffany's young pussy and suck on her firm tits in sweet remembrance of her cell buddy and then take her back to her patch on the street until Tiffany had revealed those luscious breasts and that fresh, tight, young pussy. Geraldine had immediately wanted her for keeps.

In the three years she had walked the streets Geraldine had found herself in situations she had thought she would never get out of alive. She had been beaten, fist-fucked, burnt with cigarettes, gang-banged, robbed and brutally sodomized. She had left prison thinking she was tough after having to grapple daily with the other inmates and even some of the prison guards but nothing had prepared her for life on the streets. *So* she'd deliberately fucked Tiffany hard that first night in the car to give her a taste of how tough streetwalking could be—she had been cruel to be kind. Tiffany might have quickly fallen prey to a ruthless pimp who would have thought nothing of keeping her stoned to control her.

Gerald had taken a long walk off a short pier—he had served his purpose well—fucking Tiffany hard so that she needed Geraldine's tender touch afterwards. She had kept his *cock*, just in case Tiffany stepped out of line!

Geraldine had used 'Gerald' after she had found a loophole in the system while she was a City high-flyer. She had managed to obtain fraudulent documents and buy her house with the stolen fund using the name. She'd acquired a taste for young pussy while on the inside, so on her release she started picking up young prostitutes dressed as Gerald. Usually she fucked them doggy-style in her car, paid them generously and took them back. Now she had Tiffany her life was complete. She wasn't going to let any of her tricks get their hands on Tiffany's young pussy, no fucking way. The babies could breast-feed on her sweet nipples but Tiffany's pussy was all Geraldine's. No punter was going to touch it, much less stick a finger or a cock inside it.

She was surprised Tiffany hadn't noticed the absence of stubble on her face while she'd been fucking her as Gerald. They were getting on like a house on fire—Geraldine's face, fingers or dildo constantly buried in Tiffany's eagerly receptive pussy. And Tiffany was no longer lying back and letting Geraldine do all the work; now she insisted on tonguing Geraldine's clit beautifully.

***

Tiffany was very content with her £500 weekly allowance from Geraldine. She bought herself something new every week and still managed to put more than half of it away in her bank account. Breast-feeding was no hardship and Geraldine was always there to see to her dripping pussy afterwards.

Recently, while riding in a taxi she had passed her old friend, Mary, on a street corner in broad daylight, looking desperate. She'd stopped and given her £50 to buy a ticket back to her family in Leicester. When she climbed back into the taxi she'd thanked her lucky stars Geraldine had rescued her. Life hadn't turned out the way she'd planned but she had no complaints. Geraldine was teaching her French and had enrolled her in Accounts classes. Gerald and his big penis were gone, though oddly, she missed him a little. Whenever Geraldine took her from the back, it reminded her so much of Gerald, except that Geraldine's dildo didn't fill her pussy to bursting like his cock used to. Geraldine had said he'd gotten a job overseas so she would probably see him whenever he returned.

She'd never thought that she'd enjoy sleeping with a woman but Geraldine knew how to make her feel good. Plus she didn't have to worry about becoming pregnant. She knew she would eventually leave Geraldine when her craving for a real penis got the better of her, but for now she was building her bank balance and having the greatest pleasure cumming two or three times almost every day.

***

Friday at 9pm Geraldine opened the door to best friends

Tariq and Raymond. They had come to her house to fuck her twice before and they had chosen the same meal on the menu—DP. Double penetration, double penis, double payment but same boring shit!

She wished they would just fuck each other and leave her alone! She suspected Tariq was the bigger faggot because after the first time he had never chosen her pussy again. She was convinced that he only fucked her ass so he could rub his cock against his friend's because even though he always came first, he kept his cock buried inside her to prolong contact with Raymond's cock.

They were both good-looking young men, in their very early twenties. Either could get any amount of pussy he wanted but like clockwork the last two Fridays they had come rapping at her door for a serving of DP. And Tariq, the faggot, had the bigger fucking cock—made her ass sore every time.

She was getting way too old for ass-fucking! It was time for some intervention.

"Do you guys have girlfriends?" she asked as they took their clothes off, both cocks already standing to attention.

"I have a girlfriend," Raymond replied, palming her breasts.

Tariq, the faggot, didn't answer. He stood behind her and pulled off her robe to reveal her naked body. He pressed his rigid cock between the cheeks of her ass as Raymond pressed his into her lower belly.

"Guys, it's my birthday and I don't want to go to bed with a sore ass tonight so let's try something different," she encouraged as she turned and took both cocks in her hands and stroked them. "It would give me the greatest pleasure to see you guys play with each other's cocks."

Geraldine offered Raymond's stiff cock to Tariq but he just stood looking at his friend. She grabbed his hand and wrapped it around Raymond's cock and moved it backwards and forwards. When she took her hand away Tariq continued without missing a beat.

"Come on, Raymond, you do the same for your friend."

Raymond surprised her by just grabbing his friend's cock and stroking it. Within minutes they were really wanking each other's cocks, seeming to forget she was in the room.

"Look at you guys, best buddies jerking each other off and loving it."

They stopped at the sound of her voice and she could have slapped herself. They had been doing so well.

"OK. Now I'm going to give each of you the best blowjob you've ever had," she said pushing them towards the bed.

She wanted them to cum before they remembered they were there to give her a DP. She decided she was going to start with sucking Raymond's cock because if he came there was little chance Tariq would want to fuck her ass as there would be no cock to rub his own against. She wrapped her right hand around Tariq's cock and urged him a little closer to her as she took Raymond's cock in her mouth and sucked on it until it was rock-hard again. Then she pulled it slowly from her mouth, ran her tongue around the head and offered it to Tariq. He didn't hesitate and lucky that she didn't want it back because he didn't offer to share.

She suspected that it wasn't the first time Tariq had a cock in his mouth as he pulled it deep into his mouth and lovingly cupped Raymond's balls.

She quickly moved down the bed and took Tariq's cock into her mouth. Raymond ran his hand up her leg and pushed two fingers in her pussy as he watched his friend give him head. Tariq came first and minutes later Raymond grabbed Tariq's head and pumped his cum into his mouth. Tariq pulled his head back instinctively as the first spurt of cum hit his throat, he quickly covered Raymond's cock and caught the third spurt; the second had caught him *almost* in the eye. He opened his gullet and let his friend's lovely, thick cum pour right down it.

"Well, guys, your time is up."

She'd informed Tariq when he called earlier that she only had half an hour to spare.

He paid her eagerly and she showed them to the door.

Geraldine watched them as they walked towards Tariq's Range Rover and smiled—her work was done. She would be very surprised if Raymond didn't find a cosy bed and bury his cock deep in Tariq's ass before the night was over. She would be even more surprised if they came back next Friday. She didn't mind one bit, she would lose some income but her ass would have a well-deserved rest and she would have more time for lovely Tiffany and her tight, young cunt.

***

I have used the term 'faggot' very fondly in this story, I hope no one takes offence. I think it is a rather sweet little romance and in my next book I will update their story.

*I love the word 'cunt', don't you? It has a wonderful earthy, natural sound and unlike the word pussy, there is no ambiguity when it is used. By the way, calling someone a 'cunt' is **not** an insult—it is high praise!*

*****

INDRA

"*H*i, this is Indra!" She stifled a yawn as she answered the phone on the second ring. Another two hours of this chatline shit before she could log off. She wished she'd paid more attention to the teachers in the classroom and less to the boys in the playground—if she had spent more time studying and less time fucking she would have probably managed to pass more than three GCSEs and would now have a decent job.

"Hi, Indra, this is Paul."

"Hi, Paul, you have a very sexy voice. Where are you from?"

"I'm from France," he responded with a strong British-Asian accent.

She was tempted to ask him something in French, since it was one of the three subjects she'd managed to pass at GCSE, but one more complaint and she would be fired. So she played along, "Tell me about yourself, Paul. Tell me what you look like so I can picture you as you're fucking me."

"I am 6'5". I have blue eyes and blond hair. I have a thick 8" cock and I am going to fuck you hard," he responded, sounding 5'6", dark-eyed and bald, with a cock no bigger than her little finger.

"You will rip my little pussy with that big, hard cock!" she exclaimed, holding two fingers of her left hand in the classic 'up yours' position.

"I want your pussy to bleed, and when I am done I will fuck your asshole as well!"

"No! I have never had a cock in my ass before. Will it hurt?"

"You won't be able to sit on your ass for weeks!"

The phone was disconnected in her ear.

Wanker!

It rang three minutes later. She jerked awake and yawned. "Hi, this is Indra!"

"Hi sweetheart, this is Andrew." A smooth, cultured voice caressed her ear. "Tell me what you look like."

"I'm a sexy Black woman. I'm 5'9", I have 34DD breasts, a 24" waist and 34" hips," she lied. Well, almost. She *was* sexy. She was half-Black, half-Indian, 5'7", had 34C breasts, a 26" waist and 40" hips. She had inherited her height, her smouldering eyes and her full lips from her handsome Black father and her dark skin, small nose and thick, almost straight hair from her pretty Indian mother.

"How old are you, my angel?"

"I'm 22 and definitely not an angel!"

"How naughty are you?"

"Very naughty." She loved nasty callers. It was too much of an effort to speak to the ones who called looking for romance—she didn't have a romantic bone in her body.

"I'll have to punish you for being naughty."

"Please punish me hard."

"Okay, take off your knickers," he commanded. "I am going to push some fingers into your pussy."

"I just loved to be finger-fucked!" she gushed.

"How many fingers can you take?"

"All of them."

"Can you take a fist?"

"I have never tried a fist," she replied honestly, thinking it was better to stick to the truth in case the fucker called her back.

"I am going to fist-fuck you for being a bad girl. Spread your legs."

"They are wide open, Andrew babes."

"Good girl. You are so wet I quickly get all four of my fingers inside you, going deeper and deeper each time. Can you feel them?"

"Yes, your fingers are so big," she moaned. "I don't think I can take your whole hand."

"You have been naughty. I have to punish you."

"Can't I just suck your cock instead?" She loved to mess with their fantasies.

"No! I decide your punishment. For your impertinence I force my hand deeper inside your little pussy."

"Ouch! You're hurting me. Please stop, I promise to be good next time."

"No, I am going to fist your pussy tonight. Stop struggling!"

"Andrew, my poor pussy is hurting. You are tearing it apart with your big, hard hand." She gave a few realistic moans for good measure. "But I am starting to like it. Fuck me, babes. Drive your hand right up my tight pussy."

"Hold still, I'm making a fist."

"Oh no! Your fist will kill me!"

"You've been naughty so I'm punishing you accordingly."

Accordingly? He was beginning to sound more and more like he was no ordinary punter—beginning to sound like he had a bit of dough.

"Okay, Paul darling, do whatever you want with me."

Shit! He was Andrew; Paul was the previous wanker!

"Fuck me with your fist, Andrew. I've been so very bad."

"I am thrusting it in and out of your wet pussy. You like that, you naughty girl?"

"Yes, babes, I can feel your fist stretching my tight pussy to the limit. It feels so good."

"I am really ramming my fist into your pussy now. Faster and faster." She heard him wanking himself, faster and faster.

"Yes, babes, faster and faster! Faster and faster!" she chanted and heard him groan.

She gave him a few minutes to catch himself before she breathed, "Andrew, you punished me so very well. You are the best, babes."

"Indra, I enjoyed fisting your tight pussy. What time are you online tomorrow?"

"Very late. I like to spend the day playing with myself and being naughty, so at night I can be punished."

"Okay, darling, I'll call you at midnight."

"Bye, babes." She made a kissing sound and Andrew disconnected the call.

She logged off and spread her legs. She didn't know what it was about fist-fucking that always turned her on. None of the other fantasies made her pussy wet but as soon as someone started talking about fucking her with a fist, her pussy went mad. She picked up her Rampant Rabbit and switched him on. Two minutes later she was arching off the bed, the Rabbit rampaging inside her clenching pussy as she came. She switched him off but left him buried as she logged back on. She pushed him in and out as she waited for her next call.

The phone rang almost immediately.

"You are speaking to Indra."

"What are you wearing?"

No fucking hello, how are you? Rude bastard!

"All I'm wearing is a bunny inside my pussy."

The line went dead.

Tosser!

The phone rang again.

"Hi, this is Indra!" The effort to be perky almost killed her.

"The name's Bernard and I like to fuck young girls' tight assholes."

"I am so glad because I have been dying for a man to fuck *my* asshole."

"You have never been fucked in the ass before?"

"No, my boyfriend couldn't get his cock inside my asshole because it is too tight, so he gave up and fucked my pussy instead."

"Your boyfriend is a jackass! How big is his cock?"

"He has a medium 6" cock."

"I have a fat 9" cock and I push it in young girls' tight assholes all the fucking time. You should get rid of that wanker."

"You have a 9" cock!" she exclaimed as she slid the Rabbit forward again. "That will be too big for my little, tight asshole. It will rip me apart!"

"Yes, I like to rip young girl's assholes with my big hard cock. I like to hear them cry and beg me to stop as I fuck them hard."

"Bernard, I would love to tie you up and fuck *your* big asshole hard with my Rampant Rabbit."

He hung up.

Bastard liked to give but couldn't take. Sounded like a fucking paedophile, anyway.

She picked up a frosted doughnut, took a huge bite and a mouthful of milky coffee as the phone started ringing. She picked it up on the fifth ring and said in a voice dripping with boredom, "Indra here."

"Are you a dirty fucking bitch?"

"Yes, I am a *dirty* fucking bitch," she replied, suddenly wide awake.

Oh good! A nasty caller!

"Are you a filthy *nigger* bitch?"

"Yes, babes, I am a filthy, nasty, dirty *nigger* whore—just like your fucking *mama*!" She slammed the phone down and logged off.

Racist fucker!

Shit! She had already been warned several times about losing her temper but she couldn't understand why the bastards would pay premium rate *just* to give her racial abuse. If they had any sense at all they would dial any number in a Black area like Brixton or Peckham and just curse whoever answered the phone, at local or national rate. Stupid fuckers!

Her phone rang five minutes later. She was still logged off, so she knew it was the supervisor from the chatline calling her. She didn't answer it as she lay on her bed, playing 'now-you-see-him, now-you-don't' with her best friend the Rabbit. It rang again ten minutes later and wearily she picked it up.

"Hello?"

"Indra, why did you allow the customer to get to you? You should have calmly told him to stop using offensive language and warned him you'd hang up if he continued," scolded cum-wouldn't-melt-in-her-mouth Francine.

"He didn't get to me. I just thought he'd like a little tit for tat."

"Then why did you log off right after his call?"

"I logged off because I wanted to shit."

"That's more information than I need, thank you very much."

"Sorry, Francine. I am so used to talking to the punters I forget myself sometimes."

Prissy fucking bitch! Regularly lets men shit in her mouth over the phone but gets offended when I talk about putting it in a toilet bowl where it belongs. Go fucking figure!

"So are you going to log back on, Indra? Your stats are pretty low and you only have one more day to make up your hours."

"I was just about to log on when you called me."

"Okay. Remember, Indra, we are providing a service. Our callers want you to live out their fantasies not give them abuse. And please try to sound like you enjoy what you do."

"Okay, Francine. Bye."

Indra had been planning to switch her bunny back on and let him hop all over her pussy at a nice high setting. Now she had to log the fuck back on. The job was really beginning to get on her last nerve! She had started it five months ago when a friend told her it was an easy way of making extra money. Since her parents had moved back to Trinidad, she'd used her mother's details to apply for the job so that the money she earned wouldn't interfere with her Job Seeker's Allowance. The agency had told her not to use her real name or give out any personal details, but since she'd used her mother's details she decided to use her real name as her chatline ID. The last thing she needed was to choose a fake name and ask a punter, *'who?'* when he called her by it. She was too busy trying to make ends meet to have time to remember a fake name.

At first she had loved the job, making the fuckers cum in less than three minutes even though she had been warned repeatedly that it was her job to keep them on the telephone line for as long as possible. She liked to stick her two fingers in her mouth and make sucking sounds as if she was giving them head—two or three minutes, next call. When she was in a good mood she could virtually blow fifteen to twenty men in an hour. But now the paltry pay didn't seem worth the sleepless nights and the slimy bastards giving her grief down the telephone line.

She logged back on as she hid most of the bunny in her pussy.

"Hi babes, this is Indra!"

"Is your pussy still sore from my fist?"

Paul? No *Andrew*! "Andrew honey, my pussy is still aching but it feels good."

"You remembered my name!"

Bless! He sounded so pleased!

"Babes, a girl always remembers her first fist-fucker, just like she remembers the first guy who put his hard cock in her tight pussy and ripped it open."

"Have you been naughty since?"

"Yes, I've been *extra* naughty. I let a guy fuck me in the ass with his fat 9" cock."

"You bad girl!"

"Are you going to punish me again?"

"Yes but this time I will fist your asshole."

"Oh no! His cock was so big it took him fifteen minutes to get the head of his cock past my rim and another ten minutes to get the full length inside my tight asshole. It would take at least half an hour for you to get your big hand inside me."

"I have the time, darling."

Now *that* was what she wanted to hear. If she kept him online for at least half an hour she could log off right after— job fucking done!

"Are you going to rim my asshole first? Get it nice and wet so you could stick your hand inside afterwards?"

"Yes, bend right over and spread your cheeks with your hands."

"Let me take off my thong first. Do you want me to take off my high heels as well or should I leave them on?"

"Leave the shoes on," he commanded. "What colour are they?"

"They are red, 6" stilettos," she informed him, looking down at her slim, bare feet. "I wear red when I want to be naughty."

"Yes, leave them on."

"I am holding my cheeks open, babes, slip your tongue right in that asshole and tongue it. Make it very wet."

"I am tonguing your tight asshole."

"Your tongue feels so good in my sore asshole."

"Are you going to let another man put his cock in your asshole, you naughty girl?"

"*Only* if you punish me like this afterwards."

"Right, you bad girl, I am going to start sticking fingers in your asshole now."

"Okay, Andrew babes, but start with one finger and work your way up, honey. My ass is still sore from that horrible man's big cock."

"No. I'll start with two fingers, you bad girl. There, I've stuck two fingers in your tight asshole and now I am vigorously finger-fucking you."

"Yes, babes. Yes."

"I slap your ass for letting another man fuck you. Bad girl!"

"Slap it again, babes. Harder this time."

Don't hurt yourself!

She smiled as she heard him making slapping sounds— his hand against some part of his body. She wondered if she told him to punch her if he would knock himself out.

"Now I am going to give you all of my fingers, open wider."

"Ouch! Aaaah! Sssss! Your fingers are so big and

long!"

"Yes, take them all, you bad girl!"

"Yes, babes, work them in and out of my ass."

"Now I am going to push the whole hand inside."

"Give me your whole hand, babes. *Only* you punish me like this. I love it."

When the line went dead she was surprised. She had kept him talking for an hour!

She logged off and switched the bunny on.

***

Talking about first times reminded her of Jamie Atherton, her twenty-three-year-old Biology teacher. He had walked into the class the very first day she had returned to school after the summer holidays, fresh from obtaining his teaching qualifications and she had fancied the pants off him. She had started sitting up front in the classroom just to be close to him and whenever his green eyes met hers it would send a shiver down her spine, she also noticed that he flushed every time their eyes met.

She had followed him home from school one day, walking about ten metres behind him until he got to his ground-floor flat. When she knocked on his door, only minutes after he had stepped inside, he was shocked to see her. She had slipped into the small flat while he was still trying to tell her that it was wrong for her to be there. Less than fifteen minutes later he was sitting with his head in his hands, horrified that he had taken her virginity. He had begged her not to tell anyone what happened between them or he'd be in serious trouble because she was only fifteen. The sex had been shite and she'd immediately lost interest in him.

Six months later, two weeks after her sixteenth birthday, an eighteen-year-old second cousin of her father's came over from Trinidad to stay with her parents while he was doing a short course in London. The two of them had fucked every chance they got, which was almost every day. Her parents had assumed because they were third cousins they could leave them alone together. Fools! It wasn't as if he was her brother!

After her cousin went back to the Caribbean she started picking likely candidates from the boys at school but most of them were rubbish. By the time she was eighteen she'd lost track of how many boys she had slept with. She was like a clothes peg—squeeze her head and her legs opened. At first she couldn't understand why she liked sex so much, until she met a Guyanese girl who was also half-Black, half-Indian, or *Dougla* as the girl put it. The girl confessed that *she* loved cock too and explained that mixing the two races sometimes produced over-sexed off-spring. After that Indra gave up trying to control her pussy, she let it have as much cock as it wanted—*after all*, she'd thought, *why fight nature?*

At twenty, while working on the checkout at Tesco she met a thirty-six-year-old Grenadian who came into the store to buy cigarettes. Later, the same night, as he was fucking her, she realized that the men who had fucked her best so far had all been West Indian.

Three weeks later the Grenadian walked her home at the end of her eight-hour shift. After he plugged her pussy with his shaft, he demanded that she get up and cook him something to eat. She'd said that she was tired and suggested that perhaps he could order a pizza, Chinese or Indian and have it delivered. He delivered a few sound slaps across her face and she'd gotten up and cooked him an English breakfast at ten in the evening. She debated whether or not to add some spit or pee as seasoning but decided against it. He ate heartily, gave her another good shafting and then started snoring.

When she woke up the next morning she stood looking

down at his fat face, his big, ugly cock and large beer belly as he lay sprawled across her single bed. In the three weeks he had been coming to her house to fuck her, he had never once brought as much as a bar of chocolate with him, and last night he had demanded dinner like he gave her money regularly for food shopping. The next thing she knew she'd had his lighter in her hand, his pubic hair was alight and she was yelling, "Fire!"

He had jumped out of his sleep and quickly put the flames out. She ran to the kitchen and grabbed the same greasy saucepan she'd cooked his fry-up in the night before and stood waiting for him. When he'd rushed into the kitchen she thought he was going to kick her ass for sure but one look at her set face and her hair standing on end changed his mind. He'd called her a 'crazy Coolie bitch' and left.

Her last boyfriend Rodney was Guyanese and a real fuckman. He gave her some sweet fucking but he was also fucking several other women—she had to wait in line for the sweet fucks. Six months ago she had woken up to find him gone after a particularly sweet fucking. Finding him gone in the morning wasn't unusual, he had a baby-mother whom he lived with so he couldn't stay out all night but what was very unusual was the £20 missing from her purse. She had withdrawn £50 from her Giro money earlier the same day and she hadn't spent any of it, so she knew he had stolen it. She had missed smaller notes and odd things before but she'd thought she was mistaken. Once a half-full bottle of her favourite perfume had upped and walked away. She'd thought she had thrown it out with the rubbish by mistake; he had probably taken it for his baby-mother. In effect she'd been paying Rodney to fuck her. His cock was sweet but not *that* sweet! Not her fucking hard-earned Giro money! She'd sent him a text: 'Keep the £19.50 change but never fucking come back!'

Because her pussy was greedy she had let several undesirable men fuck her: some ugly, some good-looking, some Asian, some Black, some White, some young and some old but *all* poor, stingy bastards! She decided if she could satisfy the pussy DIY she would save herself the hassle, so the first thing she'd bought with her pay from the chatline was her Rabbit. Talk about money well spent! She didn't need a man once the bunny had batteries. She kept backup batteries for her backup batteries. And backup for those, just in case!

***

As usual, as she reached over to speak to the first caller of the evening, Indra wondered what she would do if she recognized the voice or worst the person recognized hers. Brazen it out, of course! After all, which was worse calling a fucking chatline or working on one? The person at the other end of the telephone line would be the fool wasting good money not *her*.

"Hi, this is Indra!"

"Indra, I called back last night to finish your punishment but you weren't online."

"Andrew, babes, my ass was so sore I had to soak it in the bath."

Good start to the evening. It should be a nice long call.

"Is your ass better now?"

"It's a little better but I was naughty again today," she confessed. "Babes, I couldn't help myself."

"How naughty?" he demanded.

"I let two guys fuck me at the same time."

"That was very naughty."

"I was wearing my favourite high heels, black with 7" heels." Andrew seemed to have a thing about high heels. "One guy licked my feet while I was wearing the shoes but the other guy took one off and fucked me with the heel."

"That was very naughty indeed! I am going to punish that naughty pussy."

"I know, babes, I'll need a good fisting."

An hour went by without her even realizing it.

She logged off for a quick rabbit-fuck and then logged back on.

"Indra here, what's your pleasure?" She was in a surprisingly good mood.

"You bad girl, did you play with yourself again?"

"Yes, Andrew babes, whenever you punish me with your fist I get so hot I have to go stick my bunny inside me to cool down."

"Are you ready for another round of fist-fucking?"

"Babes, I'm always ready for your fist."

"Open your legs wide. Your pussy is already wet so I don't have to tongue your clit."

"My pussy is dripping. Just stick your fingers right inside me."

"I am sticking all my fingers inside your wet pussy and now I get my knuckles past your entrance."

"Oh, babes, it feels so fucking good, give me some more."

"There, I've pushed my whole hand inside you and now I am making a fist."

"Yes, babes, make that fist and fist-fuck my tight pussy."

"I am thrusting my fist faster and harder inside you and you like it."

"I love it, babes, don't stop. Fist-fuck me! Fist-fuck me, Andrew honey!" She switched the bunny on and seconds later she came with a loud groan.

"Indra, did you just *cum*?" he asked incredulously.

"Yes, babes, you were fist-fucking me so well I couldn't wait until you hung up."

"I would love to fist-fuck you for real."

"Andrew, babes, *I* would love you to fist-fuck me for real."

"Are you serious?"

"Yes." She *wasn't* but whatever floated his boat.

"Okay, I'll think of something. I will call you tomorrow, darling."

"Good night, babes. I can't wait for another fist-fuck tomorrow."

She logged off as soon as he hung up. She couldn't believe she had used the bunny in the middle of a call! Andrew didn't sound like the other punters, his voice was so sexy and sophisticated it felt more like she was having telephone sex with a boyfriend rather than a complete stranger. It was weird!

***

She walked out of the Job Centre more pissed off than usual after signing on for her Job Seeker's Allowance. The bitch behind the counter had tried to get Indra to apply for jobs she didn't want. Indra had found a reason why she couldn't do any of them. She couldn't live on minimum wage, couldn't type, couldn't use computers, couldn't travel too far, couldn't...couldn't give a damn! *Eventually* the bitch got the picture but Indra knew it was only a matter of time before they started sending her on training courses. Technically she should be actively seeking employment while receiving the fucking Job Seeker's Allowance. Just her luck to be born twenty years too late—the older generation enjoyed the dole for years without anyone hassling them, now the stress she was getting for a few measly pounds was almost not worth the bother.

Her life was shit. She needed some excitement soon or she would die of boredom.

She stopped at KFC, bought a Zinger burger and ate it as

she walked slowly home, trying to cheer herself up. As she turned the corner she admired the sleek lines of the shiny, topaz blue Mercedes-Benz SL 65 that was parked in front of her gate. She laughingly wondered if the person was there to visit her.

In her fucking dreams!

She glanced at the driver as she went past. He was a hunk! She licked her lips as she opened her gate and strolled up the short walkway. She had almost reached the front door of her flat when she heard, "Indra!"

Turning in surprise, she saw him get out of the car. He looked like a male model. About 6" tall, lean but broad-shouldered, his business suit so sharp it could cut you and every strand of his thick blond hair perfectly in place. He stopped at the gate.

What could he possibly want with her?

His dark grey eyes made her pussy jump when they met hers as she got closer to him.

"Yes?" She hoped he wasn't someone from the government coming to see if she was a benefit cheat. Nah! The government couldn't afford to buy their officials such expensive cars. "Can I help you?"

"It's Andrew."

"Andrew?" she asked puzzled. Then she made the connection and started to back away from him. The agency had assured her that the callers couldn't trace her phone number. "How the fuck did you find me?"

She couldn't believe this shit! "I'm calling the fucking police!"

"Indra, *please*." His eyes pleaded with her and she felt her pussy clench again as she stared back at him.

"What do you want with me?"

"I want to talk to you. Do you mind if we sit in my car?"

"Why should I go into your car? I don't know you."

"Indra, sweetheart, you *know* me...you *know* what I like...what I want."

Just the thought of it made her pussy instantly wet. She had imagined him older and dodgy-looking, but he looked about twenty-six and was handsome enough to give Brad a run for his money. She wouldn't mind him fucking her at all—it was about time she had some high-class cock!

"You can come inside. I'll give you fifteen minutes to tell me exactly what you want from me." She turned and walked back up the walkway. After a slight hesitation he followed her. She unlocked the door and let him precede her into her flat. "I am leaving the door open."

"That's fine."

"Sit down." She pointed him to an armchair and waited until he was seated before lowering herself on to its twin, near to the front door.

"First, let me tell you about myself. My name is Andrew Farley. I work for the Government as a telecommunications specialist. Two nights ago I secretly called you from the office instead of my home, using a very sophisticated system to override the chatline's blocking service and trace your number. If I had been caught using the equipment inappropriately, I would have been fired." He took an identification card from his pocket and held it out to her. "This is my security pass."

"That could be fake," she said scornfully, not moving to check it, in case he grabbed her.

"I am 28 years old, unmarried and I don't have any children," he continued. "I met my last girlfriend at UCL and we dated for three years, but when I was sent to Dubai on a two-year assignment she married my best friend."

"Andrew, why are you telling me all this?"

Did she give a damn about his ex-girlfriend?

"I am trying to explain why I have been calling you so

often. I used to fist my girlfriend and I have been searching for—"

"You think I'd let you *fist* me?" she asked indignantly, praying he'd say yes.

"Indra, I have been spending almost £500 a week talking to you on the chatline because you are the first person I've come across since my girlfriend who seems open to fisting. I sensed it almost from the first time I spoke to you but when you masturbated while I was talking to you, I knew it for sure. I could pay you the £500 instead."

"You want to pay to fist me?" Indra sat staring at him in disbelief. Talking to him was the only reason she was still working on the chatline. He had been calling so regularly her stats had gone through the roof—her pay had almost quadrupled. She had been really enjoying their fist-fucking chats and the bunny-fucking as soon as she hung up the phone after him.

"Please, don't be offended, I don't think you are a prostitute or anything like that. I just want to compensate you for your time," he said hastily.

"You could rip—" she began, remembering the pain her best friend's older brother had caused her when he had tried to get three of his huge fingers inside her.

"If I couldn't get my hand inside you, I wouldn't force it—not every woman can take a fist. You are young, you don't have any children—it could take a lot of time and patience to get my hand inside you. But believe me you wouldn't forget the experience. I would pay you an extra £500 if I managed to get my fist inside you and £1000 each time you let me do it again." He stood up, took a slim, expensive-looking leather wallet from his back pocket and quickly counted ten £50 notes. He put them on her side table and sat back down. "Just to show how serious I am, I'll give you £500 now. I'll come back Friday at 6 pm, if you decide you don't want to do it, you can keep the money and that will be the end of the matter. But please give it some thought, it could be mutually pleasurable."

He got up and walked through the door, leaving her staring at the notes in a stupor. By the time she caught herself and looked out, he was pulling away from the kerb. She closed the door, grabbed the money and counted it. £500—pure insanity! The notes seemed real but first thing in the morning she would take them to the bank to ensure they weren't counterfeit.

To be fist-fucked was her biggest fantasy but could she really take a fist? Andrew was sitting there a minute ago talking about taking his time, but during their conversations he always talked about punishing her, what if he tried to use force? But imagine what she could do with a £500 - £1000 a week. Give up the chatline for one and stick two fingers up at the bitch who gave her grief at the Job Centre. Hell, now that she was loaded she could pay the bitch £50 and stick two fingers *in* her. Worse case scenario she would give him some pussy if his fist couldn't fit. She was definitely going to give it a fucking try.

***

Friday at 6 pm precisely there was a knock on her front door. She opened it and he was standing outside, looking hmmm! He smiled at her as she stood back to let him enter the flat. He was dressed more casually this time but everything he wore still reeked designer.

"Hi." He gave her a single red rose and a bottle of wine in a fancy bottle carrier, and came straight to the point, "Have you decided yet?"

"Yes." No use pretending—she wanted it as much as he did. "But you better not tear my fucking pussy."

"Indra, part of the pleasure is giving you pleasure—I will not hurt you, darling, trust me." He leaned down and kissed her softly on the mouth before giving her a carrier bag with the name of one of London's top department stores embossed on it. It contained half a dozen scented candles, latex gloves and an outsized tube of lubricant. She looked at him, an eyebrow raised enquiringly.

"The candles are for creating the right ambiance *not* for insertion," he laughed. "I want you to be totally relaxed. The gloves and the lubricant are self-explanatory." He held up his slim hands. They looked manicured to the nth degree, but unlike some other metrosexuals he wasn't wearing clear nail polish. "I prefer not to use gloves, I like the sensation of skin against skin but it depends on how wet your pussy gets."

She gave a low, throaty laugh—her abundant pussy juice had put off a few small-cock men in the past. Luckily her bunny was a good swimmer, else he would have drowned by now because the more he aroused her, the more she wet his poor little head.

"Let's go to the bedroom," Andrew suggested as they stood looking at each other self-consciously.

She turned and eagerly led the way, realizing that she had missed having a man.

"Your skin reminds me of chocolate," Andrew whispered as he pulled the zipper down and slid the short denim dress off her. He put his mouth on her neck and took a playful bite. "Tastes like chocolate, too."

That would be the cocoa-butter, babes.

She unhooked her bra, slipped out of her thong and sat on the bed as he undressed. She watched him hook his thumbs in his boxers and pull them downwards. His erect cock was a total surprise. She wondered why he would want to fist a woman when the head of his hammer cock was only just slimmer than his hand. It wasn't long, about 6" but it was fat and the head fatter still. She'd had a few cocks, okay a few dozen, but she had never seen anything like it! He was tall and slim, even his hands and feet were narrow almost girlish, so where did he get a short, fat cock from?

Maybe he borrowed it from a short, fat man, she thought in amusement.

He kissed her, pressing her backwards as he climbed onto the single bed to join her. He cupped her face, pushed his tongue deep inside her mouth and rubbed his hard cock against her before he moved down to her nipples. She watched him, his blond hair falling forward as he moved from one nipple to the next, still not believing he was actually there with her. She had fantasized about him, masturbated daily thinking about him fist-fucking her. Now he was lying on top of her. Things like this didn't happen in real life.

He continued downwards, draping her legs over his shoulders, opening her pussy lips with his fingers to place his lips on her clit. She lay back and enjoyed the movement of his tongue and let her juices flow, as the sweet fragrance of the scented candles wafted around them.

"Where is that naughty bunny hiding? I'd like to meet him," Andrew said as he pushed two slim fingers inside her pussy. "Hmmm! You're nice and wet!"

She reached under her pillow for her trusty Rabbit. She always kept him at hand, just in case she had a sudden attack of horniness. Andrew pulled his fingers out and licked them as she pushed the 7" Rabbit inside her pussy and switched him on. He put his hand over hers and she let him take the bunny. He pushed it carefully in and out of her, spreading her lips and following the movement of the bunny with his eyes. "I want you totally relaxed."

It's so much better to have someone else bunny-fuck you, she thought as she arched off the bed minutes later as she came.

"Your pussy's so wet!" He pulled the bunny out and covered her body with his. "I want to fuck you first, may I?"

"Yes."

Oh God, yes! She'd thought he'd never ask! She hadn't had a real cock in six months.

He kissed her as he put the hammer against her pussy. "I don't want you sore so I will fuck you gently now. If I can't get my hand inside you, I'd like to fuck you again later with a bit more vigour."

Stop the upper-class bullshit talk and just give me the damn cock!

The hammer cleared everything in its path like a plunger in a syringe. When he slowly withdrew she gasped—the plunger was now going the wrong way!

Andrew stopped. "We will do this later. The main reason I am here today is to fist you and I want to do it in the most favourable conditions."

"OK." It wasn't so painful that she wouldn't enjoy but it would definitely make her sore and she was looking forward to the fisting as much as he was.

He slowly pulled his cock free. It was covered in her juices and he ran his hand along its length and collected most of it. "You are perfect for fisting—your pussy is just dripping and natural moisture is much better than shop-bought lubricant."

He pushed two fingers in her pussy and slowly finger-fucked her while he gently moulded her clit between the thumb and forefinger of his other hand. He slid the third carefully inside her. Her pussy ached but he wasn't really hurting her.

"This might be a *little* painful," Andrew warned as he tried to work a fourth finger past her entrance. She bit her bottom lip and held her breath. "Just stay relaxed for me, honey. If it doesn't happen today we'll keep trying."

She let out the breath she'd been holding, she'd been worried that he wouldn't come back if he couldn't accomplish the fist-fuck today. He pressed his fingers against her entrance and thrust them backwards and forwards a few times.

"You're not ready for fisting yet, but even this far is good for me—most girls won't allow it." His face was rueful as he pulled his fingers out and slid his body over hers again. "Now for the vigorous fucking I promised you."

He kissed her as he plunged his cock inside her and withdrew it quickly.

She pulled her lips away from his. "Fuck! Your cock is almost as big as your hand!"

"I'll have to fuck you often then—" he smiled devilishly, plunging his cock deeper and withdrawing it again "—in no time you'll be ready for my fist."

She held on to the headboard as he started thrusting faster. The plunger made her pussy sore within minutes but after a six-month drought she wasn't about to let that small detail mar her enjoyment of a real cock.

***

Two months later Indra sat waiting for Andrew to arrive, dressed only in a sexy red silk robe and the matching high heels he had brought on his second visit. She couldn't believe she actually had £4000 hidden in her suitcase—hopefully £5000 after she let Andrew finally fist her tonight. She had still collected her Giro payments. After all, she wasn't working—fucking Andrew wasn't a job.

His plunger had been doing a great job of preparing her pussy for fisting and by his fourth visit she'd realized that he could get his hand inside her but she had decided to play Little Miss Tight Pussy for a little longer and make some money. She wanted to visit her parents in Trinidad and maybe see if her cousin's cock with its wicked left hook was as sweet as she remembered.

Andrew claimed that he'd want to fist her regularly but who knew? Once he fisted her he might get the urge to move on. She knew from bitter experience that for many men the chase was sweeter than the capture—enough fuckers had sniffed around her relentlessly like dogs in heat, only to vanish soon after they'd had some pussy. Although, to be fair, Andrew seemed to really enjoy fucking her. Her pussy was still acclimatizing to his hammer-head cock, it made her sore every time but she would be very sad to lose that plunger. Six months ago, if anyone had given her a choice of length versus girth, she would have chosen length without a second thought—now she would have to know *exactly* how long or how fat before making a decision.

He was such a fucking gentleman; any other man would have lost patience by now but he insisted the aim of the fisting was to give her pleasure not pain. She sometimes felt guilty as she deliberately clenched her pussy muscles without appearing to do so when he pushed his fingers inside her, stopping them from going too far. The hour of Pilates she reluctantly did four times a week to control her wayward butt had given her amazing control of her pelvic muscles.

Her doorbell rang at exactly 6 pm and she wondered again if Andrew parked around the corner and waited so that he could arrive with military precision. She tottered over to the door to let him in.

Surprisingly, his hands were empty; he always brought either lingerie, luxury chocolates, perfume, wine or flowers for her. She didn't comment as she let him in.

Maybe he'd had enough.

"Hi, darling." He kissed her and then buried his nose into her neck, breathing in the perfume he'd brought her the previous week. "You look and smell incredible!"

He straightened, pulled an envelope from his pocket and handed it to her.

He was such a fucking treasure—always business before pleasure!

"Do you mind if we go to my house today?"

"Why?" She was dying to see where he lived but this was a bit sudden.

He held her shoulders and looked into her eyes. "You know you can trust me, I am not going to do anything there we haven't done before. I just want to see if a different setting would be more conducive to fisting." He kissed her again, more deeply this time as he opened her robe, cupped her ass and pressed her against his hardening cock.

"Okay. Let me get dressed."

She hurried to her bedroom and pulled on underwear, a pair of jeans and a T-shirt, stuffed an extra thong in her jeans pocket and picked up her handbag.

He smiled and held his hand out to her as she re-entered the living room.

Her next-door neighbour was watering the plants in her front garden when they came out of the flat. Her blue eyes widened in admiration as she took a look at Andrew. Then she noticed their linked hands and smirked knowingly.

"You charging by the hour now, Indra?" she shouted across the hedge.

Eat shit and die, bitch!

"I wouldn't want to put you out of business, Megan, honey," Indra replied sweetly, dying to really curse the nosy bitch out. The woman was jealous because her husband was always sniffing around Indra. As far as Indra was concerned he *too* could eat shit and fucking die!

Andrew opened the car door and made sure she was seated before coming around and slipping into the driver's seat.

Such a fucking gentleman!

She admired the sleek interior of his car, amazed by the softness and comfort of the seats. As he turned the key in the ignition and moved smoothly away from the kerb she remembered her Rabbit.

"Shit! I left the bunny!"

"I think you should leave him home, he might get jealous of the new bunny I bought you."

She laughed at the image of her bunny sulking in a corner as he watched another bunny fuck her.

They got caught in the tail end of rush hour traffic and it took them an hour and a quarter to arrive at his four-bedroom house in Holland Park. He pulled up in front of the cream-coloured building and activated the gate by pressing a button on a small square black box he retrieved from his glove compartment, they then drove up to the garage door which he opened by pressing another button. The garage was bigger than her flat. He deftly parked the car next to its bigger cousin, a black Mercedes-Benz GL 500, leaving enough room to hold a party. They entered the house through a door in the garage and she looked around the spacious living room, her mouth falling open in sheer disbelief.

So this is how the other half lived! Fuck me!

"I'll run the bath." Andrew nuzzled her neck and left the room.

He'd told her that he did some consultancy work for two of the major telecommunications companies in the UK but she had no idea he would be this loaded. His house was worth at least a cool million!

She walked up to the portrait of a couple sitting on a high-back sofa with a young boy between them. The boy was Andrew at the age of ten or eleven, the two adults were obviously his parents. Indra wondered what the stiff-upper-lipped English couple would say if they knew their son had a penchant for putting his fist in a pussy and was currently trying to get it into a Black pussy. She didn't think they would approve one bit.

"I see you've met the folks." Andrew came up behind her so silently she was startled when he whispered the words in her ear.

"Where do they live?" she asked as he moulded her breasts.

"In Cornwall, but we hardly speak to one another. They didn't like my last girlfriend because she was mixed-race."

"They wouldn't like *me* then." She could just imagine him introducing her to them, '*Mother, father, meet the woman I am currently paying to fist-fuck.*' Nice!

"I like you and that's all that matters." He hugged her briefly. "The bath's ready."

She reached for the hem of her T-shirt as he unzipped her jeans.

Sharing a bath was very erotic she discovered minutes later as she lay against him in the large, sunken bathtub.

He fondled her breasts idly. "Are you sleeping?"

"I'm wide awake." She covered his hands with hers demanding a firmer touch and he obliged by tweaking her nipples for a few minutes.

"Good. Let's go to bed." He slipped out from behind her and pulled on a large thick bathrobe. Her body felt heavy as she stepped out of the water—she wasn't used to having baths, her flat only had a tiny shower cubicle.

"Now I feel sleepy," she complained.

"Don't worry, I'll keep you awake," Andrew promised as he wrapped the ends of the robe around her. His cock stirred against her ass and she reached back to stroke it, making him groan. "Let's try the fisting before I give in to the urge to tumble you onto the floor and fuck you right now."

She smiled as he led her into his spacious bedroom; he had certainly loosened up in the weeks since he had met her—now he fucked her without asking first!

The candles were already lit and he had scattered rose petals all over the bed. In the middle of the petals lay her ultimate rabbit—the Three Way Rabbit!

"How did you know I wanted one?"

"Wild guess." Andrew smiled at the excitement on her face. "Let's try him."

Within minutes she had the bunny on the perfect setting. She handed him to Andrew and lay back to let him continue working it in and out of her pussy. As she came hard less than a minute later she knew sadly she would have to find a new, caring home for her old bunny. Three-Way was the only way!

Her pussy pulsated pleasantly. Even if she hadn't planned to let him go all the way tonight, after that fabulous bunny-fuck she would have. He moved down her body and slid his fingers inside her, one digit at a time. He got his knuckles past her opening but then it got a bit more difficult. He pressed his thumb against his palm and pushed his hand a little deeper.

"*Ah*!" That hurt a bit.

"That was the worst part…we are almost there. Breathe, sweetheart…just keep taking deep breaths."

Indra took a deep breath. Her pussy felt stretched but it wasn't painful. She felt fullness…and then a momentary easing of pressure.

"You have done it, you beautiful girl." He looked up at her, his eyes shining. He picked up a mirror from the bedside table. "See how incredible it looks."

She raised herself and looked down at the reflection in the mirror. The whole of his hand was up inside her pussy—he looked like an amputee. The contrast of his lightly tanned arm to her darker skin was awesome!

"How does it feel?"

"Incredible!"

"You are amazing. Eventually I will be able to move my fist back and forth—really fist-fuck you and you'll have the most intense orgasms. It will take a while to get you to that stage." He leaned forward and tongued her clit, and she felt her pussy pulsate around his embedded fist.

"Your hand feels as though it belongs right there."

"Yes it does but I'd better take it out before your pussy locks on to it." He pulled gently on his hand but it seemed wedged. "Relax for me, sweetheart."

Indra tried to relax as a horrible thought suddenly entered her head. *What if he can't get it out?* She had a quick, terrifying image of the two of them being wheeled into surgery for separation. Andrew seemed to sense her worry. "You are tensing up, honey, I can feel it. You've done the tough part, this is a breeze."

She forced herself to relax as he tongued her clit and made the smallest thrusting motions. Instinctively, she started to rotate her pussy against his hand as the most unbelievably delicious sensations started running through her body.

"That's it sweetheart, feel the pleasure."

He sucked harder on her clit as her arousal mounted and suddenly she exploded, her contracting pussy gripping his fist. Andrew reached down and quickly wanked his cock, shooting his load just as her pussy suddenly expelled his fist.

"That was intense." If she'd known it would be so mind-blowing she would have let him do it much sooner.

"For me, too." He kissed her softly before reaching into his top drawer. He handed her an envelope as he got off the bed. "Let me get the champagne. We have to celebrate our first fist-fuck."

She lay back against the pillows and watched him walk out of the room before opening the envelope and quickly counting her dough. It would be so easy to fall in love with him—he treated her so fucking well! The money kept her focussed—she would be foolish to think that she was anything more than a paid piece of ass.

Andrew came back with the champagne and they lay on the bed together, sipping it by the soft lights of the scented candles. She was still having mini orgasms every now and again. It was unbelievable.

"When we talked on the phone I never imagined you'd be so beautiful," he confessed as he moved her single, thick braid aside and kissed her neck. "I was expecting a much older woman."

"If I was older what would you have done?"

"I would have still wanted to fist you but I might not have fucked you."

"You would have fisted me even if I was older? Why?"

"Trying to find a woman who will take a fist is like looking for a needle in a haystack. I was getting so desperate I was almost ready to fist a man!"

"You fist assholes as well?" She turned to look at him. _Not mine!_

"No, it wouldn't be the same as a pussy."

"Good! Because no one plays around my ass!"

"Honey, if I could fist your pussy for the rest of my life I'd be a very happy man." He put his glass down on the bedside table and moved down the bed to spread her legs. He stuck his head between them but instead of tonguing her clit, he carefully opened her pussy lips with his fingers. "Are you sore or in pain?"

"No."

He slid his body onto hers. "Good. Prepare for a night of serious fucking."

"I assume you mean your cock and _not_ your fist."

"Fisting is something to be savoured; we probably won't do it again for a while." He sucked on her nipple briefly. "I want to fuck you. You'll have the devil's own job keeping my cock out of your pussy now that my fist has been inside you."

He slipped his cock inside her, buried it to the hilt and pulled it out slowly.

"Shit! Your cock hurts more coming out than going in!" She stopped him from thrusting forward again. "Come up here and fuck my breasts instead."

"Alright, we'll leave the night of serious fucking for tomorrow." Andrew laughed and moved up the bed. She pushed her breasts together, creating a snug, warm space for his cock. She gave him head intermittently as he fucked her breasts and within minutes he was spurting his cum. He grabbed some tissues from the bedside table and wiped the few drops, which had escaped her mouth, off her breasts.

Such a fucking gentleman!

He blew out the candles, climbed back into bed, pulled the covers up and put his arms around her, snuggling against her back. It was the first time they were spending the night together. Andrew's huge bed was big enough for five people, yet he was wrapped tightly around her, his hand cupping her breast. Surprisingly, it didn't feel too bad.

***

The following Friday night, Indra rested her head on a down-filled pillow as Andrew gave her the plunger from the back, the seventh night of serious fucking in a row. As he'd predicted, he couldn't get enough of her pussy now that he'd frisked it and found no concealed weapons up inside. Not that she was complaining one tiny bit.

He hadn't let her go back to her flat since he'd brought her over to his house. On Saturday he had taken her designer clothes shopping and bought her an entire wardrobe, including some very sexy lingerie. While he was at work she'd curled up in bed, flicking through the numerous channels on his TV until she found a programme or movie that caught her interest. Then, just before he was due home she would have a leisurely bath, and be waiting for him wearing one of his shirts or T-shirts, or dressed like a porn star. They rarely made it further than his living room. They had eaten out on the weekend but had cooked dinner together the rest of the week.

Earlier in the evening he had decided that they'd wait another week before they tried the fisting again. She didn't mind, the fucking was very good, her pussy was so satisfied it hadn't played hide-and-seek with the new bunny all week.

But he hadn't put any *pounds* in her hand at 6pm as usual.

It had begun—the blurring of business and pleasure and she wasn't having it! This was business not a fucking love affair!

"God, your pussy is going to kill me!" he gasped as he collapsed on to the bed beside her seconds after he had shot his cum deep inside her.

"It's a good thing I've decided to take it to Trinidad with me next week then." She uttered the words just as they formed in her head. She had enough money thanks to him; she'd book a flight when she got home.

"What?" Andrew sat up in alarm. "Darling, you *can't* go now that we have finally achieved the fisting."

"I'll be back in three month's time, you—"

"Three months! That's far too long!" he protested.

"Babes, you have fucked me and fisted me, what else is there for us to do?"

"I had planned to ask you over dinner tonight but now is as good a time as any." He reached into the top drawer and pulled out a small velvet box which he handed to her.

She opened it to reveal a beautiful square-cut diamond ring.

"Marry me?" he begged.

"What?"

"Marry me, please," Andrew repeated, his grey eyes holding hers. "Give me a month to finish my current project and we'll go to Trinidad together. We'll get married and spent our honeymoon out there before we come back to the UK."

He was fucking serious! He wanted to marry her just because her pussy could take his fist!

Go fucking figure!

***

*I hope this story doesn't scare chatline operators, it is only a work of fiction—I don't honestly believe customers can override call centres' sophisticated equipment. Well, I hope not! And, no matter how sexy the voice at the other end of the telephone line—**never** accept dates from callers!*

*****

NECTAR

I love DP. Did you ask what's DP? I hope not! If you did, you are reading the wrong fucking book! Okay, as it's you I'll break it down for you. DP is double penetration—something in the pussy and the ass at the same fucking time! I prefer two cocks but I will use a dildo if only one of my men is available or two dildos if neither is around. Once there is something in each hole I am fucking happy.

Some of you may have met my younger sister, Honey Comb, in *Bedtime Erotica*. *I* taught that bitch everything she knows. She is tame compared to me; *I* don't fucking give a damn! Both of us inherited our mother's sexy body but mine is better than hers. I have to squeeze my breasts into a 36DD bra, she can barely fill a 36D. My waist is smaller and my ass is firmer than hers. She has a little wimp called Terry; I have two lame fuckers I call Tom and Jerry. I don't even call them by their real fucking names because, like I said, I don't give a damn!

Honey says her breasts aren't sensitive, that bitch is crazy—I could have my nipples sucked all day. Shit, on Saturdays when both my men are home from work we lay up in bed and it's a mouth on each nipple until I say fucking stop! After several hours of nipple sucking I am as horny as hell so I let them both fuck me. They both have nice big cocks. I rotate them so they don't get jealous. They both like to be in the pussy because like Terry, they like to feed on my breasts when they are fucking me, but I need something in my ass so somebody has to draw the short straw.

Tom and Jerry are brothers. I think their bitch of a mother either breast-fed them too long or not at all because I have never met men like them before. I met Tom (or was it Jerry?) first. I was shopping in my local Sainsbury's when I literally bumped into him. He said, 'hello' to my breasts and since I desperately needed my nipples sucked, I invited him over that same day. Sucking my nipples is the only thing I can't do myself, my breasts are firm and round so I can't get my fucking nipples into my mouth—the most I can do is flick my tongue at them. I need hard sucking to really get me going.

Tom (or was it Jerry?) came around to my two-bedroom flat at six that evening, with a bottle of wine and a dozen red roses. By five minutes past six he was lying on top of me on my sofa tweaking my nipples through my clothes while he kissed me. He was moving too fucking slow for me so I unbuttoned my top and pulled my right breast out my bra. As he stroked it a tear rolled down his face. I asked him what the fuck was wrong. He told me that my breast was so beautiful it made him emotional. I quickly whipped the other one out to give him something to really cry about! He started sucking them greedily—one of the best nipple-suckings I'd had up until that point in my life. I was in a good mood that day so I laid him across my lap, held the breast and let him latch on and suck it like he was a nursing baby. An hour or so later, I changed sides and let him suck on the other nipple. By the time he was done I was so wet I had to dry myself off a little before he put his big cock in me. I like a cock to *hurt* me. Too much lubrication lessens the sweet-pain.

I hadn't fucked for over three months and his cock was fat. He pushed it into me so hard and fast I had to bite his shoulder to keep from screaming out. He hurt my pussy good! As soon as he was able to thrust in and out of me with a bit of comfort, he threw my legs over his shoulders and fucked me harder than anyone had in my life. I loved it! Then I turned over and gave him the ass. As he tore up my asshole I pushed a dildo in my sore pussy and came like I hadn't done in years.

I opened the bottle of wine he'd brought me while he made a call on his mobile phone. The next thing I know there was a knock on my door. I went to answer it and immediately knew it was his brother on my doorstep because they resemble each other. When he realized how freaky I was he'd called his brother to help him out because I was too much woman for him. I drank some wine as brother #2 took his turn at the breasts and brother #1 took a light doze. When I couldn't take the sucking without some fucking, I woke the sleeping brother up and let him put his cock in my ass as his brother had some pussy, still sucking on my breasts. When I came I thought I was going to die—I swear I never came so hard in my life!

They have been fucking me regularly ever since. One of them had a girlfriend but he dropped her like a hot potato the very next day—he didn't need her when he had me. I immediately gave up my rented flat and moved into their three-bedroom house. Though we each have a bedroom, we all share the same bed at night. At the end of every week I handle both paycheques. I left my job within two weeks because they look after me very well. Anyway, I sometimes stay up half the night with one or both nursing on my breasts if they can't sleep, I would be too tired to do a nine-to-five even if I wanted to. I fucking don't!

***

One Sunday I go around to Honey's and I meet Terry for the first time. As soon as I walk in the door his eyes are in my cleavage. Me, I show a lot of cleavage—I believe if you've got tit flaunt tit! Honey had told me he was a breast man so when I beg him for a lift home later that night, I tell him to come up for some coffee when we get to my house. Tom and Jerry usually drive up to Sunderland to visit their mother on Sundays so they aren't home. As soon as I close the door behind him I bare my breasts and offer them to him. He doesn't think twice, he just dips his head and takes a nipple into his mouth. Moral of this story—don't tell another woman about your man's likes and dislikes, the size of his cock or how well he fucks you, not even your own fucking sister!

Within seconds of Terry sucking on my nipple my pussy starts cramping and my legs shake so much I have to reluctantly pull away. I quickly push him into an armchair and climb on top of him, face-to-face, my nipples exactly where they need to be. I hold his head and stroke his nape as I let him suck on my breasts from just before midnight to gone two in the morning. I only stop because even with the brothers sucking on my breasts regularly, Terry makes my nipples sore. The man has a strong fucking mouth but *God* he knows how to suck a nipple!

We have a quick 69 before he goes home. His cock is nice but I couldn't let him fuck me—after all he's my sister's man and I do have some principles! Although Honey is lucky, if it was our older sister, Sugar, he would have had to put that fat, hard, long cock in both her ass and pussy before she let him go.

When we were growing up, me and Honey couldn't bring any boyfriends home because Sugar would fuck them when we weren't looking. Once, poor Honey brought a boy home with her and he asked to use the bathroom. He was taking a while so she went to see what was keeping him. She found him sitting on the loo with Sugar riding his cock like she was in a rodeo. The worst thing was that Honey hadn't started fucking yet and the boy, although he was three years older, had been a virgin too—at least he was until Sugar snapped the seal off his cock. It really pissed Honey off.

I used to let Sugar fuck my boyfriends after I had fucked them myself at least once because the good thing about Sugar is that she doesn't fuck the same man twice. So, once she'd fucked my man, he was safe from her. Letting her fuck my boyfriends was good for me too, because she would straighten out any faults they had and when they fucked me the next time there was definite improvement.

Sugar moved to St Lucia a few years ago because she wanted some fresh cock and she was told that the men there are particularly well-hung. Plus, she said she had fucked all the Black men in London and was scared she would fuck one of the ones she had already fucked, by mistake. Fucking the same guy twice is her biggest phobia. I miss her a lot because she is a cool big sister. She is four years older than me, Honey is three years younger and we all definitely get our horniness from our parents. Growing up we knew better than to enter our parents' bedroom without knocking first. All three of us look like our mother, Sweetie, and even now she is in her late-forties men's mouths still drop open when they see her. Sugar inherited our mother's plump ass, I inherited her big breasts and lucky Honey inherited both but we are all man-magnets.

Sugar always gave us advice, warning us about wasting time with little dick brothers and making us promise never to sleep with any man old enough to be our father. When I turned sixteen, she started letting me hide in her bedroom closet and watch her get fucked so I could pick up tips.

Once, this tall, well-built guy pulled out his massive cock from his boxers to fuck Sugar. I almost screamed and gave the game away. Honey and I are both 5'6", I am a size 12 and she is a 14. Sugar is 5' 4" and a size 6 but for her big ass; I was really frightened for her. She took the guy's cock in her mouth and even though she deep-throated him, there was still a lot of cock left outside. His cock kept getting bigger and harder. I swear I have never seen a bigger one! Then he picked Sugar up, his arms under her legs and put her onto the head of his huge cock. She put her arms around his neck and held on to him as he forced his cock into her. I thought he would never get it all inside her but he held her by her ass and kept banging her against him. All the while poor Sugar was moaning and groaning. I wanted to come out of the closet and kick him in the balls but the fucker looked strong—I was scared he would grab me too. Better her than me!

After several minutes of shoving his cock into her, he walked to her bed, turned her around and fucked her from behind. I swear the man was pushing over 10" of stiff cock into my older sister. She turned her face towards me and the bitch winked at me before she started moaning and groaning again. After that I started to enjoy the show, I had been too worried he was hurting her to really have a good time before. Once I knew she was okay, I put my hand in my knickers and fingered myself.

When she'd seen him to the door, she came back to let me know the coast was clear. I came out of hiding and asked her how she could take such a big cock. She told me it wasn't the biggest she'd ever had. *Girlfriend* was good!

Months later, she came home with two guys, the taller one was very good-looking. She gave me the signal to hide in the closet before she brought them up to her room. They all stripped and jumped onto the bed. The shorter guy started sucking and finger-fucking her pussy while the other rimmed her ass. The shorter guy lay back and she climbed onto his cock while the other one started fingering her asshole. When his friend came, the taller guy pulled her ass upwards and put his cock against her asshole. It was so tight his friend had to suck on her breasts and finger her clit before he got the head inside. When he had buried the full length of his cock inside her, his friend got back under her and pushed his cock into her pussy. The two of them fucked her for hours and I enjoyed every minute of it. While I was watching them I fingered my pussy, by the time they were finished my pussy was sore. It was just before I started having sex, I got so hot watching the DP I pushed my fingers deeper than I had before.

When they left she told me it was the first time she'd ever had a cock in her ass although a few guys had finger-fucked her ass before. She told me it was the best sex she'd ever had. I think that is what started my preference for DP. I told her I liked the taller guy and she told me not to worry she would bring him for me the next day.

I'd had a long bath and was sitting in the living room, reading a book when Sugar walked through the front door with him the next day. Me reading? Trust me, I had to be nervous to open a book voluntarily!

Bailey, that was his name, looked really good. Sugar took us both by the hand as she gave him a lecture.

"Bailey, my little sister, Nectar, is a virgin so treat her fucking gently. If I hear her crying or screaming I will come in that bedroom and rip your fucking balls off!" This might sound like an idle threat from a woman who was almost a foot shorter than the man she was threatening but Sugar's fierce. Men are scared of her—she has some strange power over them. "Take your fucking time, undress her slowly, kiss her, suck her nipples and her clit—make sure that she is wet before you put your big cock inside her."

"Yes, Sugar." Bailey leaned forward and kissed me. I felt it all the way to my toes. I grabbed his hand and started to pull him towards my room.

"Nectar, you sure you don't want me to hold your hand, baby?" Sugar asked as we were about to walk through the door. I shook my head and kept dragging him along, impatient to get down to some fucking at last.

As soon as we got to the bedroom, I pulled my dress off and jumped on the bed. I hadn't been wearing any underwear so I was naked and had to wait until he stepped out of his clothes. Close up his hard cock looked bigger than it had looked from the closet and I thought, *oh shit!*

He climbed onto the bed and right on top of me, then spread my legs wide, and pressed the head of his cock against my entrance. I thought he was going to fuck me without any foreplay. I was getting ready to call for Sugar when he kissed me and put his hands on my breasts. He massaged my nipples and I felt my pussy get wet. He had to feel it too because my juice was flowing right onto the head of his cock.

Up to that point I used to play with my nipples every chance I got but I had never had someone suck on them. When he put his mouth on my nipple I almost screamed! It was so different from my fingers and it sent shooting waves of sensation right into my pussy. He sucked on my nipples for a long time and all the while I was moaning softly. When he moved down to tongue my clit he looked up at me and said, "You are so fucking wet!"

Then he pushed two of his big fingers inside my pussy and sucked on my clit. I groaned and Sugar tapped on the wall and asked if I was okay. I quickly shouted, "yes"—the last thing I wanted was for her to come in and stop the fucking just when it was getting interesting.

His tongue on my clit and his fingers stretching my pussy

drove me wild and within minutes I was cumming all over them. He slid up my body and I could see from his face he meant fucking business. I looked down at his cock and it looked ready to burst.

He kissed me hard, plunging his tongue into my mouth as he quickly plunged his cock into my pussy. I must have screamed but the sound didn't get past his mouth as he started pounding his cock into me. At first it felt like he was ripping my pussy apart but after a while I began to enjoy the pain. When he realized that I wasn't going to scream for help, he took his lips off mine and bent his head and sucked on my nipples. He started to fuck me even harder as he sucked on my nipples. Made me cum again in no time, he came too.

He left his cock embedded in my pussy while he sucked on my breasts. Less than five minutes later he was fucking me again. Afterwards he told me that he had deliberately left his cock inside me after fucking me the first time just in case he couldn't get it back into my swollen pussy.

He spent the next hour sucking on my nipples. He told me I had the most suckable nipples he'd ever seen. I enjoyed the nipple-sucking and was very sad when Sugar rapped on the wall and warned me that he had to go before Mom came home from work.

He came over the next day and everyone tells you the first time is painful but no one remembers to mention the second fucking time is almost as bad! My pussy felt raw when he first stuck his cock in me but already I had started to like the sweet-pain and he didn't spare my pussy, he fucked it good.

Bailey became my first real boyfriend and it wasn't long before he started pushing his fingers and then his cock into my ass too. We used to fuck at my house while my parents were at work but one day he told me he wanted me to come over to his place. I suspected it would be for something different—I was right—it was the first time he fucked my ass. He told me that he didn't want nosy Sugar coming to rescue me before he got the chance to do it properly.

He started off with a nice long rim job and then worked his way up to three fingers before he tried his cock. At first my asshole resisted and he couldn't even get the head inside me, but he spread my cheeks further apart, spat in my ass and pressed his cock harder against my asshole until the tip slipped inside. Once he got the head inside there was no stopping him, not even me begging him to stop or at least take his time. Later he made up for his cruelty by sucking my nipples for over an hour, each side.

Bailey loved ass-fucking. I liked it better the second time, and more and more as he kept fucking my ass regularly. I measured his cock once—it was only 6¼" long and not very thick. Now I look back and think, 'how the hell did his cock give me so much sweet pain?' I guess when your pussy and ass are new, any cock feels big.

Bailey was the one who got me hooked on nipple-sucking, ass-fucking and sweet-pain. But I had to give him his walking papers when he didn't want me to stick a dildo or a vibrator in my pussy when he was fucking my ass or vice versa. He was threatened by a piece of plastic. When I asked him to bring along the friend he had fucked Sugar with, he refused point blank. He said I was his woman and he wasn't going to let another brother put his cock inside me. I had to kick him to the kerb and move on.

I met Albert on a number 453 bus two weeks after I dumped Bailey. I was horny, so I decided to give him some pussy the same night. When the man dropped his pants I almost ran away. The man had a fat 8" cock! And talk about rough lover. I like a bit of pain but he gave me more than I could handle. When we got naked, the man barely kissed me and squeezed my breasts before he started to ram his big cock into me. I won't lie, I cried like a baby. Luckily, he came before he got the full length inside me. I asked him to call a cab for me, and left before his cock got hard again.

I avoided him for about three weeks and finally Sugar asked me what was wrong, so I told her. The next time he called I was in the bathroom so she answered my mobile phone for me. I didn't know this until later but she arranged to go around to his bed-sit and give him some lessons. Two days later the doorbell rang and I went to answer it. I nearly died when I found him on my doorstep with a big box of Thornton's Classic Continental chocolates. I had given him my mobile number but not my address when I left that night—I hadn't planned a repeat performance. I was about to chase his ass when he told me that Sugar had been to see him. He apologized for being so rough with me. One thing led to the other and the next thing I know we were rolling around my bed, naked.

When the man started to kiss my neck and suck on my breasts as he finger-fucked my pussy, I thought I was fucking his twin—he was like an entirely different man. Then he moved down to lick my pussy, he wasn't very good but he gave it a good try. By then, his cock was rock hard but instead of trying to just shove it into me, he rotated his hips and eased it inside me. When he got the whole thing buried inside me I was shocked—it stretched my pussy with just the right amount of sweet-pain. We fucked twice, relaxed and then fucked again.

When Sugar came home I went to her room to thank her for talking to him for me. That's when she told me she hadn't talked to him—she had fucked him! Said he was almost a hopeless case—she'd had to work on him for over four hours. She told me if he'd had a smaller cock she wouldn't have bothered to make the effort. I was a bit miffed for about five seconds. Then I remembered she had given me Bailey and was responsible for the marked improvement in Albert's performance, so I thanked her instead. She told me I was welcome and that she would do it again any time I wanted. And she did, several times.

Albert got his walking papers less than a month later. His big cock was nice and it had my pussy occupied for a while but my ass began to feel lonely. He informed me he wasn't a 'homo' when I asked him to put his cock in my asshole. I immediately chased him. Did I look like a fucking man to him? He obviously didn't know the meaning of the word homosexual, probably thought anyone who had anal sex was one. Ignorant fucker!

Then I met Ernest, a man only a year younger than my father. He was divorced and lived on his own. I had to sneak around to his house when Sugar wasn't looking because she would have been furious with me for messing with an old cock. She had always said that old cocks blight young pussies. At first, I let him suck on my nipples, tongue and finger-fuck my pussy while I wanked or sucked on his cock—Sugar's warning had me so worried I was scared to let him put his cock inside me. I want to fuck until I'm old and grey, so the last thing I needed was a blighted pussy. But one day after he had tongued my pussy well and spent quality time on my breasts, I had to let him put his cock deep inside my pussy to scratch the itch his fingers just couldn't reach. The old cock wasn't bad. It wasn't huge but he always put my legs on his shoulders to maximize the effect. He and I fucked for almost three months and though he never pushed his cock or any of his fingers in my ass, I really enjoyed the old fucking. He was a real *sugar* daddy; he paid well for the use of my young pussy. He gave me the spare keys to his house so I could sneak in and wait for him to come home from work.

One day I let myself in, to find his son, James, chilling out, listening to some of his father's jazz. He told me his father wouldn't be home until the next day, he had gone to Bristol on business. I did try to resist him for about half an hour or so, but he was so damn *fine*! I had forgotten how hard a young cock gets and how many times in one night it can get hard, James *reminded* me. I had a conscience then—I dropped Ernest and kept fucking James. Now, I would have fucked them both—one for the *honey* and one for the *money*.

James was a player. I didn't want Ernest to find out I had left him for his son, so I let James come over to my place instead of going over to his, since he still lived with his mother and Ernest visited from time to time to see his younger son and daughter. One day I was in the cinema with Honey and the next thing I know James walks in with another woman and sits down right in front of me. Not two rows in front or three seats to the left—right in front of fucking me! I said to myself, *don't act up, it could be his sister.* Well, if she was, he was a fucking loving brother. He bent to suck on her nipple and as soon as he straightened I emptied my large Coke over his head. He jumped up ready to punch somebody. When he saw me he almost died! He started spluttering, trying to explain but the girl pushed her breast back into her bra, gathered her things and left. He had to run behind her. I calmly sat through and enjoyed the rest of the movie.

I called Ernest the next day and went around for some old dick but after James's bigger, harder cock his father's had lost its appeal. I told him I'd met someone else but I felt bad that I hadn't given him a farewell round of pussy. I spent the whole day with him and late that night he pushed several large bills into my hand, dropped me two doors away from my parents' house and that was that. I've never seen father or son again.

I went through quite a few 'tired' fuckers in quick succession, some of them so bad even Sugar's expert tuition couldn't bring them up to standard. Then I met Matthew. Girls, let me tell you something: ugly men are the best fuckers in the world! Matthew knew he couldn't do a thing about his looks so he worked on his sexual technique. The man used to make me cum and cum at will. I swear I lost almost a stone within a month of meeting him. He just kept fucking me and fucking me!

When she was old enough I let Honey watch Matthew fuck me. By then Sugar had already gone to live in St. Lucia and I felt I had to keep up the family tradition she'd started. Matthew was a freak like me; he thought nothing of bringing his friend Mark to get a piece of my ass every now and then. I was in DP heaven until one day I was lying naked on the bed, all fucked-out when Matthew and Mark started getting it on right in front of me. Mark just took Matthew's cock, still slick with my pussy juices, into his mouth and started sucking on it. I thought maybe the DP they'd just given me had messed up my mind, so I closed my eyes, counted to a slow ten and re-opened them. Mark was still sucking on Matthew's dick but now it was as hard as a rock. My mother always said, 'play dead and see what kind of funeral you'll get', meaning play along even if you are pissed off just to see what happens. So I smiled at them and let them continue to see how far they'd take their shit. Next thing I know Mark is getting up on all-fours on *my* fucking bed and *my* fucking man is fucking *his* asshole. You ever heard scunt like that! Sorry, 'scunt' is a Guyanese curse word; the only word that conveys how pissed off I was with the two fuckers.

I didn't let them finish fucking, I started to cuss and go on like a crazy fucking woman. Matthew didn't say anything; he just apologized, pulled his cock out of Mark's ass and tried to stuff it into his boxers while it was still hard, before jumping into the rest of his clothes. Mark, the bastard, asked, 'what difference does it make if Matthew fucks my asshole or his?' I explained the fucking difference—I have a pussy, he didn't. And the bitch popped his neck out and clicked his fingers and asked, "So?" You ever see such eye-pass? Eye-pass is the Guyanese word for disrespect. See how stressed the fuckers made me? I had to revert to Guyanese curse words and sayings.

I kicked them both out of my fucking flat. The bitch Mark had the nerve to tell me as he was about to leave that Matthew was tired of my pussy anyway. Huh! I sucker-punched the fucker—Matthew had to help him out to his car.

They put me completely off men. For a whole three months. I am still pissed off about the lost of 'fuckable' time. Then I met Jerry (or was it Tom?) first. They are both good men and after some of the tired-ass fuckers I've been through, I am not letting them go. Any bitch who wants either of them has to come through me to get them and I don't fight like a girl! I would do the bitch serious injury—probably take her fucking eyes out for daring to look at my men.

*** *

The brothers came back from Sunderland Monday morning, early enough to fuck me before they went to work. They are not stupid, they know a day away and I will play, with some other fucking man! If Terry wasn't Honey's man I would have definitely let him hurt me with that cock of his because she hadn't lied when she'd said it was big and rock-hard.

Their mother is a right bossy boots, that's why they have to go and see her every Sunday, rain or fucking shine. This time when they come back they tell me she is starting to fret about wanting a grandchild before she dies. Personally, I think the miserable bitch will outlive us all. They start begging me to consider giving them a child and I am like, 'okay, whatever!' I am practically married to them anyway, doing all their cleaning, cooking and fucking—having a child is the next logical step.

And the great thing is they don't care whose child it is, so the next day I come off the Pill. That evening as soon as they come home they want to fuck—nothing like planting seed to make men hornier than usual.

Two months later I miss my period and they are so happy. But now they want to treat me with kid gloves, no more DP until after the baby and no more hard fucking. Shit if I had known that pregnancy would disrupt my fucking routine I would have thought twice about it! But on the flip side they are fucking my ass more regularly now. And you know I love anal!

My new bigger breasts have them going wild. Though I don't have to, I follow the nurse's advice and work on my nipples to prepare me for breast-feeding. Her advice would generally be for women who don't already breast-feed but I thought it couldn't harm to follow the advice anyway and get them into even better shape.

***

One Sunday, about six months into my pregnancy, when the brothers have gone to visit mummy dearest, I call Terry on his mobile. He is at Honey's but I tell him to pass by my place on his way home. I just want to test the nurse's advice, you know, see if the nipples could withstand Terry's assault on them for a longer period.

When I open the door and he sees my big round belly, he looks shocked but I quickly push him into the same armchair as before and take off my shirt and bra. My breasts have gone up a full cup size and the nipples are bigger from all that rolling and massaging I am giving them. He forgets the big belly in an instant although he has to lean forward over it to get to the breasts properly.

God, he works on them good for me—I think if he had a brother I would be tempted to steal him from Honey since she can't appreciate a good nipple-sucking. But although he is better than each of my two, combined they pip him to the post. As for the nurse's advice: well, it is hard to say—my nipples are a bit tender now that I am pregnant so although I lasted about the same time as before, technically if they weren't tender I might have lasted longer.

This time Terry just tongues and finger-fucks my pussy until I cum, then leaves. Earlier when he got my phone call Honey became suspicious and he had to fuck her for the rest of the day, his cock is too sore for anything, even head. That's Sugar's advice through and through—fuck a man dry before he leaves you, so he can't go and fuck another woman. That Honey was definitely listening to her big sister! Go girl!

***

The brothers fix up my bedroom for the baby. I know it is a girl because I asked what sex it is; I don't have the patience to wait until the baby is born. I also wanted to buy the right clothes and paint the room the right colour.

My baby is due any second so the brothers are down to just tonguing my clit, rimming my asshole or gently finger-fucking me, they are really looking out for their unborn daughter's welfare and it is sweet in a way. They still suck on my nipples while I wank or suck their cocks. They'll even indulge in a little breast-fucking if only one of them is around.

When I go into labour Tom is home with me, they have been taking turns to stay home with me, just in case. He drives me to the hospital and I give birth to their bouncing baby girl in less than an hour. My mother had advised me to 'make passage', i.e. have as much sex as possible to ensure a quick, smooth delivery. I believe her advice worked.

Jerry is a little disappointed when he misses the birth by only ten minutes but I am not! He had planned to videotape the happy event while Tom held my hand. My pussy stretching to admit my daughter into the world isn't something I want a record of.

The next day they both come to see me, each bringing a huge bouquet of flowers. I see one of the nurses looking at them kind of funny when they take turns in holding and kissing our daughter like they are both the father.

I am about to say, *"Bitch, mind your own fucking business!"* when she is paged and has to leave the room. Nosy fucker! Probably can't get a man of her own, so she is pissed off because I have two. These public hospitals just can't get the staff!

I don't have any complications or stitches so I am discharged literally as soon as I push the baby out. The first night home my breasts are so heavy with milk they are like two footballs, my daughter is barely taking anything and I am producing milk for about twenty babies. That night I am sleeping between the brothers, as usual, like the cheese between two slices of brown bread. I am restless and one of them hears me groaning in pain and asks what the problem is. I tell him my breasts are too full and he wakes his brother up. I thought they were going to take me back to the hospital or something. But hell no! They just open the flaps on my nursing bra and start sucking on my nipples, drinking the milk like it is from a bottle. They give me instant relief but I have to eventually tell them to stop because they are turning me on too much!

I fall asleep happy—I had secretly worried that the brothers would cease their nipple-sucking until I weaned our daughter but they both assured me that they intend to drink whatever milk the baby left, as often as they could.

I find out their real names when I have to register the birth: Timothy and Jeffery. Exactly Tom and Jerry! I mean, they had told me their names when we had first met but I couldn't be bothered to remember them. I let the older one, Jeffery, put his name as father on the birth certificate; the next baby would have Timothy's name. It's only fair.

As soon as they come home from work each day they drink some breast milk as appetizer before they have their main meal. If they come in together, I sit in a chair and they kneel at my side and each has a nipple for himself.

Isn't it good that nipples come in pairs? Double the fucking pleasure!

After the first month I put my daughter on two bottle feeds a day just to make sure she is getting the proper nutrients because I'm producing so much milk, I am sure it's diluted. And I don't want to stop the two bigger babies taking my milk because I am having too much fun.

When our baby is two months old I can't wait any longer, I need some cock. The brothers are driving me insane with the nipple-sucking. My doctor said I should abstain from sex for about six weeks; my mother advised me to wait three months to let the pussy tighten to its pre-pregnancy state. Since my doctor is a man and doesn't have a pussy, I follow my mother's advice. I want my pussy to stay nice and tight as it is the only one I have. The only alternative is some good old ass-fucking.

I am literally waiting on all-fours on the bed when Jerry walks in. He whips his cock out and gets to my ass straight away. They know me so well, sometimes I don't even have to tell them what I want—they do it instinctively. While he is fucking my ass Tom comes home and immediately gets under me and starts drinking milk and fingering my clit.

***

I wean my daughter at three months as she's quite happy with the bottle. I know I might sound like a horny bitch and a terrible mother but breast-feeding her turns me on and I never read about *that* in any maternity book—makes me feel like a freak.

That evening it is time for some serious fucking. I suck Jerry's cock and swallow cum for the first time since giving birth and it tastes so good! In the meanwhile Tom is eating my pussy and trying to get three of his fingers inside me. He would fist-fuck me if his hands weren't so big because he loves that shit. Anyway, as soon as Jerry cums it is time to switch and I wrap my lips around Tom's cock. Jerry uses a flannel to dry up some of my pussy juice and when I sit on his cock he pulls me down onto it hard. I have Tom's cock in my throat so I can't scream but tears come to my eyes, it hurt so fucking good!

Three weeks later the brothers bring this nerdy looking guy to the house and I think they say his name is Sam, or is it Damn? Who the hell cares? He isn't my type so his fucking name doesn't matter to me. I see him looking at my breasts funny. I offer him some dinner and afterwards we are sitting around chatting when I notice he has a boner, a small one but a boner nevertheless. So I ask them outright why he is visiting and they tell me he wants to pay a hundred pounds to watch me breast-feed them. I say I'll do it for two hundred—never go with the first offer. I expect him to meet me halfway with a hundred and fifty pounds but the bastard is so eager he agrees to pay my asking price.

I grab the money and sit in my usual comfy chair. The brothers open my blouse and the flaps on my nursing bra and then kneel beside me. Technically I can wear any bra but the brothers love nursing bras and have bought me dozens of sexy ones. They also offer good support now that my breasts are heavier. As soon as they start to suck my nipples Sam whips his cock out and starts to wank. Thank goodness fucking me isn't part of the bargain because his cock is small. Unlike Sugar and Honey, I will work with a medium-sized cock but, like them, I will not give a small-cock man the time of day. You have to draw the line somewhere, and I draw it just in front of a small dick.

Then Sam shoots his fucking load all over my freshly shampooed carpet. Jackass!

When he leaves I give the brothers a slap each for telling other people about our business. They are immediately sorry and try to make it up to me. Jerry lifts me bodily and takes me into the bedroom. When we get there they strip me and Tom works on both nipples as Jerry tongues my clit and finger-fucks my ass and pussy at the same time. I just lay back and let them work hard. I am tempted to stroke Tom's cock as he sucks my nipples because it is within hand reach, but as I am punishing them, I resist. Then they switch and Tom starts to rim my asshole while he moulds my clit between his fingers. He knows that I like a bit of anal play and soon he pushes two fingers into my ass and vigorously fucks it. When I feel him trying to get a third inside me, it's too much, I need their cocks now!

Usually, I lie facing the one who is fucking my pussy while the other kneels on the bed behind me and fucks my ass. Tonight they change the plan. Tom lies down, separates my ass cheeks, puts his cock against my asshole and urges me onto it with me backing him. As soon as I have it buried inside me he pulls me back against him and Jerry dries my pussy. I know he intends to mistreat it when he pushed the flannel inside my entrance to get as much moisture as possible out of it. They like my pussy dripping wet but they know I like it a bit dry so the initial friction gives me some sweet-pain. He climbs onto the bed, puts his arms under my thighs and starts to slam his cock into me. I cum within minutes.

The brothers are just getting started. Usually they thrust alternatively but tonight they thrust in and out at the same time, like they plan to rip me apart—the best DP they have ever given me! Jerry comes first and as soon as he pulls out of me Tom turns me over and fucks my ass real hard and I cum again before he does.

Later, Tom confesses that he was the one to tell Sam about the breast-feeding so I turn my back on him and let Jerry have both nipples. I sense Jerry is feeling bad for his brother because he doesn't suck them with his usual enthusiasm.

I wake up during the night, Jerry is fast asleep but Tom is still awake, even though he tries to pretend he is sleeping when I turn to face him. I kiss the side of his face and he knows I've forgiven him. He quickly scoots downwards and goes for the nearest nipple. It is so easy to make my big babies feel bad, that's why I can't punish them for long. I know he needs something special to be convinced I have really forgiven him, so I gently try to ease him off. He clamps onto my nipple and sucks harder until I whisper what I intend to do.

I sit up against the headboard, my back supported by pillows and he lies across my lap. I hold my breast, the nipple sticking out between my fingers and let him latch on. They both love it when I hold the breast and feed them like they are new-born babies but I only do it on special occasions like holidays and birthdays or if I am in a really good fucking mood.

I stroke his head and whisper soothingly to my big *repentant* baby while he drinks his milk. I think he was scared I would have carried on the punishment for longer. A day without the breast is like a year to them.

He empties the first breast before he moves on to the

other, drinking slowly to prolong the time at my breast and all the while I am soothing him and stroking him. He even goes back to the first one when he has emptied the second but it is too soon, my breast hasn't had a chance to re-fill but there is a little there and he drinks it.

"I'm so sorry, Nectar," he whispers to me when he finally releases my nipple.

"I know, darling. I forgive you."

Then he turns me around, fingers my clit as he quickly pushes his cock in my ass, to hurt me nicely and then fucks me quietly so as not to wake his sleeping brother. Now that is self-sacrifice—he fucks my ass when the pussy is free. If I hadn't forgiven him before he is definitely forgiven now.

I love my big babies so much. As I said before, I would kill or maim any bitch who tries to fuck or steal either of them!

The next day after they leave for work I am thinking about the guy they'd brought home. Thinking about how happy he'd been just to watch. Usually, I try not to think too much—in case I hurt myself, but suddenly I get a bright idea. I did a web design class a year ago but afterwards I found it hard to get any business although I had been one of the best in the class. I had left school with nine GCSEs, all good grades but I hated studying. Yet, I was surprised how much I'd enjoyed the web design class. Though, the fact that the teacher had been a young, sexy man might have had something to do with my eagerness to learn.

Tom comes home first. I think he may have deliberately left the office early to get a head start on the breasts before Jerry. While he is having his appetizer I tell him about my idea for a web site featuring the three of us and it gets him so hard I have to get on top of him and let him push his cock inside me while he continues on the breasts. Jerry comes in while we are in the middle of it and since it is his turn to be at the bottom Tom has to make do with the ass. That's what I like about them—they never quarrel over me. They keep track of whose turn it is in the pussy and just get on with it. *Not* that my ass is a fucking consolation prize! It is just that fucking the pussy means sucking the breasts and *that* is their favourite thing.

***

Two weeks later my website is up and running—I have posted some of the footage the three of us shot on the weekend using ski-masks to cover our faces. The first day I have over three hundred and fifty requests for a one-to-one where a person can tell us what they want done and we follow instructions. At a premium rate, of course.

The brothers come home together and have dinner while I put the baby down for the night. Then we get in front of the web-cam and entertain our first customer.

His name is Ronaldo (if that's his real name—mine's Beckham!) and he is from Leeds. He wants to see the guys finger-fuck my pussy and ass as they breast-feed. Almost mission impossible! I have to slide down to the edge of the chair in an uncomfortable fucking position to accomplish this feat. Talk about getting his money's worth!

Next guy is Phillip—he wants me to squirt my breast milk right at the web-cam as if I am aiming it at his mouth. For what it is costing him I don't mind doing it but I make sure I lay some paper kitchen towels down first.

Charles wants to see the milk oozing from my breast and running down my body, I guess he wants to imagine it's his cum. This call scares me coming right after the previous one. I hasten to oblige, just in case.

Simon wants one guy to fuck me while the other kneels at the side and sucks my breast. Simple Simon didn't want much.

Then Virginia (this freaked me out—a woman!) wants

the guys to milk me like a cow. So I kneel up on all-fours and the guys lie beneath me, squeeze my breasts and catch the milk in their mouths. I sense that her parents giving her a name so close to virgin had no effect on her character whatsoever. Dirty bitch!

Bernard wants me to send him some of my frozen breast-milk in a special cold storage container he would provide. He sounds a bit like a scientist to me, so of course, I say, *"hell no!"* The next thing I know he could do a DNA test and trace me! Or clone little Nectars! I don't think so!

Ricky wants to buy the lovely nursing bra I am wearing to feed the guys for one hundred and fifty pounds. We agree on two hundred and twenty-five. Then he begs me please *not* to wash it before I send it. Why the hell did he think I was going to? He can wash it his damn self!

Anne Marie, I don't know if it's one woman or two, wants to let me know she once used to breast-feed up to ten men a day and they paid her very well for the privilege. Competitive and a show-off! I hope her breasts are now down to her feet and the bitch trips over them.

Another woman—bitches won't leave me alone— Miranda, tells me I am an abomination to womanhood. Tells me I taking a sacred part of motherhood and turning it into something sexual and perverted. So I remind the bitch it was something sexual that got my breasts leaking milk, and then I ask her when last she got laid. She doesn't answer—I think it's so long ago she can't remember. What I would like to know is how she managed to come across my website. It is *not* listed in the fucking Yellow Pages. Personally, I think she was looking for bestiality or bondage and went too far down the Bs. And she calls *me* perverted. Bloody self-righteous bitch!

***

The website is making so much money that both my men

have taken career breaks—gives them more time to fuck me. Sam still comes every Friday to pay to watch the brothers breast-feed, I felt a bit guilty about charging him two hundred pounds the first time so now I only charge him a hundred. Sometimes I sense he would like to suck on one of my nipples himself but there is no way he would ever get Tom or Jerry to give him even a few sucks, they guard my nipples with their lives.

Got a letter from Sugar today, she needs some sisterly advice. She wants to know what love feels like. She is getting the urge to fuck a man she fucked a few weeks ago. She has never felt this urge before and she wonders if she could be in love, or if it is simply because he has the biggest cock she's ever had. I am going to discuss it with Honey before I reply. I am not sure how Sugar will handle fucking the same guy twice and the last thing I would want is to see my sister in a mental institution. I am tempted to tell her not to do it, but I want her to have someone of her own. Like Honey's got Terry and I've got Tom and Jerry—the fact that the guy's name is Berry makes me think he could be the one for her.

My breasts have gone from a 36DD to a 36G, my nipples are so prominent they look permanently aroused and actually feel that way all the fucking time. The thing is: I am enjoying the brothers sucking on my breasts as much as they are enjoying my lovely milk.

There are excellent fathers to our cute, six-month old daughter who looks exactly like me. They keep talking about having a son. I tell them constantly when a woman is breast-feeding it reduces her chances of getting pregnant but can I get them to stop for long enough? Hell no!

***

The character **Honey,** *from the story* **Telephone Sex** *in* **Bedtime Erotica,** *was so fierce I felt people needed to meet her older* *sister,* **Nectar.** **Sugar,** *the fiercest of the three is too much——even for me! I never planned to tell her story but she bugged me until I relented and gave readers a brief glimpse into her life in* **Bedtime Erotica for Men.**

*****

ANTONIA

*S*he noticed the buff-looking young Black man as soon as he stepped on to the Tube at Leytonstone Station. Their eyes met and she winked suggestively. He did a slow, thorough survey of her body, his eyes widening in appreciation as he took in her short skirt and long legs. She deliberately moved across the carriage to stand just behind him, and then closer as the Tube became more crowded at Stratford. She pressed her breasts into his back as the Central Line Tube train sped through the tunnel between Mile End and Bethnal Green Stations, opening her legs as she felt his hand reach backwards and up under her skirt. She cupped his crotch as he pulled her tiny thong aside and fingered her clit. Pushing two fingers inside her, he thrust them as deep as he could without attracting the attention of their fellow commuters. She stroked his cock through his trousers. It felt huge and rock hard. Yummy!

No one disembarked at Bethnal Green Station but a few more passengers squeezed into the already crowded carriage. He continued to finger-fuck her, pressing his thumb deliciously against her clit and she came just before they pulled into Liverpool Street Station. He pulled his fingers free and she quickly tugged her skirt down as the majority of passengers surged off the carriage. He winked at her before stepping onto the platform, looking debonair in his designer suit and shiny brogues, his laptop case conveniently covering the bulge of his crotch. She leaned weakly against one of the train's fibre-glass panels and caught her breath.

She loved travelling by Tube, pressing herself against other people—men and women. There was nothing like grinding her crotch into someone's ass or having them press their groin into her behind. Most days she was fortunate to fondle a woman's breast or cup a man's cock and balls. Three months ago she had been lucky enough to have a stranger fuck her when the crowded train was held between two stations for almost twenty minutes. The short, stocky White man had been standing behind her and she'd had her hand in his fly stroking his stiff cock when the Tube driver announced there was a defective train in front. Pulling up the back of her skirt, she had placed his big, hard cock against her entrance and he had eagerly thrust it up inside her. It had been awkward and he had only managed to get about 4" of his fat cock into her but it had been intense! They had both cum before the Tube finally pulled into the next station.

***

Later that evening as Antonia grilled a tenderloin steak for dinner, she thought of the young stranger on the train. He couldn't be more than twenty-one. He wasn't good-looking but he was built. His cock must be a good 8" or more. She'd thought of him all day and her pussy had clenched every time she remembered his big fingers and the way she had cum all over them.

She'd wanted to slip her business card into his pocket and tell him to come over tonight but he was a bit young. Young men tended to cling on long after she got bored with them. She had a very low boredom threshold, one fuck and she was ready to move on. Everyone made an effort to impress when they were fucking new pussy but in less than no time they became complacent and nothing pissed her off more than complacent fucking.

She listened to a Jaheim CD as she ate her well-done steak and a large Mediterranean salad. She loved meat, especially organic red meat and long before the Atkins' Diet had become popular she'd realized pasta, potato and rice put pounds on her slender frame so she avoided them as much as she could but ate lots of fresh fruit and vegetables.

As soon as she finished her meal, she washed the dishes and tidied the kitchen, then curled up on the sofa, listening to a Luther CD with a glass of red wine.

Damn! She was going to have to masturbate tonight, her pussy was acting up. If she didn't give it something hard it wouldn't let her sleep. Her job as an investment banker was very demanding and a night without sleep could seriously affect her business decisions the next day. But she hated to masturbate alone. It was much more fun doing it while someone was watching, preferably masturbating too. Doing it on her own made her feel like a sad, lonely teenager and she was a happy thirty-year-old who was alone by choice!

She decided to have a bath and see if the pussy would relax itself and leave her alone! But no! It was still jumping when she stepped out of the water. She grabbed a dildo from her drawer and crawled under the duvet, naked. She ran her hands over her body a couple of times before she squeezed her nipples between her fingertips. She pushed one of her breasts upwards and wrapped her lips around the nipple. Every time she pulled on the nipple her pussy jumped in response. She changed nipples, tugging and nipping until she felt her pussy juice run between the cheeks of her ass.

Now she was ready for Willy, her largest dildo. Her

pussy wouldn't be satisfied with anything but Willy tonight. It would want something as close to the young stranger's cock as possible. She rubbed her clit as she pushed Willy inside her slowly. When she had buried him as far as he could go she left him there for a couple of seconds before she pulled him right out again. And again. She was going to punish her pussy for being troublesome, when she finished it was going to be sore and hopefully it would let her get some sleep.

Greedy bitch of a pussy!

***

The next day as the train pulled into Leytonstone Station she looked for the young stranger. No sign of him.

Damn! It was Friday, and if she had seen him she would have definitely let him come over to give her some of his young cock tonight. Disappointed, she pulled a book of erotica out of her bag and started reading. The next thing she knew, the man behind her was reading over her shoulder and pressing closer to her. She held the book more conveniently and backed her ass into his crotch. His cock was already hard and she rubbed herself against it. Sadly, he got off at the next stop, but not before giving her butt a nice hard squeeze.

Later that evening she was sitting in her local wine bar, looking for a prospective bed mate while she sipped a glass of dry white. Even though she had punished her pussy good the night before, it was still jumping—it wanted a real cock.

"Is this seat taken?" a middle-aged White guy asked, looking at her smoothly-shaven legs.

"Sorry, I'm expecting someone." She smiled at him regretfully. Her hungry pussy needed a young cock at the moment.

He nodded and moved away.

She pulled the novel from her bag and continued

reading. Engrossed, she was startled when someone placed a large, masculine hand on her shoulder. She looked up at the tall, broad-shouldered man smiling down at her, in total surprise for a few seconds.

"Stuart!" She jumped up and gave him a bear hug, feeling her pussy moisten and her nipples harden.

God, he looked so fucking good!

"What are you doing here?" she asked him breathlessly.

"I came for a two-day conference in Birmingham." He gave her a quick kiss. "I couldn't go back without seeing my favourite girl. I was very disappointed not to find you at home."

"You should have called my mobile," she scolded, horrified that she might have missed him.

"I would have called your mobile if I hadn't found you here."

"Let's go." She grabbed her handbag and preceded him out of the bar. "How is Misty?"

Not that she gave a damn about his wife!

"She is fine. We just had son number three."

"Maybe next time," she consoled, squeezing his hand sympathetically. He wanted a daughter desperately.

"Misty says she doesn't want any more children."

Okay enough about Misty and the rugrats. She moved her hand from his waist and tweaked his nipple. "I was thinking that I would have to come all the way over to Martinique just for a piece of your sweet cock."

"You have all these guys in London and you're missing my cock?"

"Your cock makes me feel virginal again. It's a special feeling."

If every pussy had a maximum size of cock it could cope with, Stuart was definitely hers—not even a blade of grass could fit inside her pussy when his cock was buried to the hilt.

She jumped up onto him as soon as they walked through her front door. He fumbled with his zip one-handed as she ripped open her shirt and pulled her bra downwards. He sucked her nipple into his mouth as she reached down and freed his cock. As he lifted her, she held her thong out of the way and spread her pussy lips. She groaned aloud as his thick length pushed past her entrance and slid about halfway into her pussy.

"I missed your big cock so much." She held onto his shoulders and rotated her hips to match his. Slowly, his long cock sunk deeper and deeper inside her but minutes later when they both came, there was more than an inch outside her.

"I spared you this time. Next round you get the full length," he threatened as he pulled her off him and let her slide her legs to the floor.

"I swear your cock's gotten bigger!" She laughed and he playfully slapped her ass.

She had met him two years ago at the Notting Hill Gate Carnival while he was in the UK on business. That day she'd been wearing a tiny top that barely covered her nipples and a pair of short shorts. She had been following the float playing the hottest Soca music, drinking beer and whiining like she was boneless. He had slipped his arms around her and started to match the movement of her waist. She knew right then that she was going to have him for dinner. As his cock had hardened and she had felt the size of it, she knew he would be enough for breakfast the next morning and maybe for lunch as well.

On the way to her house he'd explained that he had moved to Martinique with his wife and two sons earlier in the year and would be flying back in three days' time. She hadn't minded—no chance to get bored of him, but when he'd pulled his cock from his boxers and treated her to its full length and girth, boredom had been the last thing on her mind.

***

She poured a generous splash of Remy Martin in a tumbler for him and a glass of chilled white wine for herself, then sat on his lap, her shirt open and skirt hitched up. He sucked on her nipples and fondled her clit between swigs of brandy as they chatted about her demanding job and his very successful consultancy business in the Caribbean. Suddenly he threw his head back, drained the tumbler and got to his feet. "Let's bathe—I want to feast on your clit."

She put her half-finished glass on the side table as her pussy started jumping. Stuart loved to eat pussy. He especially loved the slightly salty flavour of hers. He'd teased her the first time he saw her clit, told her that she was over-feeding it, that it was almost obese.

They undressed as they made their way up to her bedroom. He let her climb a couple of steps, until her backside was level with his face and then stopped her. He kissed the cheeks of her ass before he separated them and fingered her asshole. "Are you going to give me a piece of this sweet ass today?"

Stuart wasn't really a 'backshot' man but they had tried anal sex the last time he was in the UK and had been forced to give up after a frustrating ten minutes.

"Unless your cock has shrunk, and my pussy tells me it hasn't, I don't think so."

He laughed and urged her up the stairs. "Your ass is just playing hard to get."

He soaped her with a flannel while she used her massage mitt on him. As she rinsed his cock off, it looked so tasty she couldn't resist the urge to bite on it. She knelt and took the head in her mouth. Stuart groaned appreciatively but after only a few minutes he quickly pulled her up and bent her over the tub—he was one of those men who liked to cum in a pussy.

"Not so deep," she pleaded as he slowly pushed his cock inside her to the hilt.

"Shhh," he soothed as he bent over, gathered her against him and thrust himself to a quick release before turning her around and kissing her. "I know that hurt you, sweetness— I'll make it up to you in a minute."

He quickly washed her pussy again and rinsed it with tepid water. Wrapping her in a bath sheet, he lifted her bodily and strode to the bedroom. He laid her on the bed and knelt on the fluffy rug in front of it. He didn't like 69s, said he liked to give a pussy his full attention when he was eating it.

She grabbed the other end of the bed and held on for dear life as he put his mouth on her clit. *This* was worth all the pain his big cock inflicted. She didn't know where he had learnt to eat pussy but she wished he would open a school and teach other men. Even she didn't recognize some of the sounds coming from her mouth. She screamed as she came hard, sitting up on the bed and holding her head. Stuart held her hips firmly anchored to the bed knowing from experience that her legs were deadly whenever she came as he ate her pussy. He released her when it was safe to do so, climbing on to the bed and wrapping his arms around her.

***

Half an hour later, she was kneeling on the bed, giving him head again. She didn't deep-throat him, instead she worked on the tip, occasionally slipping a bit of the shaft into her mouth and sucking on it before going back to tonguing the head and his balls. His cock was so big it took her pussy days to recover whenever he fucked her.

She felt his cock start to jerk before he pushed her back against the bed and quickly drove it up inside her. Not content with that, he pulled her legs upwards.

"No-oo," she groaned as it filled her to the point of pain.

"Yes, sweets, take it all." He bent his head and kissed her as he started to move his hips like he was whiining to Soca music, rubbing against her clit with every stroke. A few minutes later she exploded and he was right there with her.

"So, are you ready to let me try this ass again?" he asked, fondling her ample cheeks.

"Baby, some cocks are made for ass-fucking, yours is not one of them."

"Once I get the head past your tight rim it would be no problem."

"You could *tear* me open trying to get the head past my rim."

"Your ass is just naughty," he said as he playfully slapped it a couple of times.

"Let me give you some well-behaved pussy to make up for that naughty ass," she said as she climbed onto him and slowly sank downwards. He filled her pussy to overflowing. She bit her bottom lip and groaned as the last inch slipped inside her. She could never get used to the size of it. She lifted herself slightly and started to rotate her waist. But he wouldn't let her get away with leaving a piece of his cock outside her pussy, in the cold. He raised his hips and rotated upwards as she rotated downwards.

"Aa-ah!" she moaned as she came down against him the first time. She raised herself and came down again. His cock gave her pain like it was her first time. "Aa-ah!"

***

Stuart was flying back on Sunday morning, so early Saturday Antonia called and cancelled her appointment with Carla. The petite blonde was disappointed but agreed to come over Monday evening instead.

Antonia had a carefully worked out fucking schedule: weekdays for one-night stands if she got the inclination; Saturdays for her regular lovers—Terrence one Saturday, Carla the next, Millie and Albert the following Saturday and Caesar every fourth Saturday; she took a sabbatical from sex on Sundays when possible.

Her Saturday lovers were all past partners whom she had found exceptional in one way or other. Stuart would have definitely been a Saturday lover if he lived in the UK. He was the only person special enough for her to disrupt her schedule.

***

She and Stuart fucked all Saturday night and last thing before the cab picked him up for the airport on Sunday morning. She didn't go to see him off. No point in going all the way to the airport to say goodbye when she could say it at her front door and save herself the return journey. Instead, she spent an hour curled up on her sofa, sipping Baileys on ice from a fat tumbler, re-living the exquisite pleasure and pain his big cock had administered to her pussy, which was so quiet she had to occasionally put her hand on it to see if it was still there. Stuart's big cock always had that effect on it.

***

Carla turned up at seven Monday evening, looking radiant, her long hair in a single plait down to her waist, her masseuse uniform hugging her 5'2" frame in all the right places. They kissed as soon as Antonia pushed the door closed.

Moments later, Carla slipped out of her white uniform while Antonia pulled a folding massage table from her small cloakroom and set it up in her living room. Antonia stripped off her gown, spread a towel on the table and climbed onto it as Carla laid out a pouch containing several bottles of aromatherapy oils and enquired, "How are we feeling today?"

"Mellow." Antonia was still basking in the afterglow of Stuart's fucking.

Carla's small hands started moving smoothly, rhythmically over Antonia's body and once again she was surprised at the strength in them. Even when she pushed a finger inside Carla's pussy, the masseuse continued without breaking her rhythm. At the end of the massage, Carla sucked on Antonia's nipple as she pushed two fingers inside her pussy and massaged her G-spot firmly.

Antonia's cum drenched Carla's fingers. The first time it had happened Antonia had been sure she'd peed herself until she'd checked the fluid and confirmed it was just copious amounts of pussy cum juice.

They made their way to Antonia's bedroom, kissing and touching. Antonia immediately strapped on a dildo, pulled Carla up on to all-fours and fucked her pussy from behind, while carefully breaching her ass with a finger. When Carla came, Antonia swapped the dildo for a longer, much thinner one and lubricated it thoroughly. Carla lay on her back, her small feet on Antonia's upper chest as Antonia pushed the dildo into her tight ass, *slowly*.

When the dildo was buried deep, Carla placed her legs on the bed and Antonia kissed her as she started to move her hips, arousing all of Carla's anal erogenous zones. Carla pulled her lips away and buried her face into Antonia's neck and moaned, "Fuck my ass, Toni baby. Fuck me, please!"

Antonia gave her long, deep, careful strokes—ensuring that there would be no telltale marks on Carla's fair skin. When she heard the timbre of Carla's moans change, she reached between them and fingered Carla's clit. Instantly Carla gave a sharp scream and squeezed Antonia tight as she came.

Antonia un-strapped the dildo and they lay curled up together for a while. Usually on Saturdays Carla would return the favour; strap on and give Antonia a good ass-fucking but there wasn't time; they both had to be up early in the morning.

Antonia kissed Carla goodbye and watched as she got into her Mini and drove away. Carla loved having her ass fucked but didn't want her husband to know—once he'd told her that his ex-girlfriend was a 'slag' because she'd let him fuck her ass. Carla vowed never to give him the pleasure. Antonia used an ultra-thin anal dildo on Carla so that he wouldn't suspect a thing. But two years ago, when he had spent three months working in Australia, leaving his lovely wife to her own devices in the UK, Antonia had regularly gone to their home straight after work and seen to his wife's ass with a much bigger dildo.

***

On Thursday Antonia was standing on the Tube reading another book when someone breathed in her ear, "Hi!"

She raised her head. It was last Thursday's Finger-Fucker, himself! Her pussy woke up and did its morning stretch.

"Hello!"

The Tube was emptier than usual so there was no chance of a quick finger-fuck to start the day right.

"Do you travel only on Thursdays?" she asked him over her shoulder as she opened her purse to extract one of her business cards.

He pressed closer to her. "Yes. I have a one-day placement at a firm in the City every Thursday."

"Placement? Are you at university?"

"No. I am doing my A-Levels."

She pushed her card back into the slimline silver card

holder and asked casually, "How old are you?"

"I'm seventeen," he replied, quite proudly.

"I see." She pulled her ass away from his crotch and straightened. "This is my stop! Bye."

She stumbled off the carriage just before the doors closed, staggered weakly to one of the platform benches and sat down shakily.

What the fuck were they feeding kids these days? That fucker looked at least twenty-one! Greedy fucking pussy almost turned her into a paedophile!

***

For the rest of the day her pussy behaved itself, sensing Antonia was in no mood to tolerate any shit from it after the near paedophilia.

But on her way home Friday evening it started acting up just as she got off the Tube. Resigned, she popped into the wine bar to see if there was anyone worth pulling. She ordered a glass of white wine and glanced around while being served. Immediately she noticed an older Black woman checking her out. The woman had a streak of grey in her hair and looked late thirties, definitely over the age of consent. Antonia took her glass from the bartender and walked over to join her.

"Hi, I'm Antonia." She smiled at the woman as she took a seat beside her.

"I'm Lucille."

"Nice meeting you, Lucille." Antonia had never seen her in the wine bar before. "You live locally?"

"Yes I do. What about you?"

"I live on Culverhouse Terrace."

"I live closer. Come to my place and let me tongue your pussy."

"I love a woman who gets straight to the fucking point but are you any good at tonguing a pussy?"

"My lovers don't complain."

"It doesn't mean they have no complaints. We British never complain about bad service."

"Why don't you try me and find out?"

"Tell me a little about your tonguing technique; give me a little *oral* demonstration."

The woman opened her mouth and revealed the stud in her tongue.

Enough said!

"You've convinced me, let's go." Antonia downed her drink and picked up her jacket.

They arrived at Lucille's flat in less than five minutes and were naked in less than six. Lucille had big breasts, a trim waist and a firm behind; it was obvious she did some kind of workout regularly.

"Can I shave your pussy?" Lucille asked as they stepped out of the shower together.

"Okay," Antonia agreed. She had shaved her pussy the night before, leaving just a neat black diamond to mark the location of her precious jewel, so she knew Lucille meant everything off. She didn't mind, and the last thing she needed was for one of her pubic hairs to get entangled in Lucille's stud. She had been shaved by other people before but the last person, a clumsy oaf of a man had given her a nasty nick with a fucking safety razor. "But let me warn you—nick it and you won't lick it!"

"I shave pussies all the time. I am so good I could do it for a living."

Lucille wasn't boasting. She proceeded to give Antonia's pussy a nice, clean shave with a very expensive disposable razor. When she was finished she rubbed a light unscented gel over it.

Caressing the silky-smooth, freshly-shaven mound, Antonia commented, "So you're good with your hands, let's—"

"I'm better with my tongue," Lucille boasted as she lay back and gestured for Antonia to climb on top of her.

Minutes later Antonia's pussy was purring as the stud stroked it. She felt herself about to cum and tried to pull away but Lucille held her hips tighter and kept stroking. As her orgasm ripped through her body, Antonia involuntarily squeezed Lucille's head between her thighs. Eventually, Lucille managed to free herself and take some air in her lungs.

"Fuck!" Lucille's breathing was ragged as she sat up and glared at Antonia. "You could have killed me!"

Antonia had to stop herself laughing. If the woman had let her up when she had indicated, she wouldn't have almost suffocated. "Sorry, I should have warned you—when I am coming stand clear!"

Lucille looked ready to punch her.

"Come on, honey," Antonia cajoled. "Lie back and let me eat your pussy, baby."

Lucille resisted Antonia's attempts to push her back against the pillows until Antonia bent her head and sucked hard on one of her erect nipples. Lucille's head hit the pillow a second later as Antonia continued to suck on her nipples. It had been a while since she had some juicy breasts to suck on and Lucille's were very juicy.

When Antonia moved down to eat her pussy, Lucille sat up, reached into the middle drawer of her bedside unit and pulled out a box, saying, "I want to try my new toy."

Lucille opened the box and took out a brightly coloured dildo that reminded Antonia of a bent arm, cut off halfway between the elbow and shoulder. Antonia watched Lucille clean it with a special fluid before she inserted the shorter end into her pussy. Antonia didn't like the purplish colour—she preferred flesh-coloured fake cocks. But it felt quite good as Lucille leaned forward and sucked on her nipple as she thrust the full 7" inside her. The bulb-like shorter end seemed to be giving Lucille just as much pleasure.

Then Lucille pressed something and the dildo started vibrating, which immediately grated on Antonia's nerve endings. She didn't own a vibrator because she couldn't stand the mechanical motion. Five minutes later boredom had begun to step in as she realized Lucille intended to do all the shafting. Antonia loved sleeping with other women but she liked to get an equal share of the fucking. With men Antonia could sometimes be girly and feminine; with women her butch-queen persona reared its head—it was fuck and be fucked or forget it!

Fortunately, after cumming Lucille fell into a deep sleep. As soon as she started snoring, Antonia sneaked out of the house.

***

The next evening she went over to be fucked by Millie and Albert, an older couple she had befriended after a run in the park one Sunday morning four years ago. The Bahamian couple were in their early-forties, both incredibly fit. They had been married for almost twenty years and were childless by choice.

Millie had invited Antonia for dinner the following Saturday. Later, while his wife had been washing the dishes, Albert had been attacking Antonia's ass as she bent over the breakfast bar—with Millie's approval, of course. His first-ever piece of ass. When Millie had finished tidying the kitchen, they had all retired to the couple's king-sized bed, where Antonia and Albert had taken turns in rimming and poking fingers in Millie's tight ass. By Antonia's next visit, a month later, Albert had succeeded in breaking the rim of his wife's ass. He now took the greatest pleasure in keeping the rim fully broken.

Millie opened the door and kissed Antonia. "Hi, baby."

"Hi," Antonia responded, reaching out to tweak one of Millie's prominent nipples through the material of her burgundy satin robe.

People in the affluent neighbourhood minded their own business. During the summer months the three of them sometimes traipsed naked to the garden shed or fucked on the outdoor furniture around the swimming pool. So, still standing in the open doorway, Millie opened the robe and let Antonia suck on her erect nipple until Albert pulled them both inside, wanting to get some of the action for himself.

He handed Antonia a glass of chilled wine. She took a couple of sips and then went back to sucking on Millie's nipple as the three of them sat on a large sofa in the living room. Albert sat on the other side of his wife and sucked on her free nipple while she stroked his cock through his boxers. When she pulled it through the opening and leaned forward to gather his pre-cum he groaned, "Let's go up to the bedroom."

He stoop up, unzipped Antonia's dress and slipped it off her shoulders. Pushing the cups of her lace bra downwards, he squeezed her nipples firmly until they hardened to his satisfaction. He then cupped her left breast in his large hand, pushed it upwards and offered it to his wife. Millie sucked on it as Albert slid Antonia's thong off her legs and unhooked her bra. He spread the cheeks of her ass and pressed his hard cock vertically in the groove. She rubbed herself against it, anticipating the pleasure of having it buried inside her before the night was through. Millie moved closer, rubbing her body against Antonia's, squashing the younger woman's slim body between her and her husband's larger bodies. She kissed Antonia as she reached down to finger her clit but broke the kiss in surprise.

"You've shaved!" Millie rubbed her hands all over the

hairless mound. "It feels really smooth."

"A woman called Lucille shaved me last night." Antonia winked at Millie.

"You naughty girl, did you let her suck her pussy afterwards?" Albert demanded as he stroked her ass.

"Yes."

"Naughty! Naughty!" Albert gave her ass two light slaps.

"And I let her fuck me with a dildo afterwards."

"Bad girl!" Albert gave her a harder smack this time and her ass tingled pleasantly.

"I also let a seventeen-year-old boy finger-fuck me on the Tube last Thursday."

"Millie, bring the paddle, she's been far too naughty to be spanked with my bare hand."

Millie fetched the stout wooden beater as Albert sat on the bed and bent Antonia over his knee. Antonia loved the paddle but it was only applied when she'd been really naughty.

"How many strokes do you think she deserves for being so naughty?" Albert asked his wife, the beater in his upraised hand.

"I think ten should do. Five for letting the young man finger-fuck her and five for allowing Lucille to shave her, suck her pussy and then fuck her with the dildo."

"Okay, young lady, prepare for your punishment. One!"

Antonia held her breath as Albert brought the beater down soundly on the cheeks of her ass.

"Two!" He brought it down again, exactly where the first stroke had landed and she felt the heat rise to the surface of her skin. Her pussy juice started flowing and by the time he'd finished she was literally dripping. "I don't think she's been punished enough, I'll fuck her tight ass with the handle as well just so she understands I am serious. Pass me the lube, honey."

Albert opened her legs and rubbed his hand over her pussy. "Look at her! Her pussy is so wet her juice has dripped out onto my thigh."

He spread her cheeks and pushed two fingers into her asshole, holding it slightly open as Millie poured a generous amount of lubricant over his fingers. He pushed his fingers deeper and finger-fucked her for a while.

"Time for you to be paddled, young lady." Pulling his fingers out, he pressed the tip of the stout handle inside her. The ridges were quite prominent and each time one passed her rim it gave Antonia the most maddening, deliciously arousing sensation. Albert held her securely and deliberately spaced the insertion of each ridge, making Antonia gasp and push against the handle impatiently.

"Behave!" He slapped her ass and pulled two ridges out to tease her. "Millie, honey, a little more lube, please—she is extra naughty today, I have to really punish her tight ass."

As soon as his wife had rubbed some lube onto the portion of the handle outside Antonia's ass, Albert drove it firmly up inside her.

"Yesss!" Antonia hissed as it pierced her fully.

Albert worked the paddle backwards and forwards with increasing speed as Antonia groaned aloud and tilted her ass upwards for maximum penetration. Millie reached under Antonia and fingered her clit as her husband continued to punish her mercilessly with the thick handle of the paddle.

When he finally pulled the paddle out Antonia screamed like a petulant child. He quickly lay back on the bed and instructed, "Sit on my cock, young lady. Let me continue your punishment."

Pulling her back against him, he slipped the head of his cock into her asshole, and then held her legs together to one side so that Millie could watch as he forced the rest of his thick cock slowly inside her. Millie, who had strapped on a dildo while Antonia was receiving her punishment, slid it into Antonia's pussy as soon as Albert's cock was sheathed in her ass.

"Let's punish her good, baby." Millie leaned over Antonia and kissed her husband before she lowered her head and sucked on Antonia's nipples. Husband and wife matched their strokes as they fucked Antonia, and her moans grew louder and louder. When she came they held her close for a moment, then Millie rolled off and un-strapped the dildo. Antonia climbed off Albert's still hard cock and Millie positioned herself as Antonia had done minutes earlier. Her husband grabbed her legs and quickly worked his cock into her ass. He released her legs when he was buried to the hilt and put his hands on her soft breasts and rolled her nipples firmly, deliberately pulling them upwards away from her breasts, elongating them until they were like mini-bullets pointing up at the ceiling. Antonia watched him eagerly and as soon as he offered her one she took it deep into her mouth and sucked it hungrily—she loved Millie's nipples. She stroked Albert's balls as she continued to suck on his wife's nipple and within minutes they both came.

Later, she lay on the bed sandwiched between them, Albert behind her and Millie in front. She had grown to love them both; they were like adoring parents, though they were much younger than her real parents. The slightly incestuous feel of the sex they had together aroused her baser instincts.

***

On Wednesday Antonia went Salsa dancing. She had behaved remarkably well on the Tube, she had only sneakily fondled one woman's full breast in almost a week and felt she deserved a mid-week treat. The guys who danced salsa were usually very good fuckmates and she had tried quite a few of them. They seemed to understand that the heat generated by the dancing needed to be quickly cooled but once body temperatures had been brought to normal by some fucking—that was the end of that.

She bought a glass of dry red wine from the bar, sat at one of the tables and watched the dancers while she sipped it. A young Hispanic guy caught her eye. She had never seen him before but he was an amazing dancer. His clothes fit his slim frame to perfection and his black ponytail bounced as he danced. She finished her drink as the song ended and went to stand at the edge of the dancing area. One of the regulars immediately grabbed her hand and pulled her onto the dance floor as the next song started. Every time she spun around, her short, wide skirt flew up to reveal most of her legs and occasionally the cheeks of her ass but she deliberately didn't try to hold it down.

The Hispanic guy captured her at the start of the next song. Not only was he a good dancer but he was an excellent partner, he spun her around so effortlessly she felt weightless.

He was Brazilian, his name was Ramiro. They danced for another hour, then she told him she had to leave. He followed her to her car, spun her around and kissed her before she could open the door. He was a little shorter than she was but she hadn't realized it when they had been dancing—he was so slim he looked taller.

His English was limited but she understood him well enough to get into her backseat and spread her pussy for him. Sadly, his cock was also limited. Thankfully it didn't take him long to cum. She quickly re-arranged her clothes, smiled sweetly at him and said goodbye.

Damn! Now she would have to masturbate when she got home.

***

The next morning on her way to work, she deliberately

moved along the platform and got on the carriage behind the one she usually did. When the Tube got to Leytonstone Station she saw her underage finger-fucker get on the Tube and look around before getting off again. He stood on the platform looking disappointed.

Fuck! Now she was going to have to use the rear carriages on Thursdays!

Friday evening she turned into Culverhouse Terrace and walked straight into Lucille's palm.

"Don't you have any fucking manners?" the woman demanded angrily. "Why didn't you leave your number?"

"I would have left my number *if* I wanted you to fuck me again. I *don't*." Antonia stepped back as Lucille raised her hand again. "Look bitch slap me one more fucking time and I'll take off these stilettos and *fuck* you up!"

Lucille looked down at Antonia's 4" heels and decided that she didn't want either of them stuck in any part of her anatomy. She pushed past Antonia and stormed off.

Antonia put her hand to her chest and breathed a sigh of relief; she'd only been bluffing about the shoes. Lucille would have kicked her ass before she'd had a chance to get her tight shoes off. They were brand-new and had been killing her feet the whole day.

Lucille didn't look as though she was going to calm down anytime soon.

Shit! Now she couldn't go back to the fucking wine bar!

***

Antonia was ultra horny when Caesar turned up with pink roses, as usual. It was their private joke, he liked a bit of pink as he called it. Antonia's period was like clockwork, it came every twenty-eight days, started on a Thursday and finished on a Sunday. Caesar liked to fuck her on the Saturday when the flow had slowed significantly but not stopped. He said he liked the extra heat her pussy generated during her period.

She had already placed the special protective sheet on the bed, so they quickly undressed and jumped on it. She opened a tube of chocolate sauce and poured some over Caesar's rigid cock. He re-capped it as she started to lick him clean. He pulled her onto the bed and fingered her clit as she took his cock deep into her mouth and let her throat close over the head. She cupped his balls and let him feel the edge of her teeth. He stiffened and spurted his thick cum down her throat. Next, she lay on the bed while he ate strawberries and licked cream off her body. Then she disposed of her tampon, and let him give her a fast, furious fuck as he sat on the edge of her circular bathtub.

"Your pussy is really hot tonight," he murmured around her nipple as he moved her up and down on his cock.

She didn't mind Caesar's little pink fetish but seven years ago she had met a guy called Bradley in Faces Nightclub one Friday night. They had danced for most of the night and he hadn't wanted to let her go when the club closed. She'd explained that she had her period and he'd promptly said, 'no problem'. She'd been a bit surprised but since she was usually horniest during her period she'd welcomed some cock. They went back to her place, jumped into the shower together and fucked, standing up in the cubicle. Afterwards, she'd showered and had been about to step out to dry her body, when Bradley had dropped to his knees and started to tongue her clit. Suddenly, he had spread her legs and pushed his tongue up inside her! She'd pulled her bloody pussy away and chased the vampire from her house. He was too fucking sick even for her, and she did some freaky shit!

***

Sunday lunchtime she got an urgent text message from Alistair—he needed to talk to her desperately. She called him back immediately. "What's up, girlfriend?"

Alistair, the drama queen, started crying as soon as he heard her voice, "An ugly bitch gave Floyd head last night."

"But honey, you suck other guys' cocks all the time!" she reminded him.

"I know, but that's different!" Alistair sniffled.

He was a complete whore. He and Floyd had been together for almost two years but he still loved to suck other men's cocks. His excuse was that he had entered the gay scene a bit later in life than most gay men and he was just trying to taste the difference.

"Did you actually see the guy sucking Floyd's dick?"

"No. But I know *the bitch* did! Girlfriend came out of the loo and looked at me like she had just eaten my last fucking Rolo."

"Honey, you know Floyd loves you. When he comes home tonight give him the best head you have ever given him and stop sucking other guys' dicks!"

"I guess he does love me, doesn't he?"

"Yes he does, Sweetpea. He was the first man to fuck that sweet ass of yours and he'd never forget that. *Hell*, I was the first woman to fuck it and I never forget!"

"Girlfriend, you know how to cheer me up. Tonight, I am going to cook him a nice meal and later I am going to have *him* for dessert."

"Now we're talking! Why would Floyd want some ugly cow when he has a good-looking bitch like you?

"Toni, sweets, must dash to the supermarket to get some tiger prawns—Floyd loves them! I'll catch you later."

"Bye, Alistair."

Alistair was now one of her best 'girlfriends' but they had been lovers when they had first met. She'd been totally drunk the night she'd met him and the next morning when she'd awoken, with his hard cock pressed against her ass, she hadn't remembered his name. He had cooked her a tasty breakfast in her kitchen, and they had showered and crawled back into bed. Minutes later, as he was fucking her ass with fast, hard strokes she had warned him that she would fuck his if he continued to pummel hers without mercy. He had surprised her by saying, "Yes please!"

She'd strapped on a dildo, popped his cherry and he had almost gone crazy. Later that day he had gone home but had come back the next day for her to give him another round of ass-fucking. After plugging his ass twice, she'd told him straight, "girlfriend, you need a man." She had occasionally buggered men before but sensed that Alistair needed a real cock. She had taken him to a gay club, and introduced herself to a hunk, who looked like just the man for the job. When she told him her friend needed his ass fucked, he hadn't hesitated, grabbing Alistair's hand and leading the way to a stall in the gents.

Antonia had followed to ensure Alistair's safety but she needn't have bothered. She watched Alistair, his face red with embarrassment, willingly suck on the nice meaty cock Floyd whipped out and equally willingly, bend over for the lovely ass-fucking that ensued.

The two of them then put Antonia in a cab, while they headed over to Alistair's place, together—with huge smiles on their faces.

The whore, Alistair, had still come over for Antonia to fuck his ass a few weeks later but she'd informed him that she didn't plan on starting any new syndrome—the 'down low' was enough. Things would get way too complicated if gay men started cheating on their lovers with women!

***

Wednesday she went back to the salsa club and the first person she saw as she walked into the darkened room was Ramiro. He made a beeline for her and wouldn't let her dance with anyone else. Later she tried to explain that she had fucked him and once was enough but she couldn't make him understand. In the end she had to let him have some more pussy or she would have been there all night.

Double damn! Now she couldn't go back to the fucking salsa club!

***

Just after quarter past eight the following Saturday night Antonia's uncle Terrence walked through her front door. She was lying on the sofa, her open robe displaying her naked body as she fingered her pussy. She jumped up, threw her arms around his neck and kissed him long and lingeringly. He slipped his arms under the robe and cupped her ass.

"Up," he commanded, and knelt so that she could hook her left leg up over his shoulder. She held on to the arm of the sofa as he examined her pussy and immediately slid two fingers into her wetness. "I see you've been playing with yourself again, although I told you not to."

He pulled his fingers out and turned her around, bending her over in front of him so that he could examine her asshole. He slid a slick finger deep inside it. "Whose been fucking this ass?"

"No one, Uncle Terry."

"I wasn't born yesterday! Someone's fucked this ass quite recently and I am going to punish you for allowing it."

He pulled her upright and she eagerly hurried ahead of him up the steps into her bedroom. Shedding the robe, she climbed onto the bed and lay prone while he undressed quickly. He picked up the larger of the two tasselled whips from her bedside table and expertly brought it down on the cheeks of her ass. He continued for a few minutes, deliberately placing the blows at random.

"Now raise your hips. I am going to plug your tight little pussy, so that the next time I tell you not to play with yourself you will obey me."

Obediently, she raised her hips, groaning like the naughty young woman she was pretending to be as he pushed the thick handle into her wet pussy. She genuinely sighed as the large penis-shaped handle stretched her.

Terrence left the whip stuck inside her and picked up the other one. He administered a few more lashes to her backside, before pulling her up onto all-fours.

"I warned you time and time again never to let anyone fuck your ass. Men don't respect women whose asses they fuck! I have told you often but you deliberately ignored my advice. You have given me no choice." He poured lube onto the other handle and then pressed the end against her asshole. "This will put you off ass-fucking for the rest of your life!"

"Please, Uncle Terry, I promise it won't happen again!"

"It's too late now. When I am done your ass will be so sore you will never let anyone near it again!"

"It's too big, Uncle Terry!"

"I know, I chose it specially to teach you a lesson you'll never forget."

He slowly worked the handle into her, pulling it back a few millimetres to push it further inside her. When it was buried deeply, he grabbed hold of the one sticking out of her pussy and worked them in and out of her alternatively, slowly pushing one to the hilt while pulling the other almost out of her.

Mesmerized by the sight Terrence abruptly brought the role playing to an end by asking, "How does that feel, baby?"

"*So* good."

"Yes? How about this?" He pushed the handle to the hilt in her pussy and vigorously thrust the one in her ass backwards and forwards and then stopped abruptly.

"Don't stop," she begged, tilting her ass up even further.

"How about this combination?" He pulled them both almost out of her and then slid them smoothly back inside her.

"Yes, just like that!" She waited eagerly for him to repeat the action but instead he knelt on the bed and fed her his cock, leaving her frustrated pussy clenching around the moulded handle.

"Baby, look at you!"

She turned and caught sight of herself in the mirror. She looked like a bitch, on all-fours with the tassels hanging out of her like a tail.

"I can't wait..." Slowly easing the handle out of her backside, Terrence bent over her and deftly rammed his cock in its place and fucked her slowly with deep, firm thrusts, pushing the other handle further into her pussy with each forward stroke.

She came almost immediately, and so did he.

Terrence was her aunt's husband and he had been fucking her since she was nineteen. He was the closest she had ever come to being in love, but she often wondered if she would stay faithful to him even if he was free. When her aunt had brought him back as her new husband after a holiday in Tobago eleven years ago, everyone had been shocked. At the lavish reception her aunt had thrown two weeks later, Antonia had danced with her new uncle and felt the big bulge in his trousers that let her know he was *very* happy to meet her. They had slipped out discreetly and headed for Terrence's brand new BMW, one of the many gifts from his new wife. When he had whipped his cock out Antonia had almost screamed. She had been a tight little thing back then and they had to abandon the attempt. The next day he had sneaked around to Antonia's flat, got her juices flowing and then spent the night burying his big cock inside her from every possible angle.

After that night, he had wanted to leave her aunt Elaine but Antonia had begged him not to—her millionaire aunt would have probably paid an assassin to take them both out!

At forty-one, Elaine had looked fifteen years younger and had lied to Terrence about her true age. She had even bribed a clerk at the small registry office to aid the deception. Terrence was only a year older than Antonia and when he found out that his wife was two years younger than his mother, he had been ready to pack his bags and go back to the Caribbean. But Elaine had made him an offer he couldn't refuse: money to start his own business; her pussy whenever he wanted and other pussy if he was discreet. Antonia suspected that her aunt knew that Terrence fucked her regularly but chose to overlook the minor detail, sensibly deciding that it was better to keep it in the family.

Terrence had started using the whips at Antonia's request after she had gotten rid of Paul, an older man who used to pretend Antonia was his daughter and give her a sound whipping for missing curfew, playing with herself or simply for having a boyfriend. The last time Paul had visited he'd gotten caught up in the fantasy and become maudlin. He'd lost his erection and started begging her for forgiveness. Antonia had suspected that something improper might have occurred between him and his real daughter. She told him to get out and get therapy—she wasn't a fucking psychologist. Pretending the woman you're fucking is your daughter is one fucking thing; fucking your daughter is something entirely different! So, she had slotted Carla into Paul's vacant Saturday and put the whips in Terrence's hands.

***

Dishing up a large bowl of the steamed fish, yams, green plantains and other hard foods she had prepared for Terrence earlier in the evening and left simmering gently on the stove, she placed it on a tray and took it up to the bedroom for him.

"Baby, you know how to look after your man." He kissed her as he took the laden tray from her.

"You work hard, honey. You need to replenish your energy."

In the eleven years he'd been fucking her she didn't have one complaint. He still fucked her with the same enthusiasm as the very first time.

When he finished eating she took the tray back to the kitchen and they had a leisurely bath together. After drying her off with a soft, white towel he oiled her down with baby oil and gently stretched her bones. She had known as soon as he picked up the oil that she had to prepare for a night of intense fucking. His next words were no surprise, "I feel like really punishing your pussy, baby. I'm not leaving here until late tomorrow."

He picked her up and tossed her lightly onto the bed, then climbed onto it and took one of her nipples between his teeth, applying just the right amount of pressure to make it harden into a little pebble before moving to the other side. She reached down to stroke his rock-hard cock while he continued to tease her nipples.

Suddenly he sat up and placed her legs over his broad shoulders and put his cock at her entrance. He leaned down and kissed her, pushing her legs right back, folding her over unto herself, as his thick cock forced itself way into her pussy. His cock was not as fat as Stuart's but he used it to maximum effect and he had the stamina of a horse. He hooked his toes under the edge of the wooden footboard and raised himself on his muscular arms to look down at her pussy wrapped tightly around his cock. "You missed me, baby?"

"Yes, Uncle Terry."

"I missed you too, sugar." He treated her to some hard,

fast strokes, then paused and placed her legs on the bed. "I have to moderate the punishment, the way your pussy is gripping me I will cum again at any second if I don't take your legs off my shoulders."

She rotated her hips as he drove his cock forwards and backwards, sometimes giving her the full length in deep thrusts, at other times pulling it out completely to tease her entrance with short jabs until she was mindless. She suddenly wrapped her legs around his hips and took him deep inside her. He groaned and climaxed, lowering his sweat-drenched body onto hers, just the way she loved and she wrapped her arms around him. She stroked his head as she held him against her.

When he rolled off, Antonia got up and went to the fridge. She poured herself a glass of wine and opened a bottle of Guinness for him. He didn't often drink alcohol but he liked to have a bottle of the Stout whenever he came over to her house, said it gave him the required energy to deal with her pussy right.

"How's Aunty Elaine?" she asked as she handed him the bottle.

"Elaine's fine but she hasn't been the same since the hysterectomy."

Her fifty-two-year-old aunt had taken losing her womb harder than anyone had expected—she had started acting her age and giving Terrence her pussy sparingly because even with the use of K-Y Jelly getting his big cock inside her wasn't easy.

Antonia put on some soul music and she and Terrence lay propped up on the bed, sipping their drinks. He kissed her and sucked on her neck and breasts in between sips, his hard cock standing to attention as she stroked it. He put his half-finished bottle on the bedside table and she quickly placed the empty glass beside it.

"Turn over and give your uncle another piece of ass, sweets." She knelt on the bed and he lubricated his cock in her pussy. Spreading her cheeks he pushed it against her asshole and slid it deep before giving her a series of hard, fast jabs that had her gasping.

"Uncle Terry, you're lethal, tonight!"

"I've got a lot of fucking in me, baby—your aunt hasn't given me pussy in two weeks."

"Poor, Uncle Terry!"

"Don't feel sorry for me, sweets. I will be coming over mid-week to punish you regularly."

"Okay, Uncle Terry."

And why not?

Recently her mid-week fucks had all been disappointing. She had almost committed paedophilia, couldn't go to her local wine bar or her favourite salsa club because of her naughty fucking pussy. At least with Terrence she was guaranteed a big cock and some enthusiastic fucking. And she would be saving her poor aunt's pussy.

***

Men always assume that women don't think of sex as much as they do—they are absolutely wrong. Some of us think about sex so much we masturbate constantly when we are at home or have to go to the ladies to mop up pussy juices when we are at work. Antonia is just someone who is brave enough to give in to the urges of her unruly pussy and bad ass.

*****

SAMANTHA

"*T*hat looks too big," Valerie said uncertainly as she watched Samantha strap on a dark-chocolate coloured dildo that matched her skin tone perfectly.

"Come on, honey, it's only quarter of an inch longer and a little fatter than the one I fucked you with the last time." Samantha smiled at her encouragingly. "You know you like a bit of sweet pain."

She wished Valerie won't bitch about the size of the dildo every fucking time. So far Valerie had taken every inch she had given her and taken them hard.

"We both know once I tongue your clit nicely you can take anything I give you," she reminded Valerie as she spread her legs and rubbed her face against her pussy. "God, you smell good!"

She quickly pushed three fingers inside Valerie's pussy. Valerie groaned as they stretched her but Samantha's expert tongue on her clit made up for the discomfort, and then some. In less than a minute Valerie came. Samantha straightened up, covered Valerie's body with her own and kissed her as she reached down and separated her pussy lips.

"You know you want this dildo inside you." Samantha's eyes held Valerie's as she pushed the head of the dildo against her and pressed it inside her entrance.

"It's too big!" Valerie moaned as the dildo forced its way into her. "I can't take it."

"Just relax, honey." Samantha bent her head and wrapped her lips around one of Valerie's erect nipples and sucked hard. Instantly she felt the dildo inch further inside Valerie. She sucked harder as she thrust deeper and deeper. Finally, she pushed the last eighth of an inch into Valerie's pussy and raised her slim body off Valerie's. "Look at that, baby. You've taken it all!"

Valerie looked down and gasped in surprise—the entire dildo was buried inside her! Samantha's mouth on her nipples had totally distracted her.

Samantha kissed her as she started to slide the dildo in and out of her, gradually increasing the tempo. She pulled her lips off Valerie's, stared into her eyes and asked, "You like this big dildo, honey?"

"Yes," Valerie whispered softly, closing her eyes as she tried to bite in her moans of pleasure-pain.

"Come on, I didn't hear you. Do you like this big dildo?" Samantha pressed a little deeper on her next stroke, making Valerie wince. She gave Valerie a couple more hard thrusts then pulled the dildo out completely. "I asked you a question."

"You know I like it." Valerie opened her legs wider. "Sam, please don't tease me!"

Samantha forced the dildo into her with one quick stroke and Valerie's body arched off the bed.

"Now tell me how much you like it," Samantha panted as she increased her tempo. "Is it better than Henry's cock?"

"Oh God, yes!" Valerie gasped.

"Now, beg me to fuck you," Samantha ordered as she took one of Valerie's swollen nipples between her lips and sucked it firmly.

"Fuck me, please, Sam! Fu-ck me-ee!"

Samantha suddenly bit down on Valerie's nipple and she came instantly, raising her hips off the bed, taking Samantha, dildo and all, with her. Samantha kept the dildo buried inside Valerie and sucked on her nipple until the tremors died and Valerie collapsed weakly back onto the bed.

"God, I could watch you cum all day!" Samantha ran her tongue around one of Valerie's puckered nipples. "Ready for my cock again?"

"Yes," Valerie replied, eagerly. Although her pussy was sore, she didn't want to waste any of the precious time they had together.

Samantha turned her over and tongued her clit before she pushed the dildo between the lips of her swollen pussy and fucked her hard from behind. Valerie groaned and clutched handfuls of the sheet. When Valerie came again, Samantha lay against her for a few minutes, cupping one of her firm breasts with one hand and stroking her clit gently with the other.

"We haven't got much time left, so let's take it to another level." Samantha quickly flipped Valerie on to her back again and positioned herself between her legs. She opened the slick folds of her pussy and slid the dildo inside her with a single thrust. The pain made Valerie hiss through her teeth. Ignoring the sound, Samantha raised Valerie's legs onto her shoulders and reached between their bodies to stroke Valerie's clit as she pushed the dildo deeper.

"Fuck!" Valerie screamed and sunk her fingernails deep into Samantha's shoulder.

"Yes, baby, take this dildo all the way up in your pussy. Every fucking inch is yours." Samantha started pushing the dildo in and out smoothly, increasing the speed of her hips with every stroke.

"Oh, ye-ess! Fuck me, Sam!" Valerie pulled Samantha's

head down and kissed her. She reached between them for Samantha's nipples and tweaked them firmly until Samantha stiffened and came, burying the dildo deep, pulling another orgasm out of Valerie in the process.

Reluctantly, Valerie eased Samantha off her and got up. She went into the adjoining bathroom and quickly washed before she got dressed.

"I wish you didn't have to go back to work this afternoon." Samantha kissed her tenderly by the door. As she straightened she groaned, "God, I need to suck on your nipples just one more time."

She opened the first two buttons of Valerie's top, pulled her left breast from her bra and sucked on it while her fingers tweaked the right. Valerie moaned and cupped her head. Samantha raised her head and asked, "Are you sure you want to go back so soon?"

"Sam, I *have* to go," Valerie moaned and pulled Samantha's head back down to her nipple. Valerie's boss had already cautioned her about her extended lunch breaks—she was this close to a formal warning. Reluctantly, she pulled her nipple away from Samantha's mouth and buttoned her top. "I'll see you next week."

***

Samantha sat on her sofa and smiled after Valerie left.

It was only a matter of time before Valerie left her husband Henry. He was such a typical macho fucking man—wanting to see another woman fuck his wife—then getting jealous when the woman fucked her better than he did. The next time she was going to give Valerie the ultimate thrill—the 10" dildo she'd aptly named 'The Home Wrecker'. Once she eased that fat boy past a married woman's entrance, the husband's little dick couldn't satisfy his wife again. It might take two or three attempts to get the full length into Valerie's tight pussy but Samantha knew once she tongued her just right and sucked on those sensitive nipples of hers, Valerie would be begging for it.

Valerie's total conquest was taking a little longer than planned. Her pussy was unusually tight—it had taken Samantha three months to work her way up slowly from the medium 8" dildo she had used the first time to the 9" fat boy she'd used today. She was getting a little tired of Valerie and the woman still seemed to love her husband. Samantha needed to pull out all the stops during her next few visits because Valerie had a way of turning up unexpectedly and Samantha couldn't take the chance of Valerie meeting her other woman.

Samantha smiled again as she thought of her latest conquest—newly-married twenty-three-year-old Celeste. Celeste's husband was thirty years older than his sexy wife and only two weeks after he'd brought her to the UK he had forced her into living out his twisted fantasy—the usual one—like all the other unimaginative fools he'd wanted to watch another woman fuck his wife. When Samantha caught sight of the 5'4" slender, busty beauty she had been very happy to fucking oblige!

The old fool had specifically asked Samantha to bring a dildo when she came to his house. She had casually asked him what size his cock was—pretending she wanted to match it to the dildo. The fool had lied and said he had a 7" dick. Of course, Samantha had whipped out an 8" black dildo that looked deceptively smaller and had fucked Celeste to two mammoth orgasms while the old fart had wanked his barely 5" cock.

The following day Samantha had called Celeste and within two hours Celeste had been lying on Samantha's four-poster bed with the black dildo buried in her pussy again, talking in French. The dildo had her so sprung she had reverted to her mother tongue!

Celeste had explained that the rich old ferret had come to Guadeloupe on holiday, and seen her in a tiny bikini on the beach. He had paid her two hundred pounds to come up to his hotel room and let him suck on her nipples. After he'd finished his sucking she had told him she'd let him do some fucking for another three hundred. His cock was in her pussy before she'd finished counting the extra money!

He had paid her the same amount for the next five days, leaving the Island three thousand pounds poorer than he would have done if he hadn't seen Celeste. But when he got back to the UK he missed the young pussy so much he had flown back to the Island a month later and brought her back as his unblushing bride.

***

Celeste was standing on her doorstep dressed in a tiny top and hipster jeans, her sexy, ribbed stomach on full display when Samantha opened the door. Samantha hooked her hand in the jeans, pulled Celeste into the flat, leaned down and kissed her. She put her hands under Celeste's top and fondled her big breasts. Celeste's small nipples tightened instantly. Samantha pulled the top off and covered one with her mouth. It seemed physically impossible that a woman as slim as Celeste could naturally have 32F knockers.

"I've got a surprise for you today," Samantha told Celeste as she lifted her head.

"I love surprises." Celeste smiled as Samantha undid her jeans and pushed them down her legs. As usual Celeste wasn't wearing any knickers and as usual when Samantha pushed two fingers in her pussy she was already wet. Samantha finger-fucked her for a few minutes then straightened, took her hand and led her to the bedroom.

"It's time for your surprise."

Samantha strapped on 'Double Entry', a slim 6" double dildo, as Celeste lay on the bed, playing with her nipples and watching her.

"What's that?" Celeste asked as Samantha approached the bed.

"Come on, Celeste don't be coy. I know you have been fucked in the ass before." She had known as soon as she had seen Celeste's asshole while she was fucking her the first night that the young woman had taken a cock, or two, or three up her ass.

Samantha smeared the slimmer anal dildo with some of Celeste's juice, spread her cheeks and pussy lips, and pushed the dildo inside her. The anal attachment slid home so easily Samantha was disappointed. The old fart obviously fucked his wife's ass, regularly. She should have known! Now the old fool done gone and spoiled her fucking surprise.

"Do you want me to get a bigger one?" she asked Celeste.

"Okay." Celeste agreed, seeming as disappointed as she was.

Samantha rummaged through her drawer and pulled out another double dildo which was so equally sized it would have been hard to tell what went where if the shapes of the two prongs weren't different. 'The Double Whammer', as Samantha had appropriately named him, was for the woman who liked something beefy in both her pussy and ass simultaneously.

"This one is satisfaction guaranteed." Samantha smiled as she rubbed both dildos against Celeste's wet pussy, smearing them with her abundant juice. She spread Celeste and tried again.

"Aaaah! Mon Dieu!" Celeste turned her head to the side as Samantha got the head of the dildo in her ass.

"You okay?" Samantha asked as she pushed it in another inch.

Celeste bit her lower lip and nodded. Samantha stroked

Celeste's clit and leaned over to suck her nipples. She pushed forward another inch and Celeste moaned. Samantha kissed her neck and asked again, "Okay?"

"I'm fine, but the one in my ass is big, no?"

Samantha laughed softly. "It is only 6" inches but it has a healthy girth. I'll go slowly and trust me when I get it buried inside you, you will love it." She pulled Celeste's slim legs upwards and pushed the dildos a bit deeper. "You feel that?"

Celeste moaned appreciatively in response.

"Don't be afraid, my darling. Relax and let it penetrate you," Samantha encouraged as she kissed Celeste and slowly pushed the remainder of the dildo all the way. *This* is what she loved about Celeste; she was completely open to pleasure.

"You have taken them both, you sweet girl. Doesn't that look and feel wonderful?" Samantha raised herself slightly so that Celeste could see the dildos buried to the hilt inside her.

"Oui!" Celeste sighed in agreement.

Samantha kissed her again. "Now, honey, just lie back and let me fuck you. I want you to cum like you've never done before."

Celeste put her hands on her own erect nipples and tugged them as Samantha started thrusting. When she came, Celeste screamed out loud and tried to push Samantha off but Samantha held her tightly and kept thrusting until she came again. Then Samantha un-strapped the dildo and rubbed her hard clit against Celeste's until they both came. They lay wrapped in each other's arms until Celeste stirred.

She got dressed quickly and at the door she pushed some folded notes into Samantha's hand as they kissed goodbye. "I had great time today. I come back Friday, yes?"

Samantha nodded and Celeste slipped through the door

with a smile.

She counted the notes—not bad for less than two hours work. She had to watch herself—she was beginning to like Celeste far too much. Fucking her twice a week was *no* hardship at all. She would probably need to buy a bigger double dildo soon but the Whammer would work for another week or so, it had been a very tight fit. Friday she would fuck Celeste a bit harder than she had done today and by next Friday she would be slamming that double dildo so hard into Celeste, her teeth would rattle. God, there was nothing like fucking a man's wife—the ultimate power trip!

***

Valerie was dressed in one of her smart business suits and looked particularly good when Samantha opened the door to her the following Thursday. Samantha felt almost sorry she would have to let her go because she liked fucking the prissy woman until she lost all her inhibitions and behaved liked the horny bitch she really was. If Celeste hadn't come along she might have fucked Valerie for another six months but now she had the younger woman Valerie had lost some of her appeal. Plus Celeste was paying for her services; Valerie was far too prissy to pay someone to fuck her.

"I missed you," Valerie said as she pulled Samantha's head down to kiss her.

"Did you?" Samantha pulled her head back, avoiding Valerie's lips. "I thought you'd be far too busy sucking your husband's small cock to remember I'm alive."

"I see you're in a mood." Valerie looked hurt as she stared up at Samantha. "Do you want me to leave?"

"Forgive me, baby." Samantha quickly kissed Valerie, plunging her tongue deep into her mouth as she cupped her breasts and tweaked her nipples. "I'm on edge—I'm waiting for a reply from a publisher and it's got me in a foul mood."

She undid the button on Valerie's blouse and tried to pull both her breasts out of her bra. The underwired cups were a bit stiff but she managed to get Valerie's nipples and most of her breasts free. Samantha would usually free them one at a time but she was trying to make up for her snappy greeting. It would have been even easier to just take the bra off but she knew Valerie loved her nipples sucked this way.

"Look at those beautiful nipples *just* waiting for my mouth." She bent and rubbed her face against the hard peaks before she looked up at Valerie, whose eyes were already soft, her mouth slightly open as she sighed in anticipation.

Samantha sucked on one nipple and then the other alternatively as Valerie held onto her shoulders for support, her moans getting louder and louder. Samantha pulled her lips away just before Valerie started to climax. Samantha still couldn't understand how a grown woman could *cum* from just nipple-sucking—it was *so* high school.

"We've got all afternoon, honey. I want you to save those orgasms for later." Samantha rolled Valerie's nipples between her fingers as a small consolation and the look of disappointment faded from Valerie's face. "Take your clothes off while I keep these nipples warm."

Samantha went back to sucking on Valerie's nipples as Valerie slipped her jacket and her blouse off her shoulders but as she reached to unhook her bra, Samantha suddenly sucked hard and Valerie came instantly.

"I'll have to punish you with some *extra* hard fucking for your disobedience," Samantha threatened as she moved to the other breast. As Valerie stepped out of her thong, Samantha bit her nipple sharply and made her cry out. "That was the beginning of your punishment, are you ready for the rest of it?" Samantha held Valerie's face between her hands and stared into her eyes.

"Yes." Valerie didn't know what it was about Samantha that made her feel weak and ready to step outside the safety of her everyday life. The woman was as intoxicating as a drug.

"Welcome to the dark side." Samantha pulled a scarf from the pocket of her dressing gown and tied it around Valerie's eyes. She led her to the bedroom and pushed her onto the four-poster bed. She slipped foamed-cover handcuffs onto Valerie's wrists and attached them to the corners of the bed. "Today, I want you to just feel."

Today was the day for some home wrecking and she knew if Valerie saw him first there was no way she'd let Samantha fuck her with him. She strapped the Wrecker in place, once again surprised how heavy the fat 10" dildo felt in the harness. She could never get used to the weight although she had wielded the giant beast many times in the past.

She climbed onto the bed and pushed her fingers in Valerie's dripping pussy—she had deliberately made Valerie cum earlier. She pulled her fingers out and smeared the moisture over the dildo, opening Valerie's legs wider as she positioned herself between them. She carefully separated the folds of Valerie's pussy and put the dildo against her entrance and pushed it inwards.

"Is that the same dildo?" Valerie gasped as it pushed past her opening and left a burning trail.

"Yes, it is. You took it *all* the last time, so just enjoy the feel of it stretching your pussy, filling you up like Henry's cock could never do."

"It feels bigger this time," Valerie moaned as Samantha thrust forward again.

"That's because you are wearing a blindfold—your senses are heightened."

"It feels as if it's getting bigger towards the base."

Valerie's hands pulled against the handcuffs but she couldn't free them.

There was still half of it to go yet and Valerie was right it *was* thicker at the base.

"Let me suck on your sweet nipples." Samantha put the words to action, leaning forward and sucking Valerie's nipples hard as she rammed another half an inch inside her.

"Sam, I really can't take anymore." Valerie's lips started to quiver.

Samantha stopped thrusting forward. She had all afternoon so she could be a little patient but she was going to give Valerie all of the Wrecker before she went home to her bastard of a husband.

"Honey, you are too tense. Let me tongue your clit for a while and you'll be begging me for the full length." Samantha pulled the dildo free, dipped her head and tongued Valerie's clit. Before Valerie came Samantha stopped and pushed the dildo back inside her. It went a little deeper but not as far as Samantha had hoped. She massaged Valerie's clit firmly and got another inch inside but there was still over three inches to go.

"Let me turn you over and take you from the back. It will be easier." Samantha pulled the dildo out, unlocked the handcuffs and tried to turn Valerie onto her front.

"It will hurt more!" Valerie resisted but Samantha turned her over forcefully and quickly re-attached the handcuffs to the bed.

"Come on, Valerie. Don't be a baby!" Samantha pushed her fingers in Valerie's pussy and finger-fucked her until she was gasping. But again, just before she came Samantha pulled her fingers out.

"Sam, stop teasing me!" Valerie screamed. "You're driving me insane!"

"The sooner you get this dildo buried in your pussy, the

sooner you will cum. It is your choice, honey."

"Why are you being like this today?" Valerie asked, sounding bewildered.

"Baby, *all* I want to do is fuck you. You are the one who is being difficult." Samantha spread Valerie's legs further apart and pushed the dildo back inside her. The new position didn't make any difference but as Samantha looked at Valerie's tightly puckered asshole, she formulated a plan. Valerie's hands were handcuffed so there was little she could do. Samantha reached around and massaged Valerie's clit, getting her fingers nice and wet as she continued to force the dildo home.

Valerie moaned and put her head against the pillow as the dildo stretched her pussy further—it was splitting her apart, she really just wanted it out of her. Suddenly she felt a sharp pain and for a second she didn't know where it originated as a red haze swam behind her closed eyelids. It took a moment for her to realize that Samantha had pushed a finger into her asshole. Valerie screamed and tried to fight Samantha but the woman held her down easily.

"There now, sweetness...just relax for me...the pain will go in a minute." Samantha gently worked her finger in and out of Valerie's asshole for a while. Valerie was amazed as she felt her pussy relax. Samantha must have felt it too because she started to thrust the dildo gently back and forth again, going deeper each time.

Finally she pulled her finger out and leaned over Valerie, grasping her breasts as she kissed her neck. "Honey, I knew you could take a 10" dildo, you just had to relax."

Valerie's mind reeled as Samantha's words penetrated the pleasure-filled fog of her mind—10"! Two and a quarter inches longer than Henry's cock! It was too much! But now that it was inside her it was beginning to feel good!

Minutes passed as Samantha fucked her gently with the

Wrecker, there was a little bit left outside but Samantha was happy—the job was done.

"You like it, baby?" She leaned forward again and playfully bit Valerie's shoulder before trailing her lips to her neck.

"Yes!" Valerie hissed as the dildo filled her on Samantha's next forward stroke.

Samantha knows my body so much better than I do, she thought as the dildo glided into her pussy and out again. She couldn't feel the brush of Samantha's thighs against her own and knew there must be a little bit left to go. She tilted her hips upwards for deeper penetration, her body demanding even more of the length. Samantha obliged by plugging her pussy with the last of the Wrecker.

"It feels *so* good!" Valerie moaned as she ground herself back against Samantha.

"I want you to cum for me a couple of times before I give you the punishment I promised you earlier," Samantha told Valerie as she reached down and fingered her clit, slowly increasing the speed of her slim hips. Moments later Valerie's body convulsed as an explosive orgasm raced through her.

"Yes, baby, cum for me, cum all over this dildo," Samantha crooned as she kept up her thrusting motion, moving her hands upwards to Valerie's breasts and rolling the nipples firmly. "Cum again for me, baby."

Within minutes Valerie obediently came again, Samantha clever fingers on her nipples and the driving rhythm of the dildo in her pussy making the second orgasm even more explosive. Samantha kissed her neck again as she straightened and pushed Valerie's legs further apart and positioned herself firmly between them.

"Now I am going to really punish your pussy, baby. Brace yourself because when you cum you won't believe the rush!"

Valerie closed her eyes as Samantha started the insanely fast thrusting she had come to know and love so well. Within minutes another orgasm ripped through Valerie but she'd learned that Samantha wouldn't stop until she had at least another one and that it would be even more intense.

"Yes, honey, fuck me." Valerie leaned her head weakly against the pillow and let Samantha have her fucking way.

Minutes later, Samantha pulled the dildo out of Valerie's pussy and reached over to unlock the handcuffs before she pulled off her blindfold. Valerie blinked as her eyes adjusted to the light again. She smiled at Samantha before she looked down at the dildo still strapped in the harness and gasped in shock. It was a monstrosity!

"You put that thing in *me*?" she demanded in horror.

"Valerie, you liked it, so please don't complain." Samantha had deliberately kept the Wrecker on so the uppity bitch could see her middle-class cunt could open itself and stretch as easily as one from the ghetto.

Valerie jumped up and quickly pulled on her clothes, not even bothering to have a shower. She knew if she didn't leave immediately she would slap Samantha and that would be ill-advised; the woman was taller and stronger than she was.

Samantha watched Valerie quickly head for the door and called after her mockingly, "You'll be back! Henry's little dick can't satisfy you anymore!"

***

Valerie stepped out of her clothes and into the bath as soon as she got home. She had noticed a difference in Samantha the last few times she had visited but she had ignored it. Samantha didn't pay the same attention to her nipples or her clit as she used to, she only resorted to tonguing them when she was trying to force a dildo inside

Valerie's pussy. Yet, every time Valerie was about to leave she would open her blouse and suck on her nipples in the sweetest way, making her late for work.

In all the years they'd been married Valerie's ass had been off-limits to Henry. Yet, although she had repeatedly said that she didn't like anything anal, Samantha had pushed her finger inside her today. And, once again, Samantha had revealed another of Valerie's dormant desires. Samantha's finger in her asshole had felt better than Valerie had imagined possible—all the years she had been afraid of the pain, she hadn't anticipated the pleasure.

***

Three days later Henry came home and found the house in complete darkness. No sign of Valerie. Worried, he ran upstairs and found her in bed, naked. She was pretending to be asleep, a little note over her head which he read in disbelief: *I have swallowed my tongue. The only way to push it back out is to push your finger up my asshole.*

Henry's cock hardened immediately. He stripped off his suit and the rest of his clothes and left them in a pile on the floor as he joined his wife on the bed. When he tried to kiss her she didn't open her mouth, so he moved down to her breasts and sucked on them as he fondled her ass. He was eager to finally finger-fuck her ass but he had to be patient and get her in the mood first; one false move and it could be off.

He stayed on her breasts, his finger gently exploring the crease between the cheeks of her ass, occasionally pressing lightly against her asshole. When she started thrusting her hips back against his finger, he turned her over and rimmed her asshole as he fingered her clit. As soon as she was relaxed enough he encircled her asshole with his fingertip and then slid it inside her.

He quickly increased the tempo until he was vigorously

finger-fucking her ass. His poor cock was green with envy. Valerie must have sensed it because she reached backwards between her legs and stroked it in sympathy.

His finger was moving so smoothly in and out of her ass, he was contemplating adding a second finger when she grabbed another piece of paper and started writing.

This time the message said: *Honey, I don't think your finger is doing the trick; you'll have to use your cock. Be gentle.*

Henry's eyes nearly popped out of his head. He quickly pushed his cock into her wet pussy before pulling it out and positioning it against her asshole. He kissed the back of her neck, stroked her breasts and her clit alternatively as he gently pushed his cock into her unbelievably tight asshole. He had to pause several times to stop himself from cumming, but eventually the full length was buried deep inside her. He rested for a while before he started thrusting slowly in and out.

"Oh yes, Henry, you've done it, darling." Valerie's voice was low and edged with pain. "Now fuck my ass, baby. Fuck it hard!"

"Sweetheart, are you okay?" Henry didn't know what was more surprising: that she had finally spoken or the vulgar words she'd used.

"Yes, honey, I'm fine." Valerie's voice was muffled by the pillow she was biting down on.

His cock in her ass was making her eyes water but Valerie knew in time she would love Henry fucking her ass as much as she loved his cock in her pussy, she just had to endure the exquisite pain. She didn't intend to confess her indiscretions to Henry, the pain she suffered while he broke her asshole in, would be penance enough.

Henry still couldn't believe he was fucking his wife's ass or that she had cursed and asked him to fuck her hard. If it was a dream, he hoped he didn't awaken until he came. He quickened his stroke and forced his cock deeper inside his wife newly deflowered asshole. He had fucked dozens of women in his lifetime but none compared to his sweet wife. Now she was giving him her tight ass too! God, he loved this woman!

***

Two Fridays later, as Samantha opened the door to admit Celeste, a movement in the coffee shop across the street caught her eye. A woman was reading a newspaper, holding it very close to her face. Samantha couldn't tell if the woman was hiding her face or simply short-sighted. She dismissed it as she admired Celeste's mini dress.

"He increased my allowance, so I brought you a little extra," Celeste informed Samantha as she dragged her inside.

The rich old codger was still paying for the privilege of fucking his wife.

"For that I will give you an *extra* special fucking," Samantha promised with a smile which didn't quite reach her eyes. Her day had begun badly—she had received a rejection letter from the publisher she'd thought most likely to publish her novel, and then she had broken one of her best crystal vases. The extra money should have cheered her up but it didn't. All Samantha could think was that some old jackass was paying over twenty-five thousand pounds a year to fuck his own wife just once a week; she was a damn good writer yet no publisher was willing to pay her twenty-five pence for her debut novel.

She strapped on the Whammer and lay back on her four-poster bed, her legs on the floor. The twin prongs of the dildo looked obscene jutting from her groin like a chocolate alien being.

"I want you to sit on these dildos for me," she instructed Celeste. She felt like lying back and letting the younger woman do some work. She wanted to keep her energy for the pounding she planned for her later. Today she would give Celeste the full Whammy and sometime over the weekend she would nip out and buy a bigger double dildo for her next visit.

Celeste swung her legs over Samantha's hips and positioned herself over the dildos. Samantha moved further off the bed for leverage as Celeste tried to get the two ends inside her. The anal dildo gave the most trouble but Samantha opened Celeste's butt cheeks and forced her down on it.

"Bounce for me baby!" Samantha commanded as she slapped Celeste's ass. Celeste obediently pulled herself about an inch upwards and then came slowly back down again.

"Ooooh! The one in the ass is too big," she moaned.

"I don't care—I said bounce!" Samantha slapped her ass harder and Celeste tried again. Her slim body trembled as she came down again and she looked about to cry.

I better not push her too much.

"Okay, baby, well done." Samantha leaned forward and pulled one of Celeste's small nipples into her mouth. Celeste wrapped her arms around Samantha's neck and started bouncing up and down in small movements.

"Yes, baby, bounce! Bounce!" Samantha kissed Celeste as she held her slim hips and helped her move up and down on the dildos.

She loved Celeste for always trying to please.

"Now, let *me* bounce for you." Samantha turned over and positioned Celeste beneath her. She put her hands on Celeste's legs and pushed them back. Then she planted her feet on the floor. Her weight pushed the two dildos into Celeste to the fullest extent.

"Aaaah!"

"Take it all for me, baby." Samantha looked into Celeste's eyes and held her gaze. "I want to fuck you really hard today—really punish you. Will you let me?"

"I'll try." Celeste reached for her own nipples and rolled them.

"Yes, baby, work on those nipples for me." Samantha withdrew and plunged forward suddenly.

"Aaaah!" Celeste's body's tensed but she barely had a chance to draw breath as Samantha thrust forward and backward again in a quick motion. "Aaaah! Aaaah!"

Celeste's sounds of pain spurred Samantha on and she drove the dildo forward with more force each time—she was fucking mad at the world!

"Samantha!" Celeste slapped her sharply across the face. "Stop it!"

Samantha almost punched her in retaliation but caught herself in time. Shit! She had almost messed with her meal ticket!

"I am sorry, baby. Fucking you is so addictive; I go a little crazy sometimes," Samantha apologized. Wrapping her arms around Celeste, she kissed her gently and begged, "Forgive me, please."

"Yes," Celeste acquiesced instantly.

Samantha bent her head and pulled one of Celeste's nipples into her mouth, reaching down to stroke her clit as she started thrusting slowly.

"Good. So *very* good!" Celeste moaned. Her ass was sore but the slight pain intensified the pleasure as the two dildos slid slowly in and out simultaneously.

Samantha lifted her head from Celeste's breasts. "You know I love you, sweetie. I just want to give you pleasure in any way I can. I fuck you hard *only* because I love you."

"I love you, too."

"Sometimes I get a little jealous when I think of that dirty old man's hands all over your body. It makes me want to punish you for letting him touch you."

"Samantha, I let him fuck me so I get money for the two of us," Celeste reminded her softly, as she reached for Samantha's breasts and tweaked them. "You are the one who gives me pleasure."

The words were exactly what Samantha wanted to hear. She buried her lips into Celeste's neck and kissed the smooth column of flesh. It was the most sensitive part of Celeste's body and the younger woman reacted immediately by pulling her slim legs upwards and wrapping them around Samantha's hips. Samantha kept her lips on Celeste's slim neck, running her tongue against the soft skin as she pinched Celeste's small nipples between her fingers. Celeste was so caught up in all the sensations running through her body she seemed unaware that Samantha had increased her thrusting to almost the same pace she'd slapped her for minutes earlier.

After Celeste's third orgasm Samantha left the Whammer sheathed and stared into Celeste's pleasure-filled eyes. Celeste was still trying to catch her breath, her eyes unfocused, her body trembling in the aftermath of the last intense orgasm. Samantha's heart missed a tiny beat. Was she actually starting to like this petite woman more than she should? Celeste reminded her too much of Georgina. The married woman Samantha had fallen in love with, the woman who had refused to leave her husband even after Samantha had been fucking her for almost four years; the woman who had started all this shit; the woman who had broken Samantha's heart and made her plot revenge on all married couples; the woman who had made Samantha break up seven marriages and counting.

***

"Don't get up, I'll see myself out." Celeste bent over and kissed Samantha as she lay naked on the bed. "See you Tuesday."

"Don't let him fuck that sweet ass of yours, it belongs to

me now," Samantha commanded. "And if you are very good I'll have another surprise for you on Tuesday."

"Okay, I'll give him only pussy next time," Celeste promised as she straightened.

"I miss you already," Samantha pouted.

Celeste bent over to kiss her again. "I must go."

"I love you," Samantha called after Celeste as she walked through the bedroom door.

"I love you, too," she replied, in French, blowing her another kiss and was gone.

Valerie lowered the newspaper as Samantha's door opened. The petite woman appeared but there was no sign of Samantha. Valerie checked once more to see if there was any movement behind the curtain before getting to her feet and hurrying after the young woman.

***

The next Tuesday Samantha sat restlessly waiting for Celeste. She couldn't call the house but she was really worried. Celeste had never missed any of their appointments before. Something was seriously wrong.

When Friday came and Celeste still didn't show up, Samantha sensed that she wasn't coming back. The next week she started taking wife-fucking bookings again. She needed fresh married pussy. She regretted letting Valerie go, she could have been regularly fucking her with the Wrecker if she had kept the bitch blindfolded each time she fucked her with him. Imagine Valerie making a fuss about the size of a dildo after she'd had the entire length buried in her pussy and had loved every inch! Prissy bitch!

Two weeks later, Celeste called Samantha sounding very agitated. She told Samantha that her husband had had her followed the last time she'd gone to Samantha's and now she was almost under house arrest. She had booked a dental appointment as a ruse the next day but wanted Samantha to meet her at a small, discreet hotel where she had managed to book a room. She begged Samantha to bring all her dildos because she wanted to be fucked until she couldn't walk straight.

The next afternoon Samantha rapped on the door of the hotel room, a big smile on her face. Celeste opened the door, stark naked—looking even better than Samantha had remembered. Celeste moved backwards and Samantha closed the door behind her. Eyes devouring Celeste's sexy body, Samantha dropped her bag of tricks and bent to kiss the petite woman's full lips. Just then, someone came up behind her and pressed a handkerchief over her nose and mouth. She struggled but her limbs seemed to be made of jelly. Her last conscious thought was, *oh fuck!*

When she came to, she was naked, spread-eagle and handcuffed to a bed. She blinked when Valerie bent and looked into her eyes.

"Celeste, darling, I think our lover is awake."

Celeste came to stand at Valerie's side and Samantha wondered if she had gone mad. How the fuck did they know each other?

"I think I'll start now." Valerie, wearing just a thong, climbed onto the bed and kissed Samantha's neck before she moved down to her breasts and rubbed her face over her nipples. "I missed these," she whispered and looked up at Samantha before she took one of her nipples in her mouth and bit it firmly before she moved to the other side and did the same. Then she moved down to Samantha's pussy and rubbed her face against it. "I especially missed this."

Samantha didn't know what the fuck was going on but Valerie started tonguing her clit just the way she had taught her to and it took too much willpower not to enjoy it.

"I'll suck her breasts." Celeste, still naked, sat on the other side of the bed, took one of Samantha's nipples in her mouth and teased it, mercilessly. Working together they completely overwhelmed Samantha and she couldn't hold back the orgasm that almost blew her head off minutes later.

"Did I give you permission to cum?" Valerie demanded as she strapped on the dildo Samantha had fucked her with the first time she had gone to her flat. "Now I'll have to *punish* you."

"Bitch, don't you dare put that in me!" Samantha screamed as Valerie positioned herself between her legs. Valerie ignored her as she gathered some of Samantha's pussy juice to lubricate the dildo. She pushed the dildo inside Samantha's pussy and the flesh resisted.

"Relax for me, baby." Valerie pushed harder. "You can take it."

"If you don't get that fucking dildo out of me, I'll kick your ass!" Samantha threatened in fury. The entrance of her pussy burned like it was on fire. She hadn't had anything but a finger or two in her pussy in over two years. Georgina had been the last person to push a dildo inside her.

"You are too tense, baby—let me bite these sweet nipples for you," Valerie mocked as she pushed the dildo deeper and teased Samantha's nipple with her teeth. "It's almost inside you. Baby, I knew you could take all of it."

It was only halfway in but Valerie was teasing Samantha. She pushed it deeper and Samantha groaned. "There now, there now."

"Fuck her hard," Celeste encouraged.

"You like my big dildo in your pussy, baby?" Valerie asked. The murderous look on Samantha's face made her laugh. She cupped Samantha's face and stared into her furious eyes before she quickly kissed her chin, afraid to put her lips near Samantha's mouth in case they were bitten off. "Brace yourself because I am going to fuck you hard!"

Samantha winced as Valerie increased her tempo.

"You don't want to cum for me, baby? You don't want to cum all over this dildo?" Valerie mocked again as she slowed the thrusting. She eased the dildo out and got off the bed. "I think I am done with her now."

"Can I fuck her ass now?" Celeste asked Valerie as she came to stand beside her.

"NO!" Samantha screamed.

Celeste pushed her finger in Samantha's pussy and then tried to probe her asshole.

"Please!" Samantha begged. She had never so much as had a finger in her asshole, this was getting serious.

"You think she's been taught a lesson yet?" Valerie asked Celeste with a smile.

"I want to fuck her ass!" Celeste strapped on the black dildo that Samantha had used the day she came over to fuck Celeste at her husband's request.

"Valerie please!" Samantha begged, knowing that Valerie was more likely to listen to reason than the hot-blooded younger woman. "I've never had anal sex before."

"Baby, you don't know what you are missing! Henry fucks my ass regularly now and I love it," Valerie informed her. "He told me to thank you for opening my eyes *and* my asshole!"

"Now, my husband pays me just to suck my nipples while I jerk him," Celeste joined in. "My new young boyfriend puts his 9" cock in both my pussy and my ass for *free*."

"I think we can let her go now." Valerie looked at Samantha's stricken face and felt a wave of compassion for her former lover.

"But I still want to fuck her ass!" Celeste laughed as she stroked the dildo. "I want to make her bounce for me!"

These fucking bitches, Samantha fumed, as she watched them. *I'll kill them both as soon as they release me.*

Valerie unlocked the handcuffs on Samantha's right hand as Celeste un-strapped the black dildo and put it back in Samantha's bag.

"You can unlock the other ones yourself, get dressed and leave," Valerie instructed as she handed the key to Samantha.

Samantha unlocked the handcuffs, got off the bed and dressed in silence. Celeste and Valerie watched her warily from the other side of the room. Suddenly she started to move towards them threateningly. "You stupid bitches! I'll beat *both* of you!"

"One step closer and I'll blow your fucking head off!" Celeste drawled like *Dirty Harriett,* pulling a gun out of nowhere and pointing it straight at Samantha. "Make my day, bitch."

Crazy French-West Indian bitch!

Samantha grabbed her bag and stormed out of the room.

Valerie quickly rushed to the door and doubled locked it before she turned to Celeste, her eyes wide. "Where did you get that gun?"

Celeste pointed the gun at her and pulled the trigger. "Need a light?"

A small flame flickered at the end of the gun-shaped cigarette lighter and they fell on the bed together, laughing.

"I'll miss her," Valerie mused as she got dressed a few minutes later.

"I'll miss her, too." Celeste got off the bed too and reached for her mini skirt and short top.

"I have to take the key back to reception." Valerie kissed the young woman's cheek before she gave her a warm hug. "Look after yourself."

"I will," the younger woman promised.

Valerie turned and started walking in the opposite direction.

"Valerie!" She turned her head as Celeste called her

name.   Celeste was standing outside the room, waiting impatiently for Valerie to re-open the door.   Valerie did so, wondering what Celeste could have possibly forgotten.

Celeste opened her handbag and pulled 'The Whammer' and his smaller friend, 'Double Entry'.   "I stole them from Samantha."   She laughed as she pulled out a harness as well.

"What are they?"   Valerie looked at the oddly shaped items in puzzlement.

"Samantha never fucked you with double dildo?"

"No."   Valerie shook her head, still not quite sure what exactly she was looking at.

"He is mine."   Celeste clutched The Whammer to her chest before she offered his slimmer friend to Valerie.   "But you can have him."

"What would I do with him?"

"I'll show you."   Celeste turned The Whammer towards her groin and thrust him against her.   "Or like this."   She pushed him through the harness and strapped up.

Valerie laughed as Celeste stood in front of her, fully dressed with the double dildo sticking out in front like the horns of a rhino.   Celeste looked at Valerie and smiled.   "We have the room for the rest of the afternoon.   We could have some fun and *then* go home."

"What kind of fun do you have in mind?" Valerie asked cautiously.

"Samantha's kind of fun!"   Celeste double locked the door again and pulled Valerie towards the bed.   They undressed quickly and climbed onto it.   Celeste climbed on top of Valerie, her large breasts pressing into Valerie's.

Valerie pulled her upwards and sucked one of her nipples into her mouth while she tweaked the other firmly.   Celeste supported herself on her hands and moaned as Valerie reached down and fingered her clit.   Celeste's pussy was wet and Valerie pushed two fingers inside her.

"All four, baby," Celeste whispered as she shifted down slightly and went for one of Valerie's nipples. Valerie pushed all her fingers in Celeste's pussy and thrust them as deep as they would go.

"Me too, honey," Valerie whispered back. Celeste immediately squeezed her fingers in Valerie's pussy and finger-fucked her Samantha style, still sucking on Valerie's nipple. Valerie came seconds later.

"You want to be fucked by double dildo?" Celeste asked her, finally pulling her mouth off Valerie's nipple.

"I am not sure." Valerie wasn't convinced that the double penetration would be pleasurable. Surely, a dildo in both holes at the same time would be too much? With Henry it was usually his cock in her pussy or her ass and that felt unbelievable.

"*So* good," Celeste promised as she got off the bed and grabbed the dildos and the harness. Valerie laughed again as Celeste climbed onto the bed with the slimmer of the double dildos sticking out absurdly in front of her, looking like a skinny black rhino.

She was moaning softly seconds later as Celeste worked it deeper inside her. The two dildos rubbed deliciously against each other through the thin separating membrane as Celeste finally got the last few millimetres inside both openings.

"Is good, no?" Celeste asked as she started to thrust the dildos in and out.

"It's wonderful." Valerie couldn't believe the sensation running through her body. She reached for Celeste's nipples. In response Celeste's hips moved faster.

"I fuck you hard, yes?" Celeste asked.

Valerie nodded and opened her legs wider. Celeste proceeded to give an excellent imitation of Samantha. Valerie arched off the bed as she came minutes later. But like Samantha, Celeste didn't stop after Valerie had one orgasm; she rode her to another two before she pulled the horns free.

"Me now." Celeste lay back on the bed and parted her legs eagerly.

"Are you sure you can handle this?" Valerie asked as she strapped on The Whammer. His slimmer friend had been more than enough for her.

"Yes. Samantha fucked me with him twice." Celeste smiled as she remembered.

Valerie smeared the dildo with Celeste's juices as Celeste had done with hers. Then she pushed two fingers in Celeste's ass as Celeste had also done hers.

"He's bigger. All four, baby." Celeste raised her hips as Valerie pushed her fingers in her ass and briskly fucked her with them.

"So good, baby. So *very* good!" Celeste groaned as she rotated her hips against Valerie's thrusting fingers and played with her own clit. Valerie increased the speed of her wrist and felt Celeste's asshole softened around her fingers.

"I think you are ready now." Valerie tilted Celeste's hips upwards and placed the heads of the dildos against her. She pushed the anal dildo in a little first before sliding the head of the other into her pussy. Then she slowly pushed forward as she rubbed Celeste's clit firmly. The anal dildo made slightly slower progress but both heads were soon tightly embedded.

Celeste seemed to be in a world of her own, her head turned to the side as she repeated the words 'so good' like a litany. Valerie continued to stroke her clit as she worked more and more of the lengths inside her. Finally with about an inch to go Valerie carefully lowered her body on to Celeste's as she continued to make small thrusting movements. She turned Celeste's head gently and looked into her eyes. For the first time she realized what Samantha saw when she had looked into her eyes in the past. It was quite a rush to give someone a pleasure-overload.

She covered Celeste's lips with her as she relaxed her legs and let her bodyweight push the dildos home. Celeste's mouth opened and Valerie caught her soft moan. She gently brushed Celeste's hands aside and pinched the woman's nipples as she started to thrust the dildos in and out of her.

"Is good?" Valerie asked.

"Is *so* good," Celeste confirmed.

Valerie increased her pace. "Better?"

"Better." Celeste repeated, wrapping her slim legs around Valerie's hips.

Valerie was working the dildos smoothly in and out of Celeste now she'd gotten the technique right. "Harder?"

"Harder." Celeste arched her neck and Valerie leaned down and kissed it. Celeste immediately grabbed her tighter.

Valerie rode Celeste to two mind-blowing explosions before she pulled The Whammer free, slowly. They lay in each other's arms for a long time not saying anything, both thinking about Samantha. She had been bent on wrecking their marriages but she had opened their eyes to pleasure neither had known existed.

Eventually, Celeste raised her head and looked at the clock on the wall. "I have to go."

"So do I," Valerie responded. She would have to order a take-away; she was too sated to cook Henry's dinner.

"Maybe we do this again?" Celeste suggested as she dressed quickly.

"Maybe," Valerie agreed with a smile.

Once again they hugged as they parted, but this time they shared a long, deep kiss before they walked off in separate directions.

Valerie smiled as she thought of the Whammer's friend

stuffed into her small handbag. She was going to call him Rhino. She would hide him in her lingerie drawer and take him out as often as she could to feed him some pussy and ass. She might eventually let Henry know she had the wild animal as a pet, but for now he would be her fucking secret.

***

When Samantha got home she was *mad*!

When she opened her tool bag and discovered two of her double dildos and a harness were missing she was *madder*!

When she began to wonder what those two bitches could be doing, and possibly to each other, with the two dildos she was *maddest*!

Her pussy ached like she had just lost her virginity. She was still stunned that the two of them had joined forces against her. And then the petite bitch had pulled a gun on her! She wished she had punched Celeste the day the little bitch had slapped her. If she had known how things would have turned out she would have given Celeste the fucking of her life that day!

Well, she had done, hadn't she?

She should have made the bitch bounce some more!

Then Samantha smiled as she remembered she had Amelia coming around later for some fucking. Lovely White Amelia, who had been so scared at first to have a Black woman in her lovely White home and even more scared to have a Black tongue on her White pussy. Lovely Amelia, whose husband William must have fallen to earth from the planet Freakdom. Not only did he ask Samantha to fuck his wife in the ass while he watched; he had made poor Amelia deep-throat the black dildo while it was strapped onto Samantha before the ass-fucking. He had given his wife's ass a good hard spanking while she was giving the dildo head, calling her 'a filthy fucking bitch' and 'a dirty fucking whore' alternatively in a crisp upper-class voice.

Samantha had *only* given Amelia her card because you never know. When the woman had called her three days later Samantha had been very shocked, for a minute; she quickly recovered to tell Amelia to come around the next day with some cash.

Poor old William likes men more than he likes women but as the headmaster of a very exclusive boys' school he has to be a little circumspect. So he did the expected and married a woman but on their wedding night he spanked her hard, then finger-fucked her front and back. The next night he tongued her pussy just for the hell of it.

He loves to fuck assholes but uses a dildo to fuck his wife's, saving his precious cock for other men's anuses. Says her ass is too fat and soft—says it puts him off. The fact that she is missing a bat and a pair of balls has nothing to do with it—nothing at all.

Personally, Samantha found Amelia's ass rather nice, though reddened by William's spanking, it had taken the 8" black dildo very well on the first occasion, and had been progressing nicely ever since. Amelia, a high six-figure earning accountant, had mastered 'Double Entry' in one session, moving swiftly on to the Whammer by the next. She was due for another Whammy today.

Shit! The bitches took it!

Well, Samantha did have the 'Double Decker', the new dildo she had bought for the little bitch Celeste. Could Amelia take it? It was a huge step…hmm, maybe, if she was very, very gentle.

***

Those of you who read **Bedtime Erotica** *would have met* **Henry, Valerie** *and* **Samantha** *in the story* **Another Woman,** *which was essentially about* **Henry** *and* **Valerie.** *I felt that* **Samantha's** *side of the story had to be told.*

*****

Breinigsville, PA USA
14 October 2009
225866BV00003B/3/P